DAUGHTER OF THE SKY

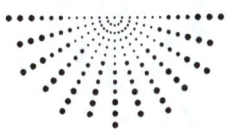

MICHELLE DIENER

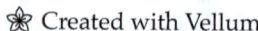 Created with Vellum

ACKNOWLEDGMENTS

Thank you to EJR Digital Art for the amazing cover, Edie and Liz for their great eye for detail and suggestions and my beta readers Jo, Julia and Bridget. As always, thanks to my amazing family for all their love and support.

To Gramps–I think of you often.

CHAPTER ONE

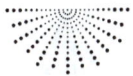

Inyoni yezulu – the bird of heaven:

The bird of heaven is said to descend from the sky when it thunders and to be found in the neighbourhood of where lightning has struck.

— THE RELIGIOUS SYSTEM OF THE AMAZULU
BY REV. CANON HENRY CALLAWAY, M.D., 1870

Lindani didn't run from anything, even a monster in the sea.

He blinked the wind-thrown rain from his eyes and leant over the cliff, his heart thundering along with the sky. A massive beast rolled in the waves, heaving in the flickering lightning light.

He raised his spear and with a crack that made him

jump, a white fork of light stabbed downward, illuminating the seascape and allowing him to see the thing clearly at last. It was not rising from the waves, it was sinking into them. He stared, transfixed, until the horror of what was happening below at last spurred him into action.

He turned on his heel and ran, shouting, down the hill to the village.

"A ship is going down."

Despite the wind, his voice must have carried because Dumisani had climbed out of the guard tower and stood huddled at the gate to receive him, wincing as the cold rain hit his face.

"A ship. A whiteman's ship. Sinking near the shore." He turned, taking his first steps to the beach, even though he knew he should wait for his father's orders. "Tell the chief!" he shouted over his shoulder.

The ship had been on its side, in its final death throes, like a buck after the second or third spear pierces its flank. Sinking down, with an acceptance of its fate.

As he hurtled down the path to the sea, excitement rose up within him. He had never seen a whiteman, never even seen one of their ships this close. They were too careful of the sharp black rocks lurking like sharks just past the breakers and did not sail too close to the shore.

He burst out of the low scrub onto the dunes and was hit by the roar of the angry ocean as it pounded the sand. Running up the nearest dune for a better look, Lindani waited for the next lightning strike. It came just in time for him to see the final spray salute of the sea as it embraced its victim and swallowed it whole.

He shivered, and wondered how many people such a big thing carried. How many souls would be joining their ancestors tonight? The storm raged on, but his sense of urgency was gone. The ship disappeared as if it had never been. And yet . . .

A huge wave crashed onto the shore, tumbling a large wooden box with it. And then another box joined it on the sand as the water sucked back, trying to hold on to its treasures. In the next flash of lightning, Lindani saw the length of the beach littered with debris and boxes.

A shout sounded to his right and he saw his father leading the men of the village onto the beach. The *sangoma*, old Mandla, jogged just behind the chief, his sharp eyes missing nothing.

Lindani ran towards them. "The ship broke up and sank, *inkhosi*."

"You should have waited for me." His father's face was stern, but Lindani knew his father would have done the same in his position, and there would be no trouble for him.

"Are there any survivors?" Mandla asked, his eyes never leaving the waves bringing their pieces of ship.

Lindani shook his head just as thunder cracked above them, making them duck. Lightning sizzled, for a moment turning the dark beach bright as day, illuminating the waves.

He blinked. There was someone in the water.

Lindani had an impression of a face, eyes closed, hands gripping a piece of board, and he didn't think, he ran straight for the sea.

He heard Mandla call out behind him, but the *sangoma's* words were swept away by the noise of the sea and the storm.

The water, usually so warm, was icy cold tonight. It pushed Lindani back, trying to stop his rescue. As he fought it, wading in to his hips, the tide changed direction, pulling on him now, greedily trying to claim another soul. He stopped and planted his feet apart, resisted the pull as he searched the foam-topped swells.

He braced himself as the next icy wave rolled in, hoping the water would bring the person to him. Something bumped against him as the water rushed over his shoulders, forcing him back. He reached out a hand blindly and caught hold of clothing, heavy with water.

He had them!

Hanging on tight, Lindani let the strength of the wave carry them both closer to the beach.

He tugged at the cloth, and a hand reached for him. Grabbed his shoulder. He pulled the survivor closer, locking arms around a slight body, and as the tide turned again he braced himself, digging his feet into the sand and straining landward.

The added weight of the slender figure in his arms made him heavier, but still the force of the water almost bowled him over, dragging him into the depths as he scrabbled to gain a foothold.

Then his father was there, and Dumisani and others, grabbing him back from the sea. They hauled both of them up past the tide line, and as lightning struck again, beyond the breakers, Lindani laid his burden down on the sand.

It was a girl, her face white as the bones of cattle baked in the sun. But it was her hair that was most different. He could not look away even when he felt Mandla come up behind him, put a hand on his shoulder.

"What will the spirits say of this, Lindani? You have stolen a bird of heaven from the sea."

He was right.

A bird of heaven had red feathers, and the hair of the girl before him, he had seen in the brief flicker of lightning, was a vivid, nature-defying, red.

CHAPTER TWO

No treaty or obligation can be binding on such a perfidious race as the Zulus, ruled by a treacherous and bloodthirsty sovereign like Cetywayo. Our future safety, as well as the voice of humanity, demand that the power of the Zulus should be broken, and that the innocent blood which is daily shed upon our borders should cease to flow.

— MR. BROWNLEE: SECRETARY FOR NATIVE
AFFAIRS, CAPE COLONY

December, 1878, six years later . . .

ELIZABETH WATCHED THE MESSENGER FROM THE MOMENT HE appeared on the far hill, standing to get a better view. He stumbled often, either from exhaustion or on the small rocks hidden in the long summer grass.

Usually, the messengers from the clan chief or the King walked in long, ground-eating strides. They didn't run.

Her heart beat a little faster and she looked down at the village below, the beehive huts in their cosy horseshoe protected by the high thornwood fence.

As the messenger came closer, he began to shout, and she heard Bheka, standing high in the guard tower, shout back.

She started down the path back to the village, running where she could, then slowed to a walk within sight of the fence, her breathing only just even as she entered the gates. By her estimation, the messenger was only five minutes behind her.

Bheka had come down from the tower to be ready to greet the messenger, and they exchanged silent, tense looks as she passed.

She skirted the inner cattle enclosure and headed to the top of the village to where the chief's hut lay. The messenger would be taken here to deliver his news. First to Lindani, and then Lindani would tell the elders, and the news would filter down to the rest of them.

"My sister." The soft voice of Nosipho called to her from the cooking fire. "Bheka says a messenger comes."

Elizabeth took a deep breath and moved towards Lindani's wife, serene and beautiful, her belly taut and round with the child she was carrying.

She nodded. "I've seen him. He is nearly here."

Nosipho beckoned her closer. "Could he be from Bangizwe's general, calling Bangizwe back to his regiment?" Her voice was hopeful as she smoothed her belly with her hand.

"Perhaps." But Elizabeth didn't think so. From the

messenger's frantic race across the veld, she guessed the message was important. Bangizwe was not so indispensable to the Zulu army that he would warrant such a fuss.

In fact, she'd come to suspect over the week he'd been visiting at the village that Lindani's uncle was smarting from the whip of a reprimand. That rather than boast of his accomplishments, he'd come here to lay low and lick his wounds.

Elizabeth shot a look in the direction of the guest hut, where Bangizwe lurked like a baboon spider in his hole. He'd taken every opportunity since he'd arrived to point out how young Lindani was to be chief, and how much older and more experienced he was.

Anything that would send him on his way would be welcome.

"The longer he stays here, sees what a fine place this is, the more he wants to be chief." Nosipho spoke quietly. "He watches Lindani with hatred in his eyes. And he talks disrespectfully of Lindani to the village elders. He tries to sow seeds of discord."

Lindani wasn't the only one Bangizwe hated. Elizabeth had felt the cold, hard edge of his looks, too. Heard the sneering insults about her white skin.

"If he is being called back to his *ibutho*, that would be very good." As she spoke, Bangizwe ducked out through the guest hut's low door. He glanced their way, and the look he sent them both was full of loathing. He crouched with the other men before the fire, looking in the direction of the gate.

"You are expecting a message?" One of the men asked him.

Bangizwe shook his head, hunching closer to the ground as he waited.

For the first time, Elizabeth wondered if this *could* be

about Bangizwe. Perhaps whatever it was he was avoiding had come to find him. Drag him back.

A praise song rang out from the gates; Bheka singing to the messenger, telling of Lindani's accomplishments.

Bangizwe's lips twisted in disgust.

And Elizabeth suddenly understood.

If Bangizwe was ever made chief, if he found a way to replace Lindani, she couldn't live here anymore.

"THE NEWS IS THAT THE BRITISH HAVE GIVEN THE KING AN ultimatum." Lindani crouched before the fire in the beer hut as Elizabeth worked, sniffing in the sweet smell of fermentation.

"What kind of ultimatum?" She stirred the boiling pot of sorghum and maize, fighting with the wooden spoon in the thick mixture, but her eyes were on him.

"There are many things, mostly nonsense things, I don't know why they are even mentioned in a serious matter like this, but the important points are that the King must disband the army, must disband the military system, and must let a British official oversee Zululand."

Elizabeth tipped forward onto her knees in surprise, nearly burning herself on her pot. "By when must he do this?"

"The silly things must be done twenty days after the ultimatum was given. Which was five days ago. The big things they give the King thirty days to accomplish." His voice vibrated with anger.

"The King would never disband the military system. It's how the kingdom works." Understanding hit her. "They know that. They know the King cannot comply. And when he doesn't . . ."

"The British will invade."

Still kneeling by the fire, Elizabeth saw something in his eyes that sent a chill down her arms despite the flames in front of her. "You think this puts me in danger," she said slowly. "Because I am British?"

"I think any white person will soon need to have sanction to stay in Zululand if their people are at war with the King," Lindani said, and there was a raw note to his words. "The messenger has already noted your presence and says he will need to report it."

"What do you think will happen?" It felt as if there was an *assegai* at her throat, it was so hard to speak.

Lindani grimaced. "I don't know. I will speak to the clan chief. He will decide if you can stay, or if we must take you across the border to Natal."

She went cold. It felt as if her chest was too tight to take a breath and to shake the feeling off she stood and heaved the heavy pot off the fire, placing it to steep in a cool corner of the hut.

She ignored the pots of grain which had already sat for a day and needed to be boiled in water, and crouched before the fire again. "What will the King do? He cannot give in to them."

Lindani laughed, but not in his usual, carefree way. "The King will never give in. He is a Zulu."

"Yes," Elizabeth said, her heart thumping hard in her chest. "He is a Zulu, and so are you. What are *you* going to do, Lindani?"

"I am going to do what the King asks of me, of course."

Elizabeth said nothing, looking him straight in the eye,

an impropriety that still scandalized the villagers, but which had always been the way between them.

Lindani sighed.

"I am going to war, my little sister. Every man who can lift a spear in this village is going to war."

CHAPTER THREE

I have no fears myself that Natal will be overrun by hostile
Zulus, but much fear that Zululand should be overrun by
hostile Britons.

— ANTHONY TROLLOPE, 1878

T he guards were looking at her.

Even though her eyes were downcast as she sat
cross-legged on her grass mat, waiting to be called by the
clan chief, Elizabeth could feel their interest.

They weren't hostile, only curious. A white woman in a
bead skirt and necklace was an unheard-of sight.

She and Lindani had left the village and walked the
seven hours to the clan chief the day after the messenger had
come, to show they had nothing to hide, and wanted only to
do the right thing.

Bangizwe had wanted to come with them, to meddle, no

doubt, or pretend some importance he didn't have, but the messenger had told him he had to return immediately to his *ibutho*, and he'd been forced to leave for the capital, oNdini, scowling and disgruntled.

She much preferred the curious gazes of the clan chief's men to his glowering.

The late afternoon sun stung her back and shoulders, and she drew up her knees, resting her chin on them.

Lindani had been summoned to the chief's hut over an hour ago, to speak on her behalf, and she couldn't understand what was taking so long.

But she was from a small village, and unfamiliar with the ways of a clan chief, who was also one of the King's most highly-regarded generals. Lindani told her he was in charge of the Zulu scouts. The King's spymaster.

She refused to allow herself to think what would happen if he ordered her to leave Zululand. She would wait and see what he said before getting worked up. And surely, one young woman was a threat to no one?

There was movement at the door, and a warrior emerged, tall and haughty.

"Come," he commanded her in a deep voice.

Stiff with sitting for so long, Elizabeth eased herself to her feet, and discovered her foot had fallen asleep.

She had to limp towards her fate.

"Sit." The warrior who'd called her stood just within the entrance.

Blinded coming into the gloom of the large hut after the brightness outside, Elizabeth blinked. She knew she had no choice but to obey, but her legs screamed at her to stand a little longer.

"*Sit.*"

A hand slapped the burnt skin between her shoulder

blades and she stumbled forward, biting her lip so as not to cry out in pain.

She knelt down, her eyes on the ground. She saw there were only two other people in the hut. Lindani sat to one side, between her and the *isiKhulu*, the clan chief, who sat cross-legged in the centre of the hut.

"Look at me."

The words were spoken in English, and Elizabeth gasped, lifting her head until her eyes met the interested gaze of the magnificently-dressed man before her.

Although he sat, she could tell he'd be as tall as Lindani if he stood, and he had the bulk and strength of maturity that Lindani had yet to acquire. The green and scarlet red *iGwalagwala* feathers on his headdress proclaimed him a very high-ranking warrior.

"Your chief says you are called Inyoni Yezulu?" The question was asked in Zulu, and the clan chief leant forward to get a good look at her. Elizabeth nodded.

"Your eyes are very green and your hair is very red." His hand reached up and touched one of the feathers of his headdress. "Your colouring is like a bird. You are well-named."

Elizabeth's heart thundered. Should she respond? She resisted an impulse to look to Lindani for direction.

"Tell me your story, bird of heaven."

"I . . ." Elizabeth took a deep breath. "My parents died in China, and I was put on a ship back to England, to live with my grandmother. But a storm blew up off the Zululand coast, and the ship went down. Lindani . . ." She did look at Lindani this time. "Lindani saved me. He saw me in the lightning light and swam out to pull me in."

"And for six years you have lived with the Zulus?"

Elizabeth nodded.

"And you have never tried to go back to England? There are many traders who would have taken you." The chief seemed bemused.

"I have always hidden from the traders. I did not want to go back. I was taken into Lindani's family as a daughter, and that is what I became. A daughter of the sky."

There was silence in the hut.

The clan chief made a frustrated movement with his hand. "You put me in a difficult position. If I send you back to Natal now, in this time of strain between Zululand and Britain, the British will use you against us. Demand some ridiculous atonement for keeping you all these years." He paused. "And yet, I cannot let you stay."

Elizabeth jerked her head up, then blushed and looked down hurriedly.

"Why not, *isiKhulu*?" Lindani spoke for the first time. He kept his voice humble, but the question alone was daring.

"Because any whiteman in Zululand risks being labeled a spy."

"I would never spy against the Zulus," Elizabeth gasped.

The chief made a humming sound, tapped his finger against his lips. "Why did you truly not return to your own people?"

Elizabeth drew in a breath. Tried to find that spark of rage within to adequately explain herself.

"My parents died by the hands of their own countrymen. Shot down by British soldiers in a street riot."

She was wrong. After all this time, she could still feel a tiny spark of rage within.

But did she really want to fan it to life again? She drew in a breath. "So much time has passed, I cannot find that same anger any more, but it was very strong when Lindani rescued me. My only other relative is my grandmother. A

14

hard, cold woman I never liked, and who never knew or liked me. There was no reason to return, and every reason to stay."

"If you truly have no love for your old countrymen, then I may have a solution, little bird."

Elizabeth saw Lindani's fists clench, saw his whole body tense, and realized he knew already what the clan chief would ask of her. And was angry about it.

"I have spies watching the British as they move towards our border, of course. But they can only get so close, and none understand English. But if I had a spy within the British camp . . . ah, what things I would know!"

Lindani looked as if he wanted to leap to his feet.

"Don't we have spies among the Zulus sent by some of the clan chiefs in Natal who want to bring down the King?" His voice was strangled.

The clan chief shook his head. "Those traitors have been sure to use only loyal men. We have not managed to get a spy in there." He paused, and looked thoughtfully at Elizabeth. "Besides, my spies watching the camps say the Natal tribesmen are treated like dogs. They do not know from day to day what is happening, and all the decisions are made in English. No, what I need is a white, English-speaking spy."

"But she is a woman." Lindani's voice was quiet. "They will know she's no soldier."

The clan chief laughed. "You have not seen a British soldier, then. They wear many, many clothes. Some of them are very young. With her hair short and clothing that is a too big for her, it could be done."

Her skin prickled, suddenly cold, despite the sting of the burnt skin on her back. She was being asked to do something big.

Something terrible.

But no less than was being asked of Lindani. Of all the men in Zululand.

The Zulus had taken her warmly to their hearts and shared everything they had with her generously. She had made Zululand her home, and now she was being called upon to help save it.

She drew herself straight, looking at the clan chief's feet. "I will do it," she said, and Lindani turned to her in horror.

She gulped down her reservations. She was either in or she was out. There was no going back after this, but then, she had little choice.

She nodded decisively. "I'll spy for you."

CHAPTER FOUR

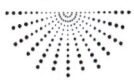

Why does the Governor of Natal speak to me about my laws? Do I go to Natal and dictate to him about his laws? I shall not agree to any laws or rules from Natal, and by so doing throw the great kraal which I govern into the water. [. . .] Go back and tell the white man this, and let them hear it well. The Governor of Natal and I are equal. He is Governor of Natal and I am Governor here.

— KING CETSHWAYO, AS QUOTED IN ONE OF
SIR BARTLE FRERE'S DESPATCHES TO THE
IMPERIAL GOVERNMENT.

The British camp lay below them, white tents stretched out across the plateau. It dwarfed the little settlement around which it had temporarily sprung.

Lying on her stomach between Lindani and Malusi, Elizabeth could not find her voice. There must be thousands of men down there. Thousands.

Not even a breath of wind stirred, and the air above the camp shimmered and danced in the heat.

"They're preparing to move out," Malusi said.

Elizabeth followed the line of his finger to a group of redcoats lifting boxes into ox wagons, their movements slow and oppressed in the furnace that was Northern Natal on a hot summer morning. Faint shouts drifted up to their spy post, just discernible over the high-pitched buzz of the cicadas.

Elizabeth hunched her bare shoulders against the sting of the sun, and wished she'd brought a springbok skin to shield her back and arms.

"Do you think Inyoni should join them before they leave, or on the trail?" Lindani narrowed his eyes, leaning forward on his forearms, and Elizabeth knew he saw far more detail of the camp below than she did.

His eyes were sharp as the kites circling above them, riding the thermals and eyeing the refuse ditch at the back of the camp.

"It will be easier to wait along the trail and slip among them during the move. Safer." Malusi cast a quick glance at Elizabeth.

"But?"

"The general would like to know what is in the despatches from this column to the others. The main general of this whiteman's army is in the camp below, and he will be instructing the other columns on their movements."

"You don't have a uniform for me yet." Elizabeth tried to force the fear out of her voice. She managed to make the words calm and smooth. But inside, her heart ran quick and erratic as a duiker. She was not a trained spy like Malusi. Not a trained warrior like Lindani.

Nothing in her life before she became a Zulu had prepared her for this moment.

Malusi's hard eyes cut across to her, and she was unable to look away.

"If you have doubts about this, if you feel you cannot do it, tell me now."

She swallowed hard. Kept her gaze steady. "It is not that I have doubts, I'm nervous. I have never lied before, never spied." She clasped her hands together. "I don't want to fail."

Watching Malusi consider her answer, she knew she had said what needed to be said. What had to be said.

Even now, she was sure, everything that came out of her mouth was reported back to Malusi's general – Lindani's clan chief. She was, after all, his most daring project. And Lindani's future and hers depended on her co-operation.

She swung her gaze back to the camp, and looking at the sheer enormity of the force massed below, grudgingly admitted the general was right on one count. She couldn't go back to Natal now without serious repercussions.

She could see the headlines. A young English girl, held in captivity, forced to near slavery by the heathens. Made to go bare breasted, uncovered except for a grass skirt. Scandalous! Let's bring these savages to heel.

"Take that sour look off your face, brother." Lindani slapped a hand on the ground before him, jerking Elizabeth out of her thoughts. "The general has put my sister in a difficult position, and has she once complained?" He shot Malusi a look over the top of her head. "Your task is to support her, not harangue her."

"I thought she meant . . ." Malusi looked away, back over the camp, and Elizabeth frowned in genuine puzzlement.

"What did you think?"

"That you were reconsidering betraying your countrymen." He spoke cautiously, as if afraid of insulting her.

He was calling her a traitor, but the insult washed over her, meaningless. She flipped her hand, as if flicking away a bothersome fly.

"I cut my ties to my country six years ago." Elizabeth stared out over the white-tented camp, away from the sympathy she knew she'd see in Lindani's eyes.

"But you must have been a child six years ago."

"I was fourteen. My parents were killed in a riot in China. Fired upon by idiot redcoats, just like those below."

A long piece of grass tickled her under the chin, and she snapped it off irritably.

"Your parents were killed by their own soldiers?"

Tension made Elizabeth draw her arms together beneath her, and she lifted up on her elbows. "They didn't know my parents were there until it was too late." She felt restless, wanted to leap up and walk, but even she knew a silhouette on the hilltop would be a bad idea. The redcoats may be idiots, but they weren't stupid.

"So it was a mistake." Malusi frowned.

"It should never have happened. The riot itself was preventable, and to fire into a crowd of men, women and children . . ." She shook her head. She would never understand it. Never.

"An empire is a very big thing to hate," Malusi said, gesturing down to the camp with its over four thousand troops. "Even one of their columns is a big thing to hate."

Elizabeth kept silent. The truth was, she hadn't touched her hatred, her deep anger, for a long, long time. Even when she'd tried to make the clan chief understand her reasons for not returning to England, she'd only felt a weak spark of it.

But seeing the redcoats, hearing the shouts of drill sergeants, had brought it back to her, almost fresh as the day she'd stepped from the pier in Hong Kong onto the *HMS Miranda*, to be sent back to England. A place she remembered only dimly. Grim skies and a pinched, hard-faced grandmother.

She waited for the anger to fade.

She hadn't fed it. She thought she'd put her hatred behind her.

But since they'd leopard-crawled to this lookout and looked down on the largest of Lord Chemlsford's columns, the anger had come rushing back, thickening her throat, burning her eyes, making her toes and her fingers curled and stiff.

Like a thousand-year old egg, she'd buried the rage and now she'd dug it back up. More putrid and foul than before.

"You are wrong about me." Elizabeth picked up the long piece of grass she'd snapped off earlier and began looping it round and round her forefinger, making the skin beneath white as she tugged.

Malusi said nothing, waiting.

"My people are not those redcoats down there. I belong to the people of the sky now." She slipped the grass spiral off her finger, watched it expand and try to reclaim its straightness. An impossibility.

Malusi was quiet a moment longer, but it seemed she had convinced him. "We may not have a uniform yet," he said at last, "but we do have other whitemen's clothes."

"Stealing secrets dressed as a civilian could get her caught before we even start. The officers will surely be more suspicious of a person out of uniform." Lindani spoke reasonably, but tension hummed off him.

Malusi pointed to the far side of the camp. "You see there, where some of the horses and the oxen are kept? I've been watching this camp for a long time, and the traders often go there, to check their animals, and to talk to the soldiers who look after the officers' mounts.

I don't expect Inyoni to sneak into an officer's tent and try to read his secrets, but listening to the gossip of the men may give us something. No matter what she hears, it will be more than we know now."

Elizabeth's heart leapt and twisted in her chest, trying to escape in terror. She drew in a deep breath, and with it came the perfume of the veld. The sweet smell of the long green grass they'd crushed beneath them, the deep, loamy scent of the soil, and just discernible, on the outer edges of her senses, the promise of rain.

It calmed her.

"How will I get in?" she asked.

"You are going to pose as a trader. Bringing meat to those skinny whitemen such as they have never tasted before." Malusi grinned widely.

"Not alone?" Lindani's voice was sharp.

"You want to go with her?" Malusi's mouth twisted in scorn. "She can't have you at her back when she infiltrates the column in uniform."

"So? Let us ease her in. And you forget Inyoni has taught me English. Two sets of ears are better than one."

They glared at each other over her head, but Elizabeth had the sense not to get between two Zulu warriors engaged in a battle of wills.

One saw himself as her older brother, her guardian, the other saw her as a tool to be used. Neither would appreciate her opinion, no matter that this was more her concern than theirs.

From the corner of her eye, she saw Malusi give a curt nod. Decision made, both men began wriggling backwards over the crest of the hill.

As she followed them, felt the uncomfortable rub of grass and stone on her bare stomach and breasts, she looked straight into the swiveling eyes of a chameleon, bright green and almost invisible in the lush summer grass. It hung by its funny, gripping hands, clasping the slender stem of a bush bent almost to the ground with its weight.

"I need to learn your tricks, *unwabo*," she whispered to it as she snaked backwards. "I'm going to need every one."

THEY TROTTED TOWARDS THE CAMP ON THE RUTTED, DUSTY track, just a young driver and his boy. Elizabeth eyed the sentries along the makeshift wall of mealie bags, rifles held loosely in their hands as they watched the cart approach.

Her hands were slick with fear, but who would know the difference in this heat?

The afternoon was drawing on, and the weight of humidity pressed like a wet blanket over her head.

Above, in a sky so big it humbled, black and purple thunderclouds mushroomed upwards.

She wondered how the sentries managed, standing out in the blistering heat with no relief, covered with two or three layers of uniform. They should have melted into puddles just after midday.

She would be wearing those same layers soon, and just thinking of it, she slipped her hand behind her and tugged at the loose cotton shirt Malusi had provided. It stuck to her back, and she pulled it away from her skin, sticky with sweat. Its sleeves were too short, and the coarse wool jacket she wore over it itched at the wrists.

She envied Lindani, sitting at the back of the cart in nothing but faded blue trousers cut off at the shins instead of his usual *umuTsha*. They'd decided the leather flap and monkey tails were too risky, that trousers made him look more like a whiteman's worker. She only hoped he looked humble enough. Servant-like enough.

He had a way of tilting his head that was cocky and arrogant, and a Zulu warrior's deep-seated confidence in his abilities. She wondered if he was capable of playing someone's worker-boy.

She began pulling back on the reins as they approached the sentry at the gates and pushed her worries about Lindani from her mind. Of the two of them, she was most likely to get them caught. A woman in boy's clothing.

"What's your business?" The sentry at the gate looked at her with eyes glassy with boredom and heat exhaustion.

"Someone ordered supplies," Elizabeth said, the English like thick porridge on her tongue. It had been weeks since she'd used it in anything but her dreams.

She didn't try to deepen her voice. She didn't think she could keep it up for any length of time. They would either accept she was a young teenage boy with a high voice, or she was lost.

The sentry waved irritably at a fly, his actions curiously slow. Every moment stretched out as fear and tension made time elastic.

"Someone, who?"

Elizabeth shrugged, using the movement to let the tension drain from her. The sentry clenched his jaw.

"Listen, boy, I can't let anyone who pleases pass in. It's a military encampment, for God's sake. Who placed the order?"

Again, Elizabeth shrugged. "I'm just the delivery boy, sir."

"Well, then you can't enter." His attempts to kill the fly became vicious and he slapped his arm a stinging blow and winced.

Relief washed through Elizabeth. She wouldn't have to do this because they wouldn't let her in. Even the general couldn't argue with that.

"Suit yourself." She began turning the horse around – a small, tough workhorse bred for these rolling hills, for the heat. Not like the thoroughbreds she'd seen the officers prance in and out of camp on.

She gave Lindani a quick look over her shoulder, but he kept his face impassive.

The beginnings of an afternoon breeze, the precursor to rain, lifted the canvas covering the two slaughtered cattle in the back of the cart as they turned, and it flapped up, snapping in the stirring air. Elizabeth gave the horse its head and leant back to help Lindani flick the cover over to keep the flies off. They'd eat well tonight, if nothing else came of this fiasco.

"Wait." The sentry's eyes were on the carcasses, and from the look on his face, Elizabeth guessed it was the best slab of meat he'd seen in a long time.

Just as Malusi had gambled, fresh meat was a hard commodity to resist.

"Someone'll have my guts for garters, turning that lot away." He waited for Elizabeth to turn the cart back, and even though she'd pulled the wide-brimmed hat low over her short cropped hair, he had obviously caught a glimpse of it. "Right-o, Red. Take the cart just within and left to the livestock pen. Ask someone to fetch the quartermaster's aide. Let them sort out who ordered this."

Elizabeth touched her hat in salute, and flicked the reins, her horse trotting past the sentry with a jerky gait.

They were in.

CHAPTER FIVE

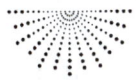

If we are to have a fight with the Zulus, I am anxious that our arrangements should be as complete as it is possible to make them. Half-measures do not answer with natives. They must be thoroughly crushed to make them believe in our superiority.

— GENERAL THESIGER, JULY, 1878, SOON TO BE LORD CHELMSFORD, COMMANDER IN CHIEF OF THE BRITISH FORCES IN SOUTH AFRICA.

It was easy to find the way. The stink of livestock was a physical presence in the camp. Choking, Elizabeth urged the reluctant mountain pony forward, her nose and eyes screwed up against the smell.

"Aye, it hits you something fierce if you ain't used to it."

A man waved her towards him, his face thin and sharp behind a scraggly beard.

Grateful for some direction, Elizabeth drew up alongside him.

A second man stepped out from a white canvas tent next to makeshift stables and open pens of oxen, a piece of paper and a pencil in his hand. "Wot 'ave we here, Smithy? A young lad bearing gifts?"

"Afternoon, sirs." Elizabeth jumped down, too afraid to look either of them in the eye. She thrust her shaking hands into her pockets.

This was close contact. Close enough to notice she wasn't a boy. Malusi had told her, over and over, that people see what they expect to see.

Short hair, tanned, freckled skin and men's clothing, a wide-brimmed hat for good measure, and no matter if you were the most alluring woman alive, no one would notice unless you drew their attention to it.

She was about to see if he was right.

"The sentry said to get the quartermaster's aide, as I don't know who ordered this." Her voice wobbled and she cleared her throat.

The first man, Smithy, groaned. "Not another one. Which quartermaster's aide? The First or the Second Battalions of the 24th Regiment? The Artillery Division? The Natal Native Contingent forces?"

Elizabeth shrugged, her heart stuttering. She had no idea about the regiments and their names. And she would soon have to pretend familiarity with it all. Not only know which regiments were part of this column, but find a legitimate place for herself among them for weeks, perhaps months.

The full scope of the task she had agreed to engulfed her,

left her trembling like a child in the middle of a thunderstorm.

"Call Rhys, of the 2nd 24ths. They're about due for some supplies. 'Aven't seen anything for 'em in a few days." The second man studied his worn, over-folded schedule for a moment. "Three, to be exact." He frowned.

"Right-o, Mr. Jackson."

Elizabeth watched Smithy dart off between two tents and disappear into the maze of the camp.

"Well, let's see what you got for us." Jackson moved to the back of the cart, and Lindani jumped down and obligingly drew back the canvas covering.

At once the flies descended, and even when Jackson flicked an arm over the carcasses, they did not move.

"Bloody flies. Cover it up again, boy." Jackson turned away, his pencil moving over his paper.

Elizabeth glared at his back, but she saw Lindani's face split with a grin.

"If they think us boys, they forget we are dangerous men," he murmured in Zulu, and she gave a reluctant nod.

Lindani saw this as a warrior's task. A test of his courage and manhood. She saw it as a nightmare.

Lindani began to drift off, down passed the stalls, towards where the farriers were shoeing the officers' mounts. Steam hissed and billowed up as they thrust their newly forged shoes into caldrons of water and it seemed to add to the sweltering heat of the afternoon.

She knew he had gone to eavesdrop, to do his job, but she wanted to call him back. Hold on to him. She jammed her hands even deeper into her pockets and kicked the boggy ground. Tried to get a hold of herself.

Jackson gave her a quick look and she watched him nervously. With every second Smithy took to return she imagined the 2nd 24ths quartermaster's aide insisting he had ordered nothing and demanding she be questioned.

Her chest felt as if someone was sitting on it, and drawing in short, choppy breaths, she began walking towards Lindani, suddenly sure they needed to get out. Get out *now*.

She stumbled, her feet clumsy with panic. The camp, with its shouting men and moaning oxen, was closing in on her, and she fixed her eyes on Lindani. How was he so far away?

"Look out."

The shout startled her, jerked her to a stop, just as a bay horse reared up and chopped the air in front of her with vicious hooves.

She gave a squeak of fear.

The officer riding it dug his heels into the animal's side and it pranced off, making for the gate.

"Are you hurt?"

Dazed, Elizabeth shook her head, looked round, straight into bright blue eyes under frowning brows.

"Th . . . thank you."

The frown got deeper at her words, and Elizabeth felt a lead weight in her stomach. The man towering over her peered down to get a closer look.

"Who are you, then?"

"Just a driver, sir. Come with some supplies." She looked away, afraid of what he would see in her eyes.

"Hey, you." The shout from Jackson was like a whip crack across her back, and Elizabeth jerked. She turned to him and began walking back, hoping, hoping beyond anything, she looked relaxed.

Smithy was standing beside Jackson, looking like the trip into the camp and back had worn him out.

"Seems the quartermaster's aide is down with a fever. Could well be he ordered this lot, but he ain't making any sense at the moment."

"Which aide?"

Elizabeth blanched as she realized the officer had followed her, was standing behind her. Watching her.

"Good day to you, Captain Burdell. Your Division's aide, sir, Mr. Rhys of the 2nd 24ths." Mr. Jackson touched his cap respectfully in salute.

"And what is it that has been brought in?"

He stepped up alongside her, and Elizabeth caught the scent of soap, sweat and leather. He wore a blue jacket with intricate black frogging across the chest over blue trousers, and while he was clean-shaven, she could see the beginnings of dark stubble on his chin.

He looked tough – hard and hardened.

"Meat, you'll be pleased to hear." Jackson looked around for Lindani, and finding him gone, flicked back the canvas himself.

"What does the quartermaster say, Mr. Jackson?" Burdell's eyes lingered on the carcasses.

"Can't find 'im, sir," Smithy said. "Looked everywhere."

"If it's possible Rhys ordered this, and no one else is claiming it, then by all means enter it against the 2nd 24th supplies. We haven't seen meat this decent in weeks."

Elizabeth's hands slowly crept out of her pockets and she allowed herself to lean nonchalantly against the cart.

"I'll sort out the paperwork, then." Jackson disappeared into his tent and Smithy drifted off down the line of horses, some with makeshift roofs over them.

Burdell stayed, watching her, his expression unreadable. "Seems you're in for a wait."

Elizabeth shrugged. Looked off down the line.

There was an uneasy silence.

"Going to find my boy," she muttered, pausing slightly on the last word. She gave him a quick nod, her eyes firmly on his boots, and sidled off towards the farriers.

She felt his eyes burning the back of her neck the whole way there.

∾

THERE WAS SOMETHING ABOUT THAT DELIVERY BOY. JACK Burdell watched thoughtfully as he scuttled down to where the farriers worked, half-hidden in the billowing steam.

The way he walked was effeminate, but Jack had taken a close look at his hands, and they were grimy and sunburned, and what little he'd seen of his face under the hat's deep brim had been brown and freckled. His stride was wide, too, no small steps.

Still, that voice, and that little cry of fear he'd made when Manning had almost run him down earlier . . .

Jack shook his head. He was wasting time. He walked down the line of livestock, following the route the delivery boy had taken, but stopping in front of a dappled grey tied to the low railing that ran the length of the pens.

"How are you doing, hmm?" He rubbed the gelding's neck and Samson nickered a greeting.

"There you are, captain." Jeff Holman came up, and rubbed Samson between the ears. "Bad news, I'm afraid."

"Lame?" Jack looked at his recently purchased horse with regret.

"Aye. Sorry, sir, I know you paid dear for him."

"Yes, I did, but that's not the most important thing."

"Would be for some, but not you, sir. You always treat 'em right."

"I don't want him becoming tomorrow's dinner for the damn swarm of locusts in this camp," Jack said. Realized too late the bitterness in his voice.

"The men got to eat." Holman shrugged.

"They don't need to eat my horse." Jack spoke with his teeth clenched. He rolled his shoulders, tried to ease the tension out of them.

"Even if you give 'im to one of the locals in the village, you can't be sure they won't send 'im to the knackers."

"No, I can't be sure, but I *will* be sure of what will happen if I sell him to the quartermasters."

Holman ran a hand down Samson's flank. "I'll try find him a home, but I can't promise."

"Fair enough."

"Going to be hard to find you another horse, sir." Holman squinted into the sun, his brow wrinkled, as if he spent his life in a bad mood. He spat on the ground. "All the decent horseflesh been bought up already. Nothing but nags left."

"Well I shall have to do without until we can find something. But as Samson is my third in a year, I've concluded these locals can see us coming, Holman."

"Aye, that they can. Highway robbers, the lot of 'em. Dare say they could teach the traders in Portabello Road a thing or two."

"Well, keep your ear to the ground for me." Jack gave Samson a last, regretful pat, and turned to go. He looked for the delivery boy again, saw him hanging on the edges of a group of soldiers grooming horses, not part of them, but listening to the conversation intently. He reminded Jack of a sparrow, poised and waiting for a chance to swoop up a crumb. Although what that crumb was, Jack was at a loss to guess.

The lad bothered Jack, and he watched him lower himself to the ground in an elegant, smooth motion, leaning against a pole while he waited.

The boy's worker approached and knelt beside him, speaking in his ear, and as one, they both looked straight at Jack. He had the sense that both started in . . . fear?

He lifted his hand in salute and walked away, putting their strange behaviour from his mind. He had other things to worry about. No horse being one of them, no more heart for soldiering being another.

CHAPTER SIX

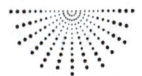

Cetshwayo hereby swears, in the presence of all his Chiefs, that he has no intention or wish to quarrel with the English.

— MESSAGE FROM CETSHWAYO TO THE
LIEUTENANT-GOVERNOR, 10 NOVEMBER, 1878

"I watched you from the hill." Malusi slapped Lindani on the back as they jumped from the cart, a grin splitting his face.

A local tribesman sat under a thorn tree nearby, although the need for shade had gone. The sky was a fear-inspiring purple, and the veld silent and still.

Every living thing that could take shelter had already found it except for the swallows, who swooped and dived at the ground.

The man beneath the tree stood and walked over to them, took up the horse's reins.

"The general will not forget your cooperation." Malusi clasped his hand. He turned to Elizabeth. "Did they pay you for the meat?"

Elizabeth drew out a small bag from her pocket and Malusi took it and handed it over to the tribesman.

"Remember, say nothing of this." He looked a moment longer than necessary into the man's eyes, and the man dipped his head, a quick, submissive gesture.

Elizabeth noticed his face was quite blank, and she felt sorry for him.

The Zulu tribesmen on the Natal side of the border were in an impossible position. Under the rule of the British, but with Zululand just a few miles and a river away.

Within easy reach of the King.

Were they as confused as the whole of Zululand at the British ultimatum that was both an outrageous demand against a sovereign state, and impossible to comply with in the time given, even if King Cetshwayo wanted to?

Which he did not.

What ruler would disband his army and turn over his country's administration to another power?

The tribesman jumped up into the cart and set off without a backward glance. He urged the horse into its fastest gait.

Elizabeth watched him go, only half-listening as Lindani boasted of the dangers of the camp to Malusi, told him what they had learned.

A single, fat drop of rain hit her cheek and ran down her face like a tear.

"Come, Inyoni."

Malusi's call drew her back to the veld.

"We're going back across the border, little bird."

Elizabeth almost sagged with relief. The thought of being back on home ground intoxicated her as much as the break in the weather. She could smell the rain, almost overwhelming in its strong perfume, and she breathed it in in huge gulps. A drop smacked her in the eye and she blinked it away, smiling.

"We need to hurry before the river swells too much with the rain."

"Then let's hurry."

~

COLIN HARRISON WATCHED HIS COMMANDING OFFICER UP ahead, chatting easily as he rode with Capt. Manning.

They were only just out of camp, the sun had barely shaken itself loose of the horizon, and already his uniform, such as it was, was stuck to him as if he'd walked fully clothed through a river. He wished for a horse, himself.

Sweat ran down his back and into his eyes, made his neck sting. The high pitched buzz of cicadas bored into his head. He looked longingly at the patches of shade made by the thorn trees scattered across the landscape.

"Look there." Harry Stokes, marching beside him, pointed to a returning picket, coming around the bend of the hill with the ease and unity of a bonded group. "I'll be. Jumping Jack isn't on a horse. He's walking with his men."

"Why do you call him Jumping Jack?" Colin squinted into the light, and saw Captain Burdell leading the picket on foot.

"Eh? Don't you know the story?"

Colin shook his head and Harry grinned. Colin rubbed his dry lips with the back of his hand and waited patiently for the story. What else was there to do in this God forsaken hellhole? It might take his mind off the heat and the blisters on his feet.

"Last year, back in the Border Wars, his company were creeping up on a Xhosa camp in the bush, when all of a sudden, Captain Jack steps on a snake. It sort of flings itself up to strike him and he jumps with it, grabs its head and throws it as hard as he can away from them, without making a sound to alert the Xhosa."

Colin was impressed. "A cool customer, then."

"Cool as they come. 'E's the kind of commander you want in the thick of battle. The kind that'll try to get you out in one piece, not dash you against a brick wall for the look of the thing."

"Not one of the upper classes, then?"

"Landed gentry, I heard," Harry tapped the side of his nose. "They ain't poor, but he's not one of those nobs with titles. He 'as the look of a lad who worked the farm about him."

They were quiet as they watched the picket disappear over a rise, making for camp.

Colin fumbled for his Oliver, hoping no more of the wood inside the water bottle had rotted off. Nothing worse than getting a mouthful of rotting wood chips to choke on when you were thirsty.

"Looks empty out there, don't it?" Harry looked off into the distance, and Colin followed his gaze. There was nothing but green grass, low bush, and thorn trees, far as the eye could see. He grunted in agreement.

"I bet it's not, though. What you reckon would happen if the Zulus all came down on Number 3 Column at once?"

"Ha, ha." Colin tried for sarcasm, but he'd thought the same thing more than once.

"Ignore him." Jenkins said, from Harry's left side. "A

right card, our Harry." He sniffed. "Chelmsford obviously thinks we can handle them."

Colin wished he could be so sure. He shrugged. "We're the ones with the rifles, aren't we?" He lifted the water flask to his mouth and steeled himself for the bits. "And the cannons." Choking, he spat out two small pieces of his bottle's inner lining.

"Yeah. Cannons that can barely make it over the ground," Harry muttered, and surreptitiously passed a silver flask of booze over. "Here, wash out the taste of that water."

"We'll hardly engage them on the move," Jenkins scoffed. "We'll find a good spot and dig in, make the blighters come to us."

"And if they don't?" Colin unscrewed the silver lid. "Cheers, mate." He took a swig of the local homemade brew and gasped. Handed back the flask with throat burning. He took a breath, thumping himself on the chest with a fist. "What if they're just like the bloody Xhosa and jump out at you. Ambush you. What if they won't fight?"

"Then we keep marching 'til we reach oNdini," Jenkins said.

Colin shook his head. "When is anything ever that easy?"

The whole unit was slowing, and Colin craned to see what was happening up ahead. It looked like the two officers had halted their mounts and were looking through their field glasses. Had they sighted the enemy?

"They've spotted some game off to the right. Some kudu." The word rippled back along the lines.

Colin saw his captain lean down and speak to his second in command, and then both officers took off at a canter.

"Aren't we on an urgent mission to guard the pontoons at Rorke's Drift?" he asked no one in particular.

"Aye. And Captain Manning's accompanying us to assess

the column's requirements at the crossing point." Jenkins lifted his eyebrows.

"Doesn't seem to have stopped either of them getting in a quick hunt." Harry's voice was deadpan.

"No," said Colin, "it doesn't." He'd seen so much of this kind of thing in the last five years, it didn't surprise him anymore.

"Step lively, lads. We want to get to Rorke's Drift before dark," the sergeant yelled from the front.

Hurry up and wait, thought Colin, bitterly. Hurry up and bloody wait.

It would all be over a year from now, though, thank God. That is, if the fever, mosquitoes or wild savages didn't get him first.

THE STINK OF MEN AND HORSES STEWING IN THE HUMIDITY HIT Jack full force as he led his company back into the Helpmekaar camp.

"The veld was better 'n this, Captain," Harolds shouted out.

"You want to go back there?" Jack called, with a smile. "Volunteer for another patrol?"

Harolds was right. The lush green summer veld was definitely better than this smelly mini-town of tents and livestock.

"Let's see if the food's improved, first," someone else said, and there was general laughter.

"Captain Burdell."

Jack looked up to see who hailed him and spied Lieutenant Chambers, the quartermaster for the 2nd 24th Battalion, sitting at a desk under the awning of his tent.

"Lieutenant." Jack saluted.

"We received some equipment while you were patrolling. I need you to sign for it." Chambers' eyes flicked from soldier to soldier, as if calculating the cost to his precious stores.

Jack ordered his men to pitch camp, then joined Chambers in his tent.

"Tell the lads not to get too settled. I hear we're moving out shortly." Chambers sounded unhappy.

Jack looked up from the list of items in his hand, and quirked an eyebrow.

"I thought the ultimatum Frere gave the Zulus only expired on January 11th."

"Yes, and I hear Lord Chelmsford intends setting foot across the border into Zululand on that very day." Chambers sniffed. "With this blasted rough country, it'll take us days just to get to the border with all our supplies, even though it's only a distance of ten miles."

Jack pressed his lips together. He was a professional soldier. He fought when he was told to. That didn't stop him coming to his own conclusions.

Chelmsford's assumption the Zulu king would not have managed to do all that was demanded of him by the date set spoke volumes. Chelmsford knew full well his demands were impossible to comply with.

A dirty way to declare war, in Jack's mind.

The thought of another round of skirmishes, scrappy and vicious, such as he'd just experienced in the Eastern Cape against the Xhosa, wearied him.

"Lord Chelmsford still with us?" Jack signed at the bottom of the list with a flourish, pressing his quill down hard as he spoke.

He hoped Chelmsford was gone. The general's presence

undermined the column commander's authority, putting Colonel Glyn in an awkward position and a foul mood. When Chelmsford was off elsewhere inspecting the other columns, things were much calmer.

"He's still here, so tell your lads to look lively."

Jack nodded but didn't reply. He handed the requisition over.

"I have the post that arrived for your men and yourself." Chambers bent down and pulled a box from a stack on the floor. "The 2nd 24th mess times are on this chit."

Jack took the schedule and the post and began making his way through the camp, his eyes on the handwriting of the top parcel in the box, addressed to him.

His sister never wrote to him, certainly never sent him anything. She was a busy mother and wife, she left the letter-writing to their mother.

With a sense of foreboding, he pulled the packet out, fiddling with the string one-handed as he walked. When he couldn't open it he lifted it to his teeth and snapped it, pulling at the brown paper wrapping to reveal a single page letter resting on top of a leather-bound journal.

Dear Jack

I am sorry to be the one to tell you the news. Mother died yesterday . . .

JACK STOPPED AMID THE NOISE AND THE HEAT AND THE STINK. Lifted his face, eyes closed, to the sky. His reason for being a soldier had just ended.

CHAPTER SEVEN

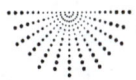

The only guarantee which we can have for the securing of peace, short of breaking up the Zulu power, is the maintenance of so large a force on their front as the Imperial Government could not keep up, or South Africa maintain. We have now such a force at our disposal; we shall never again have it. [. . .] The time has arrived for decisive action; [. . .] if it is lost, sooner or later we shall be taken at a disadvantage.

— MR. BROWNLEE: SECRETARY FOR NATIVE
AFFAIRS, CAPE COLONY

Malusi handed Elizabeth an arm-full of British uniforms and grinned. "Rather you than me in those hot things."

Elizabeth lifted a white undershirt to her nose and

sniffed. It smelled of sunshine and soap, just like her father's clothes once had. "They're clean."

She was surprised and delighted. She'd been expecting the bloodstained clothing of a man killed to provide her with a uniform. The guilt had gnawed at her since she'd agreed to this; although, if she did a good job, surely hundreds of men would die because of her?

She tried to push the guilt away, but it lay like a tough piece of meat in her stomach. Perhaps it was right that she feel it. Wouldn't it make her a monster if she did not regret the lives she would be responsible for taking?

"We stole them from where they lay drying in the grass after being washed. The whitemen playing in the water didn't even see us." Malusi looked highly amused at the thought of leaving a group of redcoats buck naked.

From the way the other scouts who'd accompanied him were laughing amongst themselves as they squatted around the fire, they found it just as funny.

Elizabeth grinned back. She liked the casual camaraderie of the scout camp, hidden behind a small hill on the edge of the Zululand border.

"Put the clothes on and I will show you how the whitemen hold their rifles." Malusi moved to join the others at the camp fire, to get something to eat after his thievery, and Lindani joined her as she shook out a pair of over-patched trousers to see if they would fit.

"I'm afraid you aren't ready for this, Inyoni." He looked at the shabby uniforms doubtfully.

"I have to make myself ready, then." Elizabeth shrugged and he reached out a hand and grabbed her chin, forcing her to look at him, at how serious he was.

"You are going to your death."

"What would you have me do?" she asked softly, trying

to keep her voice from carrying to Malusi and the other scouts joking around the fire. "Defy the general? Neither you nor I would be in favour if I did. And the general is right, if I leave Zululand and throw myself on the mercy of the British, I'll become their pawn. They'll use my being in Zululand as another way to justify this war. I'd rather be a pawn of the Zulus. At least I'm on the side of my own choosing."

"Let the British use you for more leverage. At least you'd be safe. Can one more reason for war amid all the other lies they tell make that much difference?"

Elizabeth stabbed a foot into blue trousers with red piping and hopped on one leg. "Why should I be safe when you are not? When Nosipho and everyone else in the village is not?"

"Why should we be unsafe at all?" The fight had gone out of Lindani at her mention of his pregnant wife, and his hand crept to his *isiCoco*, the ring of fibre woven into his hair to show he was married. He sank to the ground, watching her pull on a shirt. It hung mid-thigh on her, and she used the shield it gave her to modestly push her grass skirt over the trousers and off.

She would need to bind her breasts, but otherwise the uniform was big enough to hide her figure. She did up the buttons, shrugged on the jacket and crouched beside Lindani.

"I need your help, Lindani." She touched his shoulder lightly before reaching for the least holey pair of socks and smallest pair of boots.

"You have it." He scrubbed angry hands over his face. As neatly trapped by the general as she.

Elizabeth realized the scouts had gone ominously still, and she and Lindani looked toward them together.

Malusi and the others stood, transfixed, staring down the

hill. Along the floor of the valley, an *ibutho*, a Zulu army battalion, was rounding the corner, jogging as one. Precise, focused and swift. Three thousand men or more, the sweat glistening off their bare arms and chests in the sun, the civet tails of their *umuTsha* swaying in rhythm.

The front runners sang as they ran, and the warriors responded, the sound of their voices echoing through the hills.

Elizabeth shivered at their sense of purpose, at the spectacle of power.

The Zulu *impi* was on the move, called by the King. Gathering for war.

"What a sight," Lindani breathed next to her, and he seemed entranced. Drugged by the vision of devastating strength.

They watched until all they could see was the dust thrown up by thousands of running feet. How could they lose any war with such as those on their side?

When compared to the sorry, over-dressed and under-fed redcoats just across the border, it seemed impossible to believe victory could be anyone's but theirs.

"Ready?" Malusi was subdued. Awestruck. He held a rifle in his hands. "We've set up a shield over there for target practice." He pointed to an open area of veld where a shield rested against a thorn tree.

Still quiet, still gripped by the splendour of what they had seen, they waded through the long grass and stood a hundred feet from the target. Elizabeth held the rifle in her hands, smoothing her palms over the polished wood of the butt.

"This isn't the same rifle as the guards at the camp had."

Malusi shook his head.

"Where does this one come from, then?" She tugged at

the collar of her red jacket. It was only mid morning, and the heat was making her jacket itch, the sweat pooling between her breasts and running down her back. The coarse cotton of her shirt chafed against the burnt skin on her shoulders.

"This is part of the consignment John Dunn brought in for King Cetshwayo."

"John Dunn, who's gone across to the British? The whiteman who betrayed us?" Lindani took the rifle out of her hands and examined it.

Malusi nodded. "The guns he bought for the King look old compared to the ones the whiteman's army has. I think we were cheated."

"Maybe these were cheap." Lindani lifted it up, turned it over in his hands.

"Have you told the general?" Elizabeth tugged the rifle out of Lindani's grip and lifted it to her eye, looked down the sight at the target half a field away.

"I have told him. But what does it matter? Which of us like to use these things anyway?"

Elizabeth turned to Lindani. "Have you ever shot a gun?"

He shook his head. "I don't fight the coward's way."

"You should learn. You all should. You need to fight bullets with bullets." Even as she spoke, she knew she was wasting her breath. Only a battle against an army of guns would convince them.

Malusi wiped the sweat off his brow and clicked his tongue. "You are wrong, my sister. The *inyangas* are making powerful *muti*. When our shields are sprinkled with this *muti*, the bullets will not pierce them."

Taking aim, Elizabeth pulled the trigger and stumbled back as the rifle kicked in her hands. The blast startled a flock of hadedas, and they rose in a squawking, iridescent mass, pounding the air with their wings.

The three of them tramped across the green field to the shield, Elizabeth rubbing her shoulder as she went.

She saw her aim had been true. Beginner's luck, because she barely knew what she was doing.

She'd hit the shield high to the left, where a heart would be. And the bullet had gone through the hide. She lifted the shield away, and saw the bullet embedded deep in the thorn tree trunk behind it.

"This shield didn't have any *muti* on it," Malusi said defensively as she stood looking at the bullet, not saying anything.

They turned from the tree, and walked back to camp in silence.

∽

1 JANUARY, 1879

MY DEAREST CECELIA,

How are you and little Harry? I think of you both so much and wonder how you are doing.

I am well. My company has been sent ahead of the main column to a place called Rorke's Drift, which is right on the Buffalo River which forms part of the Natal border with Zululand.

There are all sorts of rumours flying around, and one is that the Zulus are going to storm across the river at any moment and invade Natal.

So my company have been sent to the border early to guard the place on the river where Lord Chelmsford plans to cross into Zululand. There are pontoons here to take the oxen that pull our wagons and the wagons themselves across, and they must be kept safe.

It is very boring, unfortunately, because we are all very much of the opinion that the Zulus are nowhere near here. We've seen a few of them, but they are cattle herders at best, and they keep to their side of the river.

One very strange thing has happened, though, which caused quite a ruckus here. After weeks of traveling from Pietermaritzburg, and then hunkering down at Helpmekaar, where the majority of the Central Column still sits, the boys and I took the chance to clean our uniforms.

Cecelia, I am sure that if you passed me in the street a few days ago, you'd have staggered back at the smell, so ripe were we all.

There was no water for washing at Helpmekaar, and our clothes were in a particularly bad state. So those of us not on guard duty went down to the river, stripped off and washed our clothes with some soap we got off the quartermaster.

The water was so lovely, and the day so hot (so strange to think how cold it is for you in Monmouthshire, and how very hot for me), we started playing about in it while our clothes dried, and we were having such laughs, it must have been quite some time later that one of us noticed our clothes had gone.

Every single last stitch!

Well, it caused much hilarity and teasing when we were forced to walk naked as babes back to the mission house at Rorke's Drift which has become our headquarters, and confess to having lost five 24th Battalion uniforms.

Even more concerning for Captain Gilford is the matter of who has taken our uniforms and what they intend to do with them.

If it was the Zulus, which we all doubt, then they are sadly mistaken if they think they can don them and pass themselves off as members of the 24th.

There are, of course, natives of this country fighting with us against the Zulu, some formed together in a contingent called the Natal Native Contingent. Most of them are sent by chiefs who have fallen out with the Zulu king, and some are from other tribes the Zulus have crushed and dispossessed at one time or another. But they all wear either their own tribal war gear, or yellow corduroy uniforms which look nothing like ours. Only someone with a white skin could get away with wearing our kit.

We think this was a prank played on us by children of a nearby village, and a few of us will go over there later today and enquire if their parents have seen the uniforms. In the meanwhile, this has turned out to be a boon for the five of us, as we have had new uniforms issued, after a few days of having to make do with anything that might cover us. Imagine me with a blanket around me and nothing else!

Now I have a new uniform, I actually feel like a soldier again, instead of a vagabond.

The messenger is leaving shortly with the post, so I will end this now with all my love and best wishes.

Colin

CHAPTER EIGHT

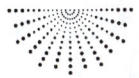

What have I done to the Great White Chief? I hear from all parts that soldiers are around me;

> — KING CETSHWAYO'S MESSAGE TO BORDER
> AGENT, LOWER TUGELA

The package lay on the small desk, and Jack had completed every duty. Not a single excuse left not to read Cathy's letter and find out what she'd sent him. He couldn't undo his mother's death by not reading the letter. Time to stop being a coward.

He walked across to his tent flap and closed it, relishing the privacy.

He'd felt sorry for Bob Harries when he'd come down with dysentery and had to be sent home, but he wasn't sorry at all to have his Bell tent to himself. This was not something to read in the company of others.

He eased into the hard wooden folding chair and picked up the thick sheet of paper his sister had written on.

Dear Jack

I am sorry to be the one to tell you the news. Mother died yesterday. I went to wake her at around eight in the morning, as she wasn't yet up, to find she had passed away in the night. Her face looked peaceful and I think perhaps that's the best way to go. Quietly in your sleep.

I know there is no way you can be home soon, if you even get this letter within the month. So I am going ahead with the burial arrangements.

Mr. Hamilton, Mother's solicitor, has been round to say I am to have some money from Father's account and Mother's jewelry. The rest of the money goes to you and of course the farm has been yours since Father's death.

Henry will continue managing it until you are able to let us know what you wish to do. He will be angry if he knew I said this to you, but I hope that you do not want to sell it. It is our home and our children's home.

I enclose a journal written by Father that I found in Mother's bedside table, which I never knew about. It seems to be a record of his time in the Punjab addressed specifically to you. Strange that Mother never mentioned it with Father dead these past six years or more.

There are many things to do, and I must finish off now. I know you will be as grief-stricken as we are, and our only comfort is knowing Mother had a good and happy life.

Best regards and much love,
Catherine

JACK LEANED BACK, HIS FINGERS TAPPING THE LETTER LYING ON his desk. It was so very much like Cathy. Practical, to the point, almost unemotional.

Mother's last letter had been full of local gossip and news of Cathy's children, it seemed impossible to believe she could be gone. Her smile and her calm had once seemed eternal.

He glanced at the date on Cathy's letter. His mother had been dead nearly two months and he hadn't known it.

Guilt needled him.

He'd put a distance between them these last few years. A distance he'd never explained or tried to bridge.

With her so fiercely proud of him, he couldn't be honest with her about his growing disillusionment with the army. But he could not lie either, so he'd said nothing.

His heart felt hollowed out, and he wanted to run or ride, fast as he could, out into the open bush.

He bowed his head, forcing his drumming fingers and tapping foot still, thinking to pray, but no words would come. He'd gotten out of the habit of prayer or thought of God. Living in the veld, fighting the Xhosa, had taken up everything in him.

He thought of his mother's face, rosy-cheeked and lined, her eyes sparkling. He hoped there was a heaven. That she was in a happy place.

Then he reached forward, took up the dark blue journal his sister had sent him, and plunged into his father's hell.

ENTRY WRITTEN SEPTEMBER, 1871

I WATCH YOU HELPING SID OUTSIDE WITH THE FARM, JACK, AND

I have the feeling I would do anything to keep you from the army. I'm writing this in part to dissuade you, in part for my own, personal, reasons.

I have medals for my service, but I also have a piece of shrapnel in my lung, and when I have to go inside, like now, and sit by the fire with nothing to do but watch you and Sid work, I wonder how I can keep you from taking up a commission.

You don't have to get your hands dirty, but you do anyway. You get stuck in. You're not one to sit around and watch others work. Seeing that, I know you would make an excellent officer and I spend my time occupied in thinking of a way to prevent it.

The short answer is, I can't. I've seen that look in your eye when I talk about farming being a noble occupation, and a vital one. Seen you thinking of a blue officer's coat, with a smart gold belt.

I know you have to make your own mistakes. I made enough of my own in my time.

Perhaps you will indulge your old man's reminiscence of his misadventures?

When I went off to fight the Sikhs, I believed we were off to bring an upstart people to heel. I never thought about the wrong or right of it, I never thought of our heavy guns against their light ones.

And all that said, for all their inferior weapons and the supposed superiority of the British in every way, the Sikhs still gave us a hiding at Chillianwallah. The worst hiding the British army has seen for a long time.

They beat the arrogance right out of me.

CHAPTER NINE

Until made a military depot [the Helpmekaar camp] consisted of two houses. Now there is a Govt. Store and white tents now dot the hill top. It is cold at night with as far as I have experienced it hot sun and cool breezes by day.

— AN ENTRY IN THE DIARY OF LT. COGHILL,
COL. GLYN'S ORDERLY OFFICER.

He had thirty minutes before the start of the special lunch the 1st Battalion had organized – a lunch that was directly to do with the contents of the journal in Jack's hands.

He'd joined his father's old battalion, and he'd always had a vague knowledge of what had happened to the 24th Regiment during the Second Sikh War. And a very specific knowledge of what had happened to its soldiers. He had only to look at his father, old and tired before his time, for that.

Around him, his fellow officers started making their way to the mess tent, but rather than wait in cramped, airless conditions for terrible food, Jack set his chair in the shade of his tent and opened his father's diary. Since he'd started the journal last night, if felt as if his father was alive again, so clearly did his voice come through the pages.

He'd had an evening picket duty, and no time since he'd woken this morning to look at another entry, but he was surprised at how eager he was to read more.

His father had been vague about his engagements with the Sikhs when he was a boy, trying to discourage his interest, he understood now.

But instead it had made the whole thing more mysterious, more exciting. His father should have spoken up, rather than kept quiet.

It seemed his father was speaking up now.

Entry written October, 1871

We were so green, all of us. There was a suppressed excitement at being in India, out on an adventure.

We were such fools.

We had heavy gun power and the skills to fire them, but that was about our only claim to superiority. That and the fact that we were supposedly a cohesive force.

The Sikh Army had been betrayed by their own leaders in the First Sikh War, and there was not much love lost between some of the divisions under General Shere Singh in this Second Sikh War. Afterwards, we heard some of the divisions did turn coat and fight for our side.

As it was, before we saw action we were happy to be fighting under Gough. The little Irishman was a soldier's commander. He would run around in the thick of battle dressed in a white coat. His battle coat, he called it, to draw enemy fire away from the men and to him.

He always kept our needs in mind, and we would have done anything for him.

We did do anything for him – even when he ordered us to attack the Sikhs, hunkered down with guns in entrenched positions, head on.

Jack closed the book.

Would he do anything Chelmsford asked of him? Or Glyn?

He looked up at the dirt-speckled canvas of his tent awning, opaque with sunshine, and considered.

He would have to, but he didn't have the same blind loyalty his father wrote about. That innocent enthusiasm for the fight, the hero-worship of the men in charge, had been chiseled off him, one painful tap at a time.

All he had left was the oath he'd sworn to fight and obey orders. And the responsibility for the lives of the men he commanded.

It was a hollow motivation. And if weighed on a scale, it was to his men, to individuals, that he now gifted his loyalty.

The level of sound in the mess tent rose – a sure indication that lunch was almost ready – and Jack reluctantly put the journal away and made his way to it.

He took his place on a wooden crate as the column

commander, Col. Glyn, stood and tapped his glass with a spoon for silence over the rowdy crowd. The 1sts had done what they could to accommodate the officers of both battalions of the 24ths for this luncheon, and Jack was impressed with their inventiveness.

"I would firstly like to thank the officers of the 2nd 24ths for accepting our invitation. It has been a long time since the 1st and 2nd battalions of the 24th Regiment have served together in the field. The last time was in India, and although none of us present today were members of this regiment during the Second Sikh War, we remember the tragedy of the Battle of Chillianwallah with much regret and sad hearts."

A round of hear, hears went up and then true silence fell over the group.

"To lose so many men and officers in a single maneuver was a dark moment in this proud regiment's history. Exactly a week short of thirty years ago, nearly half our number were cut down by the Sikhs. I would propose a toast to those who fell at Chillianwallah. May it never happen again."

"Chillianwallah," Jack toasted, along with the others, "may it never happen again." He looked around the room, at the raised glasses and the sombre faces. Wondered if he was the only one here who thought the toast was in vain.

It would happen again.

He knew his fellow officers too well. Knew the type of men who commanded them.

It wasn't necessarily the 24ths that would suffer – hopefully fate wouldn't be so cruel as to visit that kind of massacre on them again – but someone would, somewhere. They were meddling in enough places for it to be only a matter of time.

He flung the last drop of his drink down his throat and realized he was sick of himself. Sick of his own ill-humour.

He thought back to the day his cynicism had been sharpened to a fine point six months ago, in the undulating hills of the Eastern Cape. The incident that had changed him forever.

He remembered the gunfire, the shouting, and then the sharp, stinging pain of a bullet in his shoulder. How the ground seemed to rush up at him.

He was about to call out when a Xhosa warrior burst from the bush and leapt over him. The man halted his flight and turned back, and Jack thought it was all over.

The warrior leant over him, close enough for him to see the complex bead necklace at his throat, and then spoke in broken English, no doubt learned on the diamond mines.

"Why are you trying to break us, whiteman? Do you not have enough of everything already?"

Before Jack could reply, the man spun around and raced across the small clearing. Just before he disappeared into the bush, Jack heard the crack of rifle fire and saw the warrior's body jerk. Saw him fall.

A man truly broken.

"Don't look so down, old chap." Major Carr slapped him lightly on the back as he passed. "The beef goes down all right if you chew it enough."

"This is beef, sir?"

Carr laughed and moved on.

"Well, no need to think this campaign will be anything like the Punjab, eh." Sitting next to him, Timothy Shaw waved his fork in the air. "The Sihks had guns. This lot haven't even got those. They don't even have any decent rifles if the intelligence is accurate." He speared a piece of beef. "Poor buggers don't stand a chance."

CHAPTER TEN

It is necessary that the Zulu army, as it is now, shall be disbanded, and that the men shall return to their homes . . .

— PART OF FRERE'S ULTIMATUM TO KING
CETSHWAYO, 11 DECEMBER, 1878

The lanterns swinging from the ox-wagons of the column stretched out like a Chinese street decoration, but crouched up against a thorn tree, Elizabeth could hear there was no joyous festival being held on the track below.

In contrast to the Zulu *ibutho* they'd seen four days ago, running swift and sure, this army looked in disarray, a stumbling parade of wagons, cattle and men.

The pre-dawn sky rang with shouts and swearing as the men struggled to get the wagons over the rough ground. Two had already lost a wheel and they were still in sight of the lights of the Helpmekaar camp.

Last night there had been another massive thunderstorm and the dust had turned to mud, the track to a boggy mess. As if nature herself was impeding the British advance.

The time had come. She needed to slip among the redcoats before dawn broke, under cover of the sharp, chill darkness – the only time of day wearing the layers of uniform was welcome.

She turned one last time, looking up the hill where she knew Malusi and Lindani lay, watching despite the dark to make sure all went well. More a gesture than anything else, for even if they could see what was happening below, there was nothing they could do to help her if she was discovered.

She was on her own. She'd known she would be from the beginning. She rose cautiously, running clammy palms along the sides of her trousers, and began to pick her way down the short incline to the track below. The hill was treacherous with mud, and she was forced to slide from thorn tree to thorn tree, ducking to avoid the vicious thorns of their branches.

Her boots felt strangely uneven, the red mud caked under them so thickly it was like a second sole. She reached the bottom and stumbled behind a cart with a stuck wheel, the oxen dragging it through the mud and lowing as they took the strain.

"Hey, you."

Elizabeth almost fell full length into the slush as she tripped over her fear.

"I need a hand with the ammo."

She turned, saw an officer holding a lantern, its light illuminating a sharp nose and brown, floppy hair. Quick grey eyes narrowed as she hesitated.

"Yes, sir," she replied.

"Well, then, jump to it. And where is your helmet?"

Her helmet! She'd left it on the hillside. "I don't know, sir," she whispered.

"Well, see you find it." The man eyed her critically. "My God, Her Majesty must be desperate to take them so young. You don't even need to shave yet, boy. Sounds like you could still be singing the high notes in the church choir, eh?"

Elizabeth bit her lip.

"Well, we need to unload this cart, so I want those ammo boxes transferred to this wagon in double time. Which company are you?"

Heart in her mouth, Elizabeth moved past him and grabbed the first box of ammunition. "I'm the replacement quartermaster's aide for the 2nd 24ths, sir. The former one is down with a fever."

"Are you, by God?"

Elizabeth didn't need a sixth sense to know she'd made a terrible mistake. His tone was sarcastic, disbelieving, and every instinct she had screamed at her to bolt. But she couldn't run. She needed to see this through.

"Yes, sir." She brazened it out, throwing the ammo box from the crippled wagon onto the cart behind it, and the officer winced.

"Be careful with that. If the bullets dent, they jam in the barrel."

"Sorry, sir."

"It just so happens I am Lieutenant Chambers, quarter-master for the 2nd 24ths, and your new boss. Now who the hell appointed you my aide and didn't bother telling me about it?"

Elizabeth slammed another box of bullets into the cart, untwisting her tongue.

"Captain Burdell, sir." She was digging a hole for herself. It was getting deeper by the minute, but if Chambers would just go off in high dudgeon to find the officer who had taken such an interest in her a week before, she could disappear. There were four thousand troops here, there must surely be a place she could hide.

Giving up, going back to Malusi, wasn't a choice.

"But I just saw him," Chambers spluttered, no longer as sure in his anger as he had been when faced with Elizabeth's glib reply, and her heart sank lower.

Just her luck and Burdell would be–

"Ah. Burdell. Come here, there's a good chap."

Four thousand men on the move in terrible conditions in the dark, and she chose to join them at the very place Captain Burdell lurked like a tripwire.

Her mind went blank and her body began to shake. She darted a look back to the bush. Would Chambers come after her if she ran?

He clamped a firm hand on her shoulder and the thought shriveled and died.

"What is it now?" Burdell's voice held the edge of a man nearing the end of his patience and he loomed out of the shadows, his face half-lit by Chambers' lantern. This summons was the last of many straws, by the sound of it. Or rather, the second last.

Elizabeth had no doubt she would be breaking the camel's back.

She'd been a spy for five minutes and she was already a failure.

The only way out now was pleading. Or running.

Chambers shoved her in front of him, and she lifted her gaze to Burdell's, saw him suck in a breath at the sight of her, his body stiffening.

"Do you know this boy?" Chambers asked him.

Burdell nodded, a deep frown creasing his brow.

"Well, he tells me you assigned him to be my aide. What the hell is going on?"

Burdell's jaw dropped.

Charlotte looked up at him, with no attempt to hide the desperation and fear she felt. It would sway him to help her, or it wouldn't, but she had nothing to lose.

Although why would he help her? Why on earth would he?

"I . . . heard Rhys was down with a fever." Burdell spoke slowly, his eyes never leaving her face.

"Well, yes. Damned inconvenient, not that it's his fault, poor chap."

"Er, this boy is . . . my new batman, and you know I prefer to do mostly for myself, so I thought I'd loan him to you during the day. Help you out until someone officially assigns you a replacement."

He ran a hand through his hair, dark as the shadows that surrounded him, as if questioning his sanity. "Sorry I didn't mention it before, totally slipped my mind earlier in the chaos." His hand moved vaguely to indicate the men and wagons passing to their right.

"That's jolly decent of you, Burdell." Chambers released his hard grip on her shoulder, and Elizabeth suppressed an urge to rub it. "An extra pair of hands will come in useful. Much obliged."

"Think nothing of it." Burdell's eyes were fixed on her, holding her gaze. They glittered in the lamp-light, unreadable.

"Well, if you're happy for me to have him now, I'll put him to work." Chambers lifted up another box of ammo and handed it to her, and Elizabeth pretended it weighed nothing as she hefted it across from the crippled cart to the wagon.

"Most certainly." Burdell quirked his lips. "I won't need the little blighter 'til tonight, anyway, but I just need a quick word with him, if you don't mind?"

Chambers waved expansively, and a large, strong hand snaked out and grabbed Elizabeth's forearm. He jerked her across the track.

They had to weave through the men and the carts streaming in full flood along the makeshift road, and she was pushed and jostled into him, bumping into his back. She tried to jerk away, almost bending backwards, afraid he would feel her breasts, but his stride did not falter, and he dragged her a little way into the bush.

"Now is not the time, but I expect an explanation." He spoke so low, she shouldn't have been able to hear him over the noise, but she could.

Very clearly.

She nodded and he gave her another piercing stare.

"Don't make me come and find you, either. Because I will."

Elizabeth jerked her arm back, stared at him, speechless.

He gave her one last, hard look, and dove into the river of men and wagons. Elizabeth stood a moment longer, trying to make sense of it.

By some miracle, Burdell had saved her skin. She couldn't fathom why, but there would be an accounting tonight.

From the look in Burdell's eyes, Elizabeth was quite sure he'd track her down to the very depths of hell, if he had to.

A MAN COULD GO ALONG, AND GO ALONG, GENERALLY unhappy, getting closer to the edge, and then suddenly, he was there. Right there, able to fall either way, and frankly, the dark, shadowy side was by far the more tempting.

Dark and wild, able to make him feel again. Although Jack's first plunge into lies and treachery may well get him court-martialled.

The death of his mother, the discovery of his father's last missive to him, the depth of fear and pleading in a pair of huge green eyes . . . he must be getting soft.

Swayed from his better judgment by some boy up to no good–

Scratch that. Jack knew he was a she. He'd tried to over-ride his senses with his eyes, but it was no use, and crossing the track with her breasts pressing against his back, with those few moments alone in the bush, had confirmed it.

Outwardly, dressed in her soldier's uniform, with her cropped hair, no doubt she did look like a boy.

A very pretty boy, but the eye and the brain had a way of glossing over anything that didn't quite fit. But, for Jack, there was something about her. He didn't know what it was, but no amount of layers, sunburn or grime could hide it.

He knew it was why she'd attracted his attention the first time he'd seen her.

"Burdell."

The call came from Shaw, astride his mount and forcing his way through the crush. Jack had to tip back his head to look at him.

"You're a way off from your men."

"Chambers needed a hand." Jack shrugged.

"And instead of asking one of your men to help him, you did it yourself." As usual, Shaw's tone was dry enough to turn this boggy mess into hard-packed earth.

"Just as easy for me to do it as anyone else."

Shaw made a face, as if to say it was useless talking to

him about such matters and pointed up ahead. "It's going to be a long day."

Another wagon had lost a wheel.

"Well, we've been on the move for two hours and we've made all of a quarter of a mile, haven't we?" Jack kept his voice light, but he was in a strange mood. Unsettled and dissatisfied, even though he'd taken his first leap into the dark unknown.

"You're a lot more flippant these days, Jack." Shaw waved a hand at him and rode off, his company just in sight.

Jack made no move to pick up his pace and catch his own men. He'd get there soon enough, especially at the rate they were moving.

It was worse than a flippant attitude. Since he'd been injured in the Cape he'd lost more than his respect for the army and his commanding officers. He'd lost his belief in what his country stood for.

∼

Entry written November, 1871

WINTER ALREADY HAS THE FARM FIRMLY IN ITS GRIP, AND MY lungs cannot last long before letting me down. Even though you're only sixteen, Jack, I can see the man you are going to be when you help Sid with some of the jobs. You'll be a right lad with the ladies, make no mistake. I feel thin and withered when you come tramping in, bringing the cold air and the smell of the farm with you.

You remind me of myself in India. Striding about, full of pep and energy. Eager.

We had no idea what was coming. How ridiculous our assumptions were.

The first major setback of the campaign was at Ramnagar. Gough was desperate to engage the enemy, but he'd been ordered not to cross the Chenab River. There was a heavy concentration of British forces laying siege at Multan, and Dalhousie, the Governor General, wanted Gough to wait until the siege was over and the siege army had rejoined Gough's column before taking on the main Sikh army.

Eager for action, Gough decided to take on a small detachment of the Sikh army at Ramnagar, on the south bank of the Chenab, so he wasn't technically disobeying orders.

But underestimating the Sikhs completely, he ordered troops in without much reconnaissance. He may as well have signed their death warrants, as unknown to us, Ramnagar was covered by the Sikhs from across the river by two heavy gun batteries and another on a small island in the middle of the river. As our cavalry horses got stuck in the sand, they and their riders were cut down. The losses were terrible.

Gough at his impetuous worst, Shere Singh at his wily best.

It was a lesson Gough wouldn't really take to heart until it was far too late.

CHAPTER ELEVEN

The Zulu tribe, originally insignificant, was raised to become the greatest native power in Africa, south of the Zambesi River, by the ability and military talent of Tshaka, one of its chiefs. The genius, instincts, and traditions of the people are all military; the nation, which is less than seventy years old, had become a compact military engine before the years of its existence had numbered twenty, and its very life depended at that time of its history upon the perfection of its aggressive and defensive powers.

— DESPATCH TO THE EARL OF CARNARVON
FROM SIR T. SHEPSTONE, ADMINISTRATOR
OF THE TRANSVAAL, JANUARY 5, 1878

"You joining us, or running along to your Ma, lad?" The soldier who called to her was standing around the fire with his mates, and Elizabeth ducked her head as eight pairs of eyes turned her way.

No.

She couldn't stand out. She couldn't be the outsider she felt.

"My Ma makes better food than the swill they're feeding me here, so I'd rather be running along to her," she called back from her perch on a rock, just within reach of the fire's glow. Her heart pounded so hard in her chest, they could surely hear it.

They laughed. Stopped watching her so intently.

"My Ma too, come to think of it," another of the men said, "and I never thought I'd be longing for *her* home cooking."

"Ah, Her Majesty's infantry. Take the Queen's shilling and learn to appreciate the comforts of home through the sore lack of 'em."

The men laughed again, out of proportion to the joke, and Elizabeth guessed there was more than just tea in the mugs they held in their hands.

"Aye, you'll never see that on a poster."

"Too right."

The men were relaxed now, turned back to the fire, and Elizabeth slipped off, moving into the darkness between two camp fires.

She wanted to avoid Captain Burdell, but she knew with certainty he'd come looking for her if she didn't find him, and she was afraid of what he'd do or say if she pushed him that far.

She moved between the tents of the common foot soldiers, towards the comparative luxuries of the officers' quarters.

The 2nd 24ths officers' mess tent was well-lit and the

sound of murmured conversation and the occasional bark of laughter drifted from the open flap.

Finding nowhere to sit that wasn't boggy, and too exhausted to stand, Elizabeth gave up and sank down, cross-legged, near the entrance to wait for Burdell. Her legs quivered with relief.

She tipped her head back, easing her neck and shoulders, and looked at the rain-cleared sky, thick with stars. For some reason, it made her want to cry and she bent her head forward, the tips of her fingers digging into the damp, spongy ground, wet from an afternoon shower.

Her uniform was damp from the rain, too, and the smell of wet wool filled her nostrils. The fabric clung, clammy and itchy, to her skin, and she loathed it. Wished to pull it off and let the cool night air flow over her.

Becoming a Zulu had unlocked a delight in physical sensation her earlier upbringing had done its best to suppress. Running out in the rain, feeling it streaming over her naked breasts and arms, or lying naked with her friends, chill from the sea, on the hot golden sand to bake in the sun like a lizard.

She would never have known these things had she not begged Lindani's father to allow her to stay in his chiefdom. Had Mandla, the sangoma, not decided she was a sacred bird of heaven, and thus a gift from the ancestors.

She would always be grateful.

Drawing up her knees, she used them as a place to rest her head, and closed her eyes. Chambers had kept her working almost without rest, and she had never been so physically tired in her life.

She hoped Burdell finished his fine dinner soon because –

A pair of well-polished black riding boots met her at eye-level.

"Been waiting long?" Burdell dropped to a crouch beside her, taking her by surprise, the warm leather and wool scent of him tickling her nose. His shoulders blocked her view of the stars and his eyes did not waver from her face.

Her mouth went dry. She shook her head, and swallowed hard.

"Come on then, we'll talk in my tent."

He rose, held out a hand, but Elizabeth ignored it, illogically afraid he would somehow feel she was a woman, with that one touch.

Where did she get these fancies?

He waited for her to scramble to her feet, saying nothing of her refusal of help, then turned on his heel and led the way.

With every step, Elizabeth forced her numbed mind to go through the excuses she had thought to use through the day.

She had to get it right, or she was exposed.

"I don't bite." Burdell's voice was amused as he waited for her in deep shadow.

I bet you do.

She stopped dead, surprised at how instantly the thought popped into her head. How . . . sexual it was.

She looked down at her feet.

"My tent is through here." He turned again, and negotiated the hazard of tent pegs and ropes, moving easily through them in the dark.

He must have eyes like a cat, she thought, tripping after him.

It was quiet here, the other officers all still socializing and drinking their fine wines and brandies in their mess. She was glad. She wanted no one overhearing her efforts at lying to someone whose only crime was to dig her out of her own hole.

Can't be helped.

Elizabeth knocked the guilt that rose up with the club of self-defense.

He was waiting for her again. This time, next to his tent. He held open the flap and she slipped in.

"I've been looking forward to this little talk all day." He dropped the flap behind them and moved with sure, confident movements into the pitch dark.

She said nothing, standing just within his tent as he lit a lamp. As the wick took, the light touched his face, highlighting the sharp contours of his cheeks and nose, the wings of his brows.

He blew out the match and looked at her, and his face had lost all traces of friendly bemusement.

"So tell me, what the hell are you playing at?"

"Playing at?" Despite steeling herself for this, she stuttered, her words tripping over themselves. It was going to be as bad as she feared.

"I mean, what the hell is a woman doing out here in the middle of bloody nowhere in a war zone?"

THE NOTION SLOWLY CREPT OVER HER AS SHE STOOD IN SILENT despair that just because he knew she was a woman didn't mean he assumed she was a spy. She was white, English; it was possible it would never cross his mind – anyone's mind – that she'd spy for the Zulus.

"My brother, sir." Hope lent a tremor to her voice. Elizabeth had pegged Burdell for a gentleman from the moment she met him. If she could fake tears, it would be easier to convince him, but she was no actress. Instead, she let her shoulders droop.

"My brother joined the 24ths. My mother died recently, and if I can't find him, my uncle inherits my family home, and I'm out in the cold."

"So you travelled all the way to Natal to find him?" His voice was explosive, and she winced at the thought of anyone coming to investigate.

"I had no choice. The army said he wasn't enlisted, so he must have joined up under an assumed name. This seemed the only way to find him." She made her voice soft, hoping to quieten him without actually telling him to pipe down.

"Good God." Softer this time, but still too loud.

"Will you turn me in?"

"I don't know, Private – I don't even know your name."

"Elizabeth . . . Bird."

He rubbed a long finger against the side of his temple, as if he were developing a headache.

"Please don't report me, sir. I don't think my brother is here. Maybe he deserted, especially if were under a false name, but there is no way I can get out of the column now, we've gone too far. I'm stranded in Natal until I can sneak on a ship home. If they discover me, they'll just throw me out the army, they won't care I'm in a strange country."

"I'm well aware of that." He spoke through gritted teeth. Shook his head. "And now you've involved me." He rubbed his hand through his hair again, just as he'd done this morning. "No one but myself to blame there."

"What are you going to do?" She whispered it, not because she wanted him to speak softer this time, but because she could hardly bear to hear the answer.

"I said you were my new batman, so that's what you'll be. And as for offering yourself as a replacement for Rhys, that was your own mistake, and probably punishment enough for all your sins."

74

Suddenly, he lifted a wooden folding chair and placed it before her, waiting for her to sit before sinking down into a second one.

"I really can be your batman, sir, if you tell me what to do." It added another layer of authenticity to her life in the camp, and Elizabeth couldn't help her eagerness.

He leant away from her, horror on his face. "Absolutely not. Do you know what the duties of a batman involve?"

Elizabeth shook her head.

"Helping me dress."

She said nothing, incapable of a response, and the silence stretched out between them.

"Exactly," he said at last. "You've forced me to choose between my duty and your well-being. I won't add to it by having you try to shave me every morning. Having you sleep in the tent will be bad enough."

"You will let me sleep in the tent?" She could hardly breathe with relief. Sleep with the one person who knew she was a woman? Sleep on the spare camp cot she saw folded in one corner instead of the damp ground? Share with only one person instead of seven smelly foot soldiers?

She wondered what he wanted out of it.

"You can't sleep with the enlisted men." He crossed his arms over his chest and scowled. "For a start the tents are already assigned, you'd have to find one that doesn't have its full quota of eight, and that'll draw attention to you. And then, of course, there is the small fact that you're a woman."

His voice twisted on the last word. He drew a shuddering breath and rubbed at his temple again. "If you think my conscience could allow me to send you out, vulnerable to God knows what amongst the enlisted men, you have no idea who you're dealing with."

An honorable man, she almost said, but didn't. "Thank you." She'd never meant it as much as she did now.

"Just keep your head down and don't attract attention."

"I'll be as invisible as possible," she said earnestly, "I promise I'll be no trouble."

He let out a laugh.

"Miss Bird, since the moment I set eyes on you, you've been nothing *but* trouble."

CHAPTER TWELVE

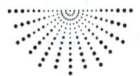

First comes the trader. Then the missionary. Then the red soldier.

— ZULU KING CETSHWAYO KAMPANDE

"Aaaah."

Jack raised an eyebrow at Elizabeth's groan. She had one boot off, and was tugging off the other. She caught his quizzical look and turned away, her face flushed.

"I'm not used to wearing shoe– boots."

She wiggled her toes through her socks, and he felt an almost unpleasant sensation of desire stir within him.

"Do you have any bags?"

She shook her head. "Just the clothes on my back."

Jack got up and rummaged in his chest. Took out a sleeping shirt, hand embroidered by his mother.

"You can have this to sleep in." It should be suitably

voluminous on her. She looked set on undressing, and he had to remind himself she wasn't a private. Didn't know how things were done.

The enlisted men slept in their uniforms. Lived in their uniforms. Which is why they looked like an army of vagabonds.

He held the nightshirt out and she stared at it, making no attempt to take it from him, as if confounded by the garment.

She looked otherworldly with her short, jagged hair and her big green eyes, some strange magical creature, suddenly dropped into reality.

"Thank you."

She rose from Bob Harries's abandoned cot and gently tugged the garment from his hand, then stood there, waiting.

"Sorry. I'll step outside while you change." He hadn't blushed since he was a lad, but he felt the heat in his cheeks and hoped the dim light hid it.

He walked out into the cool, clear night and wondered what in hell he was going to do.

Clasping his hands behind him, he rocked on his heels and tipped his head back to look at the sky. To keep quiet about a woman masquerading as a private was most definitely an offense. To speak up would ensure her being booted out of camp, and at most escorted back to Helpmekaar. From there, she'd have little or no options. But to allow her to continue with them . . . well, he'd be complicit in taking a woman onto the battlefield.

"I'm ready." Her voice was low and he clamped down hard on his back teeth. Her soft call sounded like a woman calling her lover to bed.

How long had it been since he'd slept with a woman?

Not since his injury in the Cape six months ago. Not for a good six months before that.

Like a man going to his last supper before execution, Jack walked reluctantly back into his tent.

∽

THE SMALL MISSION STATION OF RORKE'S DRIFT WAS AT LAST IN sight. Poised at the top of the Nostrope Pass, Elizabeth saw the winding Buffalo River and the green hills of Zululand spread out before her. Far in the distance, the peak of Isandl-wana rose out of the hazy plateau.

Excitement surged in her chest and she jumped over a rock in the path. Home had never looked more beautiful.

How would the British ever win this war? They could barely move their troops and supplies ten miles in three days. And Elizabeth knew the terrain got no better over the border.

"Jumping for joy, is it?" Private Johnson called from the ox-wagon behind her.

"The end is in sight, Johnson."

"Not the end, the beginning," Johnson muttered.

"At least it's the end of this trip." She grinned, too happy to let anything get her down. "We'll get some rest down there."

To her right, a mounted company of the Natal Native Contingent came past in their yellow uniforms. They were hailing each other in Zulu, and she looked at them longingly. Wished she were part of their circle, even though they were the enemy.

There were many men here who were from Natal; white farmers, and tribesmen sent by chiefs who wanted to see Cetshwayo crushed.

They were joking as they rode about having Zululand in sight. About the land and cattle that would soon be theirs.

"Wish you knew what they were saying, eh?" Johnson called to her.

Elizabeth shook her head. She understood all too well. They were poorly provisioned and poorly equipped, and if that didn't tell them how little their safety and comfort meant to the men who asked them to risk their lives for a British cause, they deserved what they got.

She shrugged her shoulders, forcing their problems from her mind. Tonight she would see Lindani. They'd agreed it was too soon to meet before then, had set the time and place before she'd even joined the column.

She missed him, missed speaking in Zulu.

Too many times to mention she'd heard the tribesmen in the Central Column speaking in the Zulu tongue, and found it hard to respond to Lieutenant Chambers in English.

"Bird. Less daydreaming, more working," Chambers yelled from his horse, riding between the wagons to check their progress down the treacherously steep road. "If you don't keep up, these wagons will arrive before you."

Not bloody likely, Elizabeth thought, but jogged obediently forward, resting her hand on the side of the ammunition cart. The whole cart bounced wildly as the driver hit a rock, forcing her to step away.

Chambers gave a squawk of distress. "I've told you to be careful with the ammunition," he shouted at the driver, galloping forward. "I don't want those bullets damaged."

Elizabeth stopped short. Chambers had said that to her before. The first time she'd met him.

"Bird, move your bloody arse. We need to get down there before the rest of the wagon train, and believe me, we'll be working way past sundown."

Johnson passed her in his wagon, and the look he sent her was conspiratorial. He made a gesture at Chambers' back that tugged a smile on her face.

She started moving forward again, her mind a swirl of damaged bullets and jammed guns. Of the pride of the British arsenal – useless.

ELIZABETH WANTED TO GO HOME. SHE STOOD, SWAYING WITH exhaustion next to her cot, and longed for it. Longed for sitting around the fire with the women and sharing stories of the day's work, of the children's exploits.

She shivered in the evening air as the stranglehold of heat began to lift, cooled like feverish flesh against the black satin of night.

If she could only talk to Lindani, ask if he had any news of home, she was sure this terrible fatigue that clung to her would lift.

Her nerves were stretched tight under her skin, making her jump at everything, making her hands flutter in fear at every meal, every time Chambers or one of the men looked too long at her face. She walked with her head down wherever she went, sure everyone was watching her.

She craved a moment of rest from being Private Bird. Surely even ten minutes of being Elizabeth, the bird of heaven, would ease the dread?

And what of Elizabeth Jones?

The question made her freeze mid-sway.

She had put Elizabeth Jones aside long ago. The young girl who was proper, obedient. Beloved child of Jonathan and Elaine, now lying in a grave in China. What life would Elizabeth Jones have had if she had reached England?

She slipped out of her jacket and flicked it with a snap to get rid of the dust, dismissing the twists of her exhausted mind. Despite how badly she longed to be home, to see Lindani, she was barely capable of putting one foot in front of another.

She couldn't sneak out now anyway, she reasoned, sitting with a groan and pulling the boots from her aching legs. Most of the men were still talking around the campfires, and she was too afraid someone would see her. Might as well get a bit of sleep first.

Her hand moved to the buttons of her shirt. Oh, to take off these terrible, terrible clothes. Layers of sweat-soaked fabric that clung to her, dragging her down. If only she could. The coarse rub of cotton and itch of wet wool, gone. The thought of it made her rest her hand on the button long after she'd decided she could not risk it.

She lay her head on the pillow, and drew her legs up to her chest, then stretched them out.

It had been a long day. So had every day, but helping Chambers organize the stores as they set up camp had been backbreaking.

Tonight, she had no reserves left.

As she sunk into sleep, she tried to think of Lindani, but instead, Jack Burdell's face came to her, lit from below by a lamp in the darkness, his stern brows almost meeting in a frown above his straight nose as he turned towards her, his eyes as blue as the Zululand sky.

THE WHISPER OF CLOTHES BEING REMOVED WOKE HER. SHE CAME to suddenly, with heart thundering, panic-stricken as to how much time may have passed. She made no sound or movement, lying still, her eyes half-closed as she watched Burdell in the weak candlelight.

His back was turned to her and he lifted his shirt over his head. She saw the sweet dividing line of his spine, the wide, muscular set of his shoulders, marred at the top by an angry scar.

And suddenly she felt weak.

Burdell had come in late every night during the awful trip from Helpmekaar to Rorke's Drift. When he spoke to her, which was as little as possible, he angled his body away, his eyes almost never meeting hers. And yet in the few times their gazes did clash and jerk away, there was a heat. An energy that made Elizabeth hot inside and as eager as Burdell to escape the confines of the tent, the forced intimacy, and get as far away from him as possible.

He unbuckled his belt and stepped out of his trousers, standing only in his drawers. She saw his hands go to his waist to unbutton them, watched as he began to slip them off, then stopped mid-thigh, cursed softly, and pulled them back on.

He was keeping them on because of her presence in his tent, she realized. She also realized something else. The Zulus were right to focus on the back of the upper thigh as an area of sexual titillation. She felt a curious, tight sensation in the pit of her stomach. She closed her eyes, and lay quietly, listening to him complete his bedtime rituals.

She would never look at him in the same way again.

At last, the deep, steady breathing from Burdell's side of the tent allowed her up from her cot. She bit down on a groan as she sat to pull on her boots, her body heavy, aching in every joint and muscle.

She hoped Lindani and Malusi were still waiting for her.

She had no idea of the time, but sensed it was long after they'd agreed to meet.

She edged off the low bed, careful to stop it creaking, and went to stand at the tent entrance, straining to hear any sound. Someone sniffed loudly close by. A hacking cough, from too many nights spent sleeping on rain-soaked ground, came from a few tents down.

Someone muttered close by and there was a rustle of clothing. Changing her mind, Elizabeth went to the back of the tent, lay down and rolled under the canvas.

Burdell's tent was at the edge of the camp, and she scrambled to her feet and slipped through the last few tents. Malusi had instructed her to head upstream and her way was lit faintly by the waning half moon, hanging clear in a sky that still harboured some of the rain clouds from the storm earlier.

Somewhere in the veld an animal hooted, a whoop of surprise or fear. It sounded close, but perhaps it came from the other side of the river. Most animals steered clear of the massive tent settlement, afraid of the noise and smells.

Even so, as soon as she was out of earshot of the camp, she trod loudly through the long, green grass to scare away the snakes, for once grateful for her boots.

She followed the river, cut deep in its bed of orange rock, until the camp was no long visible behind her.

She whistled, the sharp, carrying sound of the herd boys.

For a moment, there was silence, and then the whistle was answered. She saw Lindani's head pop up from the steep riverbank wall, saw the flash of white from his eyes and teeth. He pulled himself up easily, gracefully, and stopped short of her. She could see he was angry for the wait, his scowl exaggerated in the moonlight.

"What went wrong?" He looked over her shoulder as if expecting trouble, then focused on her face. "You look ill."

"Just very tired." She yawned and rubbed her eyes. "I fell asleep waiting for the camp to quieten down so I could come to you."

"You're working hard?" Lindani frowned.

"It is not the work, although it is hard. It's the lying. I want to answer people in Zulu, thank people the Zulu way, use Zulu expressions. I have to constantly guard against myself."

Lindani opened his mouth to reply, but before he could say anything, another head appeared over the river bank wall.

"Get out of the moonlight." Malusi's tone was hard.

Elizabeth shared a look with Lindani that was part embarrassment for their obvious mistake, part resentment. They turned and jumped down the bank to join Malusi.

Crouching under the overhang, shoulder to hip with Lindani, already damp with spray from the river, her fatigue lifted.

She was among friends at last.

CHAPTER THIRTEEN

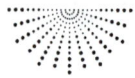

In conducting operations against an enemy like the Kaffir or the Zulu, the first blow struck should be a heavy one, and I am satisfied that no greater mistake can be made than to attempt to conquer him with insufficient means. He has the advantage of being able to march in one day at least three times as far as the British soldier, and has no commissariat train to hamper him. Unless, then, his country or stronghold is attacked by several columns, each strong enough to hold its own, moving in from different directions, he has always the power to evade the blow and prolong the war to an indefinite time . . .

— LORD CHELMSFORD TO THE BRITISH
SECRETARY OF STATE

"There are five columns in the whiteman's army. But the general must know that." Elizabeth drew five lines in the wet sand with a piece of stick, squeezed in close between Lindani and Malusi. Her voice was drowned by the rush of the river flowing right at their feet.

After a long drought, the wet season had come with a vengeance, and the river was swollen and brown with the dust of hills too long without rain.

"Tell me everything. The general can take what he doesn't know from that." Malusi edged back as the river lapped even closer to the bank.

Elizabeth nodded. "Two of the columns are not considered actual attacking columns. They are mostly made up of men from the Natal Native Contingent to support the three main columns."

She eased herself down and sat on the damp sand, her legs too tired from her day to remain crouched for long.

"Of the three attacking columns, my one, Central Column, is the one chosen to take on the main Zulu army."

"So the general was right." Lindani sounded pleased.

"Yes. These men are fighting fit. They have been fighting in the Cape, and they aren't green recruits. They have battle experience."

That silenced both Lindani and Malusi, took some of the excitement out of them. None of the young men of their generation had gone to war. As far as that went, *they* were the green recruits. Not the British.

"Their guns are very good, also." Elizabeth knew she must press this point home, but most likely they would ignore it. "Much better, much more powerful, than the one I shot the other day in the veld. And they have rocket batteries, cannons. Big seven pound guns. We don't have anything like that, do we?"

Lindani waved her statement away.

"No." She could hear the fear in her sharp tongue. "Don't dismiss the guns. Although I heard something today that has given me an idea. A way to jam some of them."

Lindani reached out a hand, gripped her forearm. "Don't do anything to give yourself away. Your function is information, not sabotage. Don't take risks."

Elizabeth nodded slowly. "Agreed, but if the opportunity presents itself, I will take it."

Lindani clicked his tongue, but he didn't pursue it.

Malusi eyed her speculatively. He would not object to her sabotaging the whitemen's weapons if she could get away with it, of that she was sure.

"Why are they waiting on the border?"

"They're waiting for the ultimatum to expire. They plan to cross over into Zululand the day it does."

"And after that?"

Elizabeth gave a snort. "It will take them days just to cross the river. It took us almost a week to move the column ten miles. But I think they intend to set up camp on the other side and carry out reconnaissance before they decide which direction to take."

"So the *impi* still has time to gather at oNdini and perform the war rituals?"

Elizabeth nodded. "You must tell the general, Chelmsford doesn't know us. He thinks we won't fight. He thinks we are like the Xhosa. That we will ambush and raid, but never fight army to army."

Lindani's teeth gleamed white in the darkness. "Then this Chelmsford can expect a big surprise."

~

A SMALL SOUND WOKE HIM. THE SIGH OF CANVAS LIFTING, letting in a draft of cool, rain-scented air that brushed over his cheek, soft as a kiss, and as refreshing.

He was immediately alert, but he kept his breathing slow and even.

There was a creak from Elizabeth's cot, and the furtive sound of clothes being removed.

Opening his eyes just enough to see the outline of her in the darkness, tugging off her boots, he relaxed his body, reveling in the warmth of his blanket, the relative comfort of his cot.

He wondered where she'd been. To the latrines, most likely.

There was a rustle of fabric again, and he closed his eyes, unable to see clearly in the darkness anyway, preferring to imagine her taking off her redcoat, sitting in her thin white undershirt.

Now she would be lifting the white shirt over her head, tugging at the bindings to free her breasts.

He heard a shuffle, and her cot creaked loudly. He decided she was wriggling out of her trousers, perhaps, like him, keeping her drawers on because of his presence in the tent.

He was worried about her.

He'd noticed her face was pale under her sun-browned skin, and dark bruises underscored her eyes. Her short-cropped hair often stood on end, dark red and spiky, as if she'd been pulling on it.

The hollows under her delicate cheekbones looked deeper, her uniform seemed to hang on her even more loosely, as if she were losing weight. Like a fey creature, slowly diminishing in the human world, unable to exist among men.

Every day since she'd joined the column, she seemed to sink deeper into herself. Tonight, in the brief glimpse he'd had of her before dinner, she'd been dragging her feet, as if every step was an effort.

She was exhausted. That was at least part of it.

He probably hadn't helped the matter. He certainly hadn't offered any support or friendly conversation, but he'd done it to protect himself and her.

He was too afraid of forgetting himself amongst the men. Treating her like a woman, or addressing her as Elizabeth in an unguarded moment and being overhead.

Better to keep a distance.

He'd offered her the safe-haven of his tent and the promise of silence, but he could see it wasn't enough.

Chambers was working her into the ground and perhaps Jack could do her one more favour. Tell Chambers that for one day, he could not offer his batman's services.

It was probably unreasonable to demand the day be tomorrow, or maybe even the next day, given they were setting up camp, but he would ask for Fremaher to be released from her duties the day after that.

It was a small thing, but it was something he could easily do, something that would give her some respite.

The relief he felt at his decision surprised him, made him realize Elizabeth Bird had been on his mind more than he'd realized – more than he'd admitted.

He heard her breathing even into the rise and fall of sleep, and buried himself deeper in his blanket. Once she looked less strained, less vulnerable, perhaps her hold on his thoughts would lessen.

He hoped so.

CHAPTER FOURTEEN

War is a lion on whose back you fall, never to get off.

— OLD ZULU SAYING

A raucous flock of hadedas gave the sun away as it tried to sneak silently into the world.

But Lindani had no need of the noisy birds. He'd been staring at the sky since he'd lain down to sleep in the scout camp. Watched it turn from black to inky blue, to pale gold.

Inyoni's face, drawn and troubled, haunted him, and he could not get to sleep.

He didn't think the clan chief had truly thought her a danger to Zululand. He'd seen an opportunity and used it. Used them both.

Unable to lie any longer, Lindani rose and took up a gourd to get water at the small stream, swollen as a tick on a cow's back with the summer rain.

As he crouched down and dipped the gourd into the fast flow of the water, he wondered what Inyoni was doing. How she had even managed to walk back to the camp the night he and Malusi had seen her was beyond him. Not since he'd pulled her out of the sea, half-drowned, had she looked so ill.

They had been away for two days, carrying her information to the general, and he'd feel better if he could see her in the camp. See her coping. He stood, hefting the gourd in one arm. Between Malusi and himself, they could go down to the river and watch for her. Malusi could mutter about it all he wanted – she was his source of information, and his responsibility, too.

Even if they could not speak with her, at least Lindani would feel he was doing something.

He'd given his mother and his wife his word that he would not let harm come to her, but he knew with uncomfortable certainty he had no power to help her if she was in danger.

The best he could do was watch over her, and if she did come to harm, revenge her on the battlefield.

He went cold at the thought. He'd saved her life once. Now, because of him, her life was in danger again. Caught this time in a sea of men. A tidal wave of rifles and guns.

Wading in to save her this time would be suicide.

"WANT A NIP?"

Elizabeth regarded the smudged silver bottle Jenkins held out to her in his grimy hand and tentatively took it from him. The strongest drink she'd ever had was the beer she'd made in Lindani's village and she felt no need to change that. But to refuse would be too notable.

"T'won't kill ya," he laughed.

She made a face. "I'm not sure about that." She did not also mention that it was eight in the morning, and the thought of home-brewed rotgut did not appeal. Jenkins would not understand that reasoning. She gathered it appealed to most soldiers, most of the time.

"God, yer a strange 'un. What you doing 'ere, eh? Fancy accent like yours, you could work as a clerk or summfink."

Elizabeth lifted the flask. "Looking for adventure."

Harry Stokes came up behind her and plucked the flask from her hand. She felt a surge of warmth towards him for taking it before she'd been forced to have a sip.

He took a gulp and smacked his lips. "What adventure would this be? The nightly adventure of braving the latrines with the hope no beastie or snake is lying in wait? Or the simple adventure of taking dinner every night an' 'oping to God it won't kill you?"

"Something like that." Elizabeth stood, noticing how black her nails were.

She looked down at her feet. Her boots were red-caked with mud, and her trousers were encrusted with it.

She suddenly couldn't stand it anymore. Couldn't cope with the dirt. She had to be clean.

"I have things to do for Captain Burdell." She gave them both a friendly nod.

"Not working for Chambers today?"

Elizabeth shook her head. "Captain Burdell needs some things seeing to." As she walked away from the fireside where she'd eaten her breakfast, she still could not believe her day stretched out before her, all her own. Even the thought of it, arranged a few days in advance, had helped her get through the days in between.

She'd kept her gratitude to Burdell to a murmured thanks, but in truth she'd felt like weeping with relief.

Burdell rarely even spoke to her directly, and yet, he'd noticed her fatigue. Her shock at how close she must look to losing her grip frightened her enough to make her response to his kindness subdued.

And just as he'd taken note of her, she'd noticed his restlessness, his constant need to be in the thick of work.

He volunteered for more pickets than any other officer.

He was out on one now, and she could please herself. And it pleased her very much to get clean.

THE RIVER ROARED LIKE A LION FURTHER DOWN, THE SOUND A backdrop to everything else, but here, where the curve of the river swung round in a wide, lazy arc, ample as a woman's breast, it was almost silent in comparison.

Elizabeth stood quiet, looking behind her for a few more minutes, making sure there was no one following her.

The silence stretched out, and with a flash of dazzling green and yellow, a sunbird swooped onto the thick, spike-lined leaf of a nearby aloe and ruffled its feathers.

She was safe.

She sat and pulled off her boots, tucked them behind a bush. In her stocking feet, clutching the nightshirt Burdell had given her in one hand and steadying herself with the other, she half-slid, half-leapt down the bank.

She got to work unbuttoning her clothes.

One by one they landed in a pile on the rocks, the nightshirt joining them, and then she stretched, naked for the first time since she'd joined Central Column. Free for the first time.

Crouching, she rifled through the clothes until she found her trouser pocket, and pulled out the soap she'd taken from Burdell's supplies. She'd left him a note, explaining, even though he would have said she could have it if he'd been there. She did not doubt it, and did not think he would be anything but embarrassed not to have offered it to her sooner.

She smiled. There was a hardness in Burdell's eyes despite the fact he stopped her heart every time she looked at him, and yet, there was also a respect and an ingrained politeness in him she was sure he'd suffer torture before abandoning.

A man of many sides. Of unplumbed depths.

She shivered, even though the heat roiled above her head, radiating off the hot red earth, and the sun bit into her arms and shoulders.

She looked down at her naked body, and wondered what it would feel like to have Burdell's hands on her breasts, or sliding down her sides to pull her close.

She lifted a palm to a hardened nipple. Dropped her hand, her heart thundering in her chest.

She would make herself mad if she pursued this attraction. Encouraged it in herself.

Grabbing up her bundle of clothes, she waded into the quick-flowing water and found a smooth rock just above the surface to wash them on. She began beating and rubbing them against it, as all good Zulu daughters know how.

The action soothed her, and when they were clean, she scrambled up the bank to drape them over bushes before leaping back down into the water and ducking completely under.

The current dragged her backwards, towards the camp, and she anchored her feet, lifting up with the water breaking over her back and shoulders as she pushed against it until she reached her wash rock.

She soaped herself, rubbing her scalp until her hair squeaked in protest under her fingers.

When she was clean, and the soap was nothing but a sliver, she held the rock, letting the current drag her feet up and under her, so she was weightless.

It felt good.

"Inyoni."

Lindani's shout jerked her head up, shocking her out of her calm. Heart thundering, she stood, waist-high, her mouth open in astonishment to see him, hunkered down on the other side of the river.

"What is it?" She could only think of Nosipho, perhaps she'd gone into early labour? Or another column had invaded, somehow overrun the village . . .

Lindani made a down motion with his hand, shaking his head. "Nothing is wrong. I came to see if I could check on you at the camp. See if you were all right. And here you are." He laughed suddenly, relief in the lines of his body as he flopped down on the rocks.

She must have looked closer to the edge than she thought the other night for him to put himself in danger. To brave a close-up look at the Rorke's Drift camp.

"I was given time off." She spoke in Zulu, and kept quiet about Burdell. Something told her Lindani would worry more if he knew an officer had seen through her disguise.

"Good. You needed it."

"What in God's name . . ?"

Lindani jerked his eyes up from hers, over her shoulder, and Elizabeth spun round.

Standing on the bank, her jacket in his hand, was Jumping Jack Burdell.

CHAPTER FIFTEEN

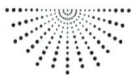

In the event of an advance being made into Zululand it is I consider very probable that a large number of Cetewayo's subjects may wish to avoid fighting, and may desire to come across our border for protection – Every reliable account from that country shows conclusively that Cetewayo is most unpopular, and those who are best informed regarding the state of feelings in Zululand are of the opinion that an internal revolution is not only possible but probable –

— CHELMSFORD'S CORRESPONDENCE, 30
OCTOBER, 1878

J ack brushed his fingers over Elizabeth's note in his pocket and stared at her, naked to the waist – and below, for all he knew.

Her eyes were wide, but she made no maidenly move to

cover her breasts; there were no shrieks of modesty from Private Bird.

He'd come upon her having a conversation with a cowherd, easy as you please, in that same state, and he felt a fierce heat in his cheeks and down his neck at the thought of the lout looking at her. He lifted his hand to his revolver pouch on his belt.

The Zulu called something to Elizabeth in his own tongue, and as she turned back to him, Jack took a good, hard look at the man, but there didn't seem anything disrespectful in the tone of his shout, and Jack realized perhaps between them, he was the one closer to wearing a leer.

His hand dropped from his sidearm.

With a cheeky wave, the Zulu rolled off into the bush, and Jack heard him running away, whistling for his herd. He steeled his features, composed himself, so when Elizabeth turned back, his face was a careful blank.

And *still* she did not cover herself.

By God – would it be up to him to turn from her?

Not that her turning would be much better. The sweet curve of her back, the dip of her waist, had riveted him, and he'd only realized she was in conversation with someone on the other bank a few moments later.

They stared at each other, the sound of the water rushing between them giving him a sense they were in limbo. Out of time.

He'd seen fear, then anxiety in her eyes at first, but now he could not read her.

Unable to stop himself, he dropped his gaze to her body, slim, firm, high-breasted, and drank her in. She made a sound, and he lifted his gaze back to her face, saw she had at last noticed the heat in his eyes.

Her nostrils flared and she moved towards him, each step slow and deliberate in the strong current.

He wanted . . .

What did he want that she could give him? A brief escape? He'd still be an officer when he woke. Having her, involving her, would only complicate things further.

She pulled herself out the river onto a rock below him and scrambled to her feet, the water streaming off her, glittering like fish scales in the bright sun.

She lifted up her hand, and hardly able to understand it, understand anything, he grabbed it and pulled her up the bank.

She stood, naked and dripping, directly in front of him and snatched her coat out of his hand, and at last he saw the outrage in her face. And a trace of fear.

He stepped back in surprise.

"Looked your full, sir?"

She was dripping wet, her hair short and spiky, standing almost straight on her head.

She held her jacket up against her. It only covered her to her hips and her long bare legs sparkled with water drops.

"I'm . . . sorry," he murmured, only half-repentant. He was a man, after all. A man who hadn't seen a naked woman in nearly a year. Good God, she was spitting like a cat that he'd looked at what she'd seemed only too happy to display.

"I forgot . . ."

She was going to say more, some cutting remark, but obviously thought better of it, her eyes jerking to the left, away from him. She drew in a breath.

"Where I come from, men don't stare at women's breasts that way. I forgot that. Forgot you would consider it my duty to cover myself, not yours to turn away."

Her remark hit him hard. It *had* been his duty to look

away. The right thing to do. But since he'd met her, when had he once taken the sensible, virtuous option?

"All men look at women's breasts that way," he said. "No matter where you come from."

Perhaps she'd been in shock, seeing that Zulu on the other side. He winced. Had he been leering while she was struggling with fear and panic?

She said nothing in response, just turned her back to him, collecting her clothes from the bushes, and giving him a glorious view of her naked arse.

He felt light-headed.

It was either run towards her, or away.

Jack tried to call a farewell, but he was only too aware it came out as some sort of squawk, as graceless as the cackle of a guinea fowl.

As he turned blindly from her, he realized he'd asked her nothing about the Zulu man who'd called to her, but he didn't care about that any longer.

He only cared about getting his hands on the globes of that arse, or getting Elizabeth Bird as far away from him as possible.

But nowhere, he realized as he stumbled over a rock in the path, would be nearly far enough.

ONE MOMENT, BURDELL WAS STANDING BEHIND HER, THE NEXT he was gone.

He called something unintelligible as he stumbled away, and unhooking her trousers from the sharp branches they'd become hooked on, Elizabeth turned to see him hurrying off down the orange-red slash of path through the long grass.

It was the first time she'd seen him move without looking like a leopard on the hunt. Purposeful and graceful.

Relief made her shake.

She'd had to tread a fine line with the men on both sides of the river. For if Burdell had so much as laid a finger on her, Lindani would have been across that river with his *iwisa* raised, ready to knock his brains out. And since he'd whistled to Malusi as he pretended to run off, her spymaster would probably have taken his *assegai* out and joined him to finish the job.

She hung her clothes on the bushes again – no sense putting on wet clothes if there was time for them to dry. When she was done, she found a grassy stretch of river bank and sat down with her knees drawn up in front of her, to wait for Lindani. That he would come was not in doubt.

She'd been frozen by his parting words. Pretending a cheerful farewell, he'd told her the smallest indication from her that she was in danger, and he'd be across to kill the whiteman.

He'd thought her cover was blown, had frowned at her quick shake of the head, the flick of her eyes telling him to get lost. But he'd done it. Thank goodness.

Thank goodness, too, Burdell had also done what she wanted, which was leave her alone. How she'd managed to send him off, she had no idea. Was only grateful that it had happened.

Lindani and Malusi's heads popped up from the river bank, their crossing as silent and invisible as a crocodile. Their faces were of a piece, set in lines of anger and fear.

"That was very foolish." Malusi looked hard, furious, and she was reminded he was not her friend. She was only a tool to him.

"You must never take off your soldier's clothes."

"He's right." Lindani clicked his tongue. "Now that whiteman knows you are a woman."

"He won't say anything." Elizabeth closed her eyes against the flicker and jab of the sun off the water, and rested her chin on her knees, watched bright orange spots dance over her eyelids. "He found out I was a woman the first day I joined the column."

"What?" Malusi's shout was uncharacteristically incautious. She raised her head and he shot her an angry look as if it were her fault he was losing his usual control.

"It was the best thing that could have happened." Elizabeth held his gaze. She deserved his respect; had done a good job. "I told him I was looking for my brother, that I was destitute. He believed me, smoothed my way in the camp. I'm sure I'd have been discovered before now, if not for him."

Malusi sat beside her, all traces of anger gone. "Has he been able to give you any information?"

Elizabeth felt bile rise in her throat, but she shook her head and kept her expression under control. "He is not part of the general's staff. And he is often on picket duty. We don't see each other often."

"Yet he came looking for you today." Lindani, unlike Malusi, did not appear overjoyed by this development. He looked suspicious, and the hard look was still in his eyes.

"I took something of his, and left a note explaining why." Elizabeth shrugged. "I don't know why he came looking for me."

But she was lying.

She did know.

Maybe knew as she wrote the note. Could she be that much of a mystery to herself?

"I know why." Lindani watched her, too much

happening behind his eyes. "I saw the way he looked at you. These whitemen cannot control their lust. Their woman must wear clothes from neck to toe, I hear, because even the sight of an ankle makes them lose their composure."

"Captain Burdell didn't touch me." Elizabeth heard the defensiveness in her own voice.

The silence stretched out between them. A lot had been said in those few words.

"We must go." Malusi broke the tension. He smiled. "Use this officer as much as you can, Inyoni. You are right, it was a stroke of luck." He leapt down the bank.

Lindani gave her a troubled look. "You are in very deep, my little bird." He turned from her and jumped down the bank after Malusi, and Elizabeth watched them half-swim, half-wade across.

She rested her head back on her knees and closed her eyes. Even though she was clean at last, Malusi's parting words made her feel dirty all over again.

∽

10 January, 1879

Dear Cecilia

We were joined by the rest of the Central Column a few days ago, and that's the end of our peace and quiet. It's like Helpmekaar all over again, although at least this time we have the river running right beside us.

We are not allowed to cross over into Zululand before the ultimatum expires tomorrow, so we have nothing much to do except clean our guns and get up to mischief. There have been a number of floggings already, as the men get their hands on a locally brewed gin called Cape Mist and get drunk and disorderly.

Some of the companies prefer to patrol up and down the river, and how I wish I could join them. The peace of the open veld sounds just the ticket right now, with the tents lying almost on top of each other, and tempers getting as hot as the weather, and as violent.

I don't think a day passes that a storm does not break in the late afternoon or early evening, and the river is swollen to capacity. These storms are quick and wild. Thunder, lightning, sometimes even hail, and this lasts for an hour, perhaps two. When it clears, everything is thoroughly drenched.

I cannot tell you how I wish for the cool, misty rain of home. The gentle waves of raindrops beating softly on the windows of our little cottage, the fire crackling and a lovely dinner in the oven.

If you could see the conditions here, the wet ground we sleep on, the terrible food, the sun so hot, when it shines down on the wet ground you can see the steam rising from it, like hot water in a kettle.

Lord Chelmsford thinks that we will be in for a warm reception by the Zulu army tomorrow, and that they will oppose our crossing their borders.

If this is indeed their plan, they are well hidden and we have not so much as seen one of them. In fact, just two days ago, on Wednesday, a sentry called that he could see men on horseback approaching from the Zulu side of the river, and we all rushed down to the drift to see who it could be.

It was a few men from Colonel Wood's column. They had crossed over the border a few days before, and these men, commanded by Captain Barton, had been out on reconnaissance. Encountering no opposition, they pressed on all the way to us, a ride of some thirty miles, meeting with no one but friendly herdsmen and villagers along the way. Because it had grown late, they stayed the night and returned to Wood's column the next morning.

The boys know, though, tomorrow is when the war starts in earnest, and there is a quietness to the camp there hasn't been before.

I send you and Harry my fondest wishes and love. Please remember me to your mother and father, and I will no doubt write soon with great stories of our victory.

Yours etc.

Colin

CHAPTER SIXTEEN

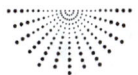

The crossing of the drift was executed under the eye of the General, who was attended by a numerous and brilliant staff, and it was most successfully carried out; although several minor accidents occurred, neither horse nor man came to grief.

— FROM THE WAR CORRESPONDENT OF THE
NATAL MERCURY, JANUARY 13, 1879

J ack was back.

Elizabeth heard the picket come in around lunch time, as ever led by their stomachs. She kept heaving the boxes onto a wagon for tomorrow's crossing, but her cheeks started up a slow burn and her hands shook.

She was still untangling her feelings from yesterday, trying to sort through what had happened.

She was a savage.

At least, that's what these oafs in camp would call her if they knew how she lived up until a few weeks ago. Bared to the waist, covered only by a fringe of grass or a small skirt of beads.

And no one, not even the few men who'd eyed her with interest in the village, had ever looked at her the way Burdell had.

Like he wanted to consume her.

He had looked, in that moment as he pulled her up the bank, more savage than any Zulu warrior she had ever seen.

She shivered. If Lindani hadn't been watching from the bushes, what would she have done?

Her mind slid away from the question, and latched on, instead, to the new level of tension in Burdell's tent since yesterday.

Some unacknowledged awareness of each other had thickened the air whenever they were together before, driving them both as far away from each other as their duties would allow. But now it weighed them down. A few minutes of being in the tent together felt like a ten mile hike carrying a heavy pack.

Elizabeth slammed the last packing case from her pile into the wagon and sat down on a crate in the supply tent to catch her breath.

Her eyes moved, of their own accord, to the boxes of ammunition for the 2nd Battalion's Martini-Henry rifles. So far, she had been too afraid of discovery to open the boxes and tamper with the bullets.

Now, in the few days she'd spent at Rorke's Drift, she knew her reluctance had another cause. She was getting to know these redcoats, and while most of them were opinionated, oafish and crude, she had discovered they were not, at heart, bad men.

Her mouth curved into a wry smile. Malusi was right when he said even a single column of the British army was a big thing to hate.

Too big for her.

To deliberately sabotage their guns was hard to contemplate, and she had to keep a mental image of Lindani, flung back like a ragdoll under fire, firmly in her mind to consider it at all.

"We seem to be on schedule here, well done, Bird." Chambers strode into the tent, ticking off his list.

"Sir." Her voice was hesitant. She clenched her fists on her thighs.

Chambers looked up from his board impatiently.

"Some of the ammunition boxes seem a little worse for wear, sir. Perhaps I should open them and check the bullets aren't damaged?"

"Good God, boy, have you any idea how long that could take?" Chambers' eyes were wide.

Elizabeth shrugged her shoulders. Shook her head.

"We've got too much to organize. Perhaps later, in the evenings when we've crossed this cursed river, although God knows I hardly need to find more work for myself." Chambers turned and left as abruptly as he'd come, muttering under his breath as he stalked off.

Elizabeth stood, her hands on her hips. If she was caught opening boxes now, after this short conversation, Chambers would think she was being diligent. It would cover both the getting into the boxes and the damage to the bullets.

And that was all she needed.

His tent was quiet.

It was just after supper, and Jack had seen Elizabeth going into one of the store tents, no doubt hard at work for Chambers in preparation for the crossing tomorrow.

It was the only time he had seen her since returning from his picket duty and he was sure she was making as much of an effort to keep out of his way as he was to keep out of hers.

If he didn't look, he wouldn't be tempted to touch.

It was the only thing he could think of to get him through this. That, and as many night patrols as he could wrangle.

If he was going to be a fool, he was going to be one only in his head, and not even there, if he could help it.

For once, the men were bedding down early. The tents were due to be struck at 2:30am the next morning, and everyone was to start moving over the drift at 4am. Only the coughs and sniffles of the men settling down disturbed the peace tonight, and it was barely seven.

He took off his boots and reached for his father's journal, eager to get back to it after too many days without the chance to read.

ENTRY WRITTEN DECEMBER, 1871

YOUR MOTHER DOESN'T UNDERSTAND MY ANGER. MY VIEWS ON the Empire. She thinks I'm being treasonous when I talk about Chillianwallah, about the Mutiny many years later, and how we comported ourselves as a nation. She cannot accept my certainty that the world will look back on our actions and will not view us kindly.

She hasn't seen her best friend ripped to shreds by a bullet, to fall face first into boggy water, all because of an over-inflated sense of our own superiority. All because the action, the picture of bravery, was far more important than the men expended to paint that picture.

After the disaster at Ramnagar, Gough was cautious and we waited for the heavy artillery to join us.

We sat around, gloomy and depressed with the loss of good men. Friends. It seemed to everyone a senseless action that gained us nothing, lost us much, and served only to show our lack of intelligence and planning.

But eventually the heavy artillery arrived, and we made preparations to take on the main Sikh army. Gough had perked up by then, and his enthusiasm infected us again.

He sent a force to cross the Chenab, to flank Sher Singh, and take him by surprise, while pretending that the bulk of the British forces were still opposite the Sikh army at Ramnagar.

But again, our intelligence was not up to scratch, and Thackwell, in charge of the ambush force of 7,000 men, could not find the ford he was supposed to use, and ended up having to go further upstream to find a place to cross.

By then, Sher Singh's spies had told him of Thackwell's force, and at that point, Singh could have dealt us a severe blow, had he crushed Thackwell immediately. Gough would have been left with severely depleted troops and almost no choice but to retreat.

But Singh's caution saved us.

He secretly withdrew his main army north into an easily defended position, while engaging both Gough and Thackwell with small forces which both believed was the whole of the Sikh Army.

Despite the fact that if Singh had pushed us, we would have toppled, he still came out the victor that day.

Again, we were fooled by a steadfast belief in our superior cunning and tactics. I wonder if we will ever give our enemies their due?

THE ZULUS WEREN'T GETTING THEIR DUE, JACK THOUGHT — IF they had any to get.

He wouldn't know.

He hardly knew anything about them. Perhaps hadn't wanted to, now he thought of it.

It was too depressing, going in to crush a nation just because they happened to be in the way. The less you knew of them, the easier it was to follow orders.

He glanced across at his pocket watch, and saw it was already eight. What could Elizabeth be doing for Chambers this late?

He sat slowly, gripped with a feeling in his gut he couldn't explain. He wanted to find her. He wasn't even going to pretend it was to stop Chambers working her into the ground, although that is the excuse he would use.

Distance.

He'd wanted it, but suddenly, he realized the futility of it. Found it harder and harder to care about its importance.

Standing, he slipped on his jacket and headed out into the quiet night to find her.

"ELIZ . . . PRIVATE BIRD?"

Elizabeth froze. She lifted guilty eyes as Jack Burdell peered into the munitions tent.

"Captain Burdell." He must surely be able to hear her heart thumping, the husky fear in her voice.

"I just wanted to check you are all right. We strike tents

in less than eight hours. Chambers can't be that disorganized that you're still working now, can he?"

"No." Elizabeth thanked fate or luck that she had just finished with one box, and was about to start on another, although she hadn't broken in to it yet. "I'm finished now."

He looked at her face, and she was sure her conscience wasn't inventing his suspicious look.

"What was it you were doing?"

"Coming over the pass, the munitions wagons went over very rough ground, and some of the boxes were thrown about. Lieutenant Chambers was concerned some of the bullets may be damaged. We're checking to make sure that isn't the case."

"Well," Burdell paused. "That is really very conscientious of Chambers. I commend him for it."

"I'm sure he'll say he's just doing his duty, sir."

"But you're not, are you?"

He couldn't possibly know how true that was.

"Sir?"

He looked sharply at her, perhaps thinking she was poking fun speaking to him as a private to an officer, but the truth of it was she had become a private. It was the only way to survive. He held her gaze for a beat before he relaxed again.

"You are working as hard as if you really are a private."

"That is the only way I won't be discovered, sir. By behaving as I am expected to."

Burdell sighed, his face softening, and rubbed a hand through his hair. "What am I to do with you? Can I really let you travel into enemy territory with an invading army?"

She had to fight hard to keep her face impassive. "You know there is no choice. The alternative is to walk to Pieter-maritzburg on foot. Alone."

"That is the only thing that prevents me from reporting you." He held out his hand to help her up, and she took it, letting him lift her from the low munitions box she sat on.

It was a foolish thing to do, on both their parts, because as he drew her up, she knew he was lying.

Saving her from being tossed out on her ear may be part of his reason for keeping quiet, but it wasn't the only one. She saw the hunger flare in his eyes as he pulled her up until she was almost touching his body.

It was the river all over again. Only this time, without two murderous chaperones watching from the sidelines.

For a moment, neither said anything, their breathing loud in the tent. He lifted his other hand, held it still a moment, and then pushed a piece of hair off her forehead. His fingers trembled as they moved across her temple.

He stepped back, releasing her hand.

The brief lowering of his defenses and then raising them again threw her into confusion, left her reeling within.

She thought he wanted nothing to do with her, even though their attraction to each other was like a living thing between them. A third person in the tent at night.

Why had Burdell changed the rules?

She sneaked a look at him, her face hot from her thoughts, but he'd moved to the entrance, was holding the tent flap for her, polite and very much the gentleman.

She ducked under his arm into the rain-cooled night air. It was drizzling, the feather-light drops welcome on her cheeks, cooling them.

"We might as well be in England, all the rain we're getting," Burdell said, so English, discussing the weather after looking at her with eyes that could scorch off her clothing.

She murmured her agreement, although the last time

she'd seen England was when she was ten, and she barely recalled it. He didn't care what her answer was, anyway.

"Get a good night, what's left of it," he said at the tent entrance, not entering so she could change. "You're working far too hard."

Of everything he'd said tonight, she was sure this was something he did mean. He admired her for her hard work.

"Good night," Elizabeth called softly, and felt the guilt sink to the pit of her stomach.

The only thing she'd worked hard at tonight was ensuring the death of Jack's men.

CHAPTER SEVENTEEN

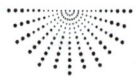

What do you come here for? We don't want you. This is Zululand. Keep to your own side. *(The call of an old Zulu woman to soldiers of the British Army.)*

—W.E. MONTAGUE, CAMPAIGNING IN SOUTH
AFRICA: REMINISCENCES OF AN OFFICER IN
1879

The boom of guns woke her.

Two shots loosed at the empty, opposite bank of the Buffalo River to signal the start of hostilities.

Bleary-eyed, Elizabeth sat up and wished these things did not have to take place in the middle of the night. Wished she had more sleep. Wished today was over already.

She knew full well the Zulu *impi* was at oNdini, that there would be no resistance to today's invasion.

She looked across and saw Jack was already up and out, and adrenalin shot through her. She would be late.

She scrambled for her clothes, hauled on her boots, and did a quick sweep of the tent, scooping up what little she had and bundling it together in the sack she'd misappropriated from stores for her personal belongings.

She rolled out the back of the tent and stood for a moment in thick mist, light-headed with tiredness. She had to lean forward, hands on knees, to get her bearings, before heading for Chambers' tent.

He was in fine fettle when she found him, shouting instructions to the drivers.

"Bird. I was about to come and find you." He beckoned her closer, and slipped her a piece of bread, buttered on one side and folded over on itself, like a sandwich. "We won't be getting much in the way of victuals today, lad, but I reckon you need something to run on, because run you will."

"Thank you, sir."

Almost perpetually hungry since she'd started working for him, Elizabeth gave Chambers her widest grin and bit heartily into it.

"We've got 4500 men moving across the river today, and by this evening we have to feed them and give them a tent over their heads."

"They'll help us, though, won't they?" Elizabeth spoke around a mouthful of bread.

"Some. But the general wants everyone ready in case of attack. Much is on our shoulders." He turned and looked towards the river. "And we'll have Glyn and the general keeping a close eye, no doubt." His words were quiet.

"What do you think of all this, sir?" Elizabeth couldn't stop herself. "Do you think it's right?"

"Right to invade?" Chambers looked at her strangely.

117

"They're a bunch of savages, Bird, who could use a lesson in civilization."

He turned to go, and Elizabeth dropped the last bit of her bread on the floor. Ground it under her boot.

❧

WITH A FULL MEAL IN THEIR STOMACHS, SITTING IN THE officers' mess after a day without rations, most of the officers of 2nd battalion looked decidedly less fractious than they had earlier.

Jack admitted to a bit of hunger-induced temper himself today, as the trying task of moving thousands of men, oxen and supplies over a river in full flood wore everyone down.

His company had been assigned to help the quartermasters, and it had been wet, hard work.

Watching the slight figure of Elizabeth Bird running to and fro for Chambers, carrying, organizing and working herself to a standstill, had made him all the more harsh with some of the louder complainers in his company.

If a slip of a girl could do it, so could they.

He winced at every load she'd shouldered, forcing himself not to go up and snatch it from her.

Not a good idea, for either of them.

He hoped she had not injured herself, but he feared she had. She'd worn a scowl all day.

"Right, gentlemen." Major Carr cleared his throat, bringing Jack back from his thoughts. "Congratulations on a hard day's work, well executed."

The laughter and the noise died down.

"Some of the column will be marching on Sihayo's stronghold tomorrow at 5am, as you know. The General has asked us to provide a captain to command the 1st Battalion of the 3rd Natal Native Contingent, and four companies of the 1st 24th will be accompanying them. The following captains and their companies of the 2nd 24th will leave three hours after the 1st 3 NNC and the 1st 24th as a reserve force."

Jack heard his name called as part of the reserve, and there were shouts of disappointment and mutters of discontent from those not chosen to go. He edged out of the crowd, and slipped into the night, still cool and wet from the evening shower.

He could hear the laughter and conversation of the enlisted men, but knew Elizabeth would not be among them. He watched her when he could, unable to help himself, and saw how she dipped her head, nodded and smiled, but never made eye contact with the men. Never invited more than passing comments.

To him, her femininity was so obvious, it was astonishing he was the only one to see through her disguise. And yet, thank God for their blindness.

He hesitated outside his tent, then cleared his throat to give her warning that he was entering.

She lay on her cot, still, but with eyes open.

"Are you part of the force tomorrow?" she asked him as he stepped inside, her voice so soft he barely caught her words.

He nodded, astonished at the leap his heart gave at the thought she was concerned for him. He eased down onto the folding chair at his desk. He really should write to his sister. Let her know his intentions on the farm.

"I'm part of the reserve force. Probably won't see any action."

"Who is Sihayo, that everyone knows his name? It's all they could talk about around the fires at supper."

"Sihayo's sons were named in the ultimatum Lord Chelmsford sent to the Zulu king. They crossed the border into Natal a few months ago, chasing after some of Sihayo's wives who had run away from him. They dragged the women back and killed them. The Governor of Natal wants them tried for murder."

She looked shocked, and he felt a stab of guilt. This was no conversation to have with a young woman. It was improper. Yet so was sharing his tent, and they'd done that every night since he'd found her.

She may not be a proper miss, but he would be wise not to treat her like the young lad she pretended to be.

In his mind's eye, he saw her as she had been at the river, and clenched his hands.

"Since when has the Governor of Natal cared so much for a few Zulu women?" Her words were sharp. Bitter.

He acknowledged the truth of what she said with a reluctant nod. "I have no doubt it's merely part of the excuse to invade. They wouldn't have raised an eyebrow if they hadn't thought they could work it to their advantage." Jack moved his writing paper around the desk with his fingertips. "I also saw the rough maps we're working with. Sihayo's stronghold lies in our path. We have to deal with him now or we'll have him to our back as we move forward, which is hardly good tactics."

She made a noise, as if too tired to answer.

"You look exhausted, and I'm not surprised." He noticed her boots were off and so was her coat. She'd unbuttoned the top of her white shirt, and he jerked his eyes away from her neckline, made himself look down at the blank paper in front of him.

"Exhausted or not, I have one more thing to do for Chambers." She sat up slowly, as if her body hurt, and pulled on her boots. When she stood, she staggered slightly, and concern for her warred with his need to have her out of his tent. As far away from him as she could get.

"You'll have an easier time of it tomorrow, I hope," he said gruffly. "Don't let Chambers work you too hard."

It was a ridiculous thing to say. Chambers could and would work her as hard as he wanted. She had no power over him.

Nevertheless, she merely gave him a half-hearted salute and limped out of the door.

Strangely, he felt no better when she'd gone. Only a terrible need to call her back.

～

ELIZABETH STOOD JUST BEHIND THE SENTRY AND WORRIED HER bottom lip with her teeth.

Now they were on the Zulu side of the river, it seemed the British were taking sentry duty more seriously. There would be no strolling casually out of camp and back again when she pleased anymore.

She needed a good reason, and one she could use more than once, for going out into the veld.

Why would someone go out at this time of night?

The only thing that came to her was the wildlife, and she remembered hearing the men joking about one of the officers, an amateur naturalist who kept halting his company while on patrol to inspect or capture insects and to bird-watch.

"Evening," she called brightly, moving forward into the sentry's line of sight. "Nothing out there, I hope."

"Not that I've noticed. Hey, where you think you're going, then?"

"Heard of Lieutenant Dartmouth, have you?" Elizabeth didn't stop, walking to almost beyond the reach of the lantern light.

"Yeeees." The sentry narrowed his eyes, trying to recall the name.

"Mad as a hatter. Wants me to go out into the veld and look for nocturnal insects for him. Seems the officers are being briefed or some such, and he can't go himself."

"That one! The one what keeps looking at birds and creepy crawlies?"

"Yeah. I'll let you know if I see anything suspicious."

"If your throat ain't been cut," the sentry muttered. "Mind 'ow you go, then."

"Cheers. And don't shoot me on my way back."

Elizabeth gave a half-wave and headed straight into the bush, hoping Lindani and Malusi were nearby. She didn't dare whistle like last time, it would carry too much.

Instead, she started singing, softly as she could, a praise song to Lindani's father, keeping a lookout as she did for any beetles.

It would not do to return without at least one.

Clouds blew, dark and fast, across the sky, and there was almost no moonlight to see by. She wove between the aloes and the thorn trees, keeping her distance from the sharp branches and sharper thorns, stamping hard on the ground with each step to frighten any snakes that might be hiding away.

She heard a rustle in the grass and hoping it was a beetle, crouched down, straining in the darkness to see.

"Inyoni, what are you doing?"

Elizabeth let out a yelp at the fierce whisper, and fell over.

"You stopped my heart for a moment." She felt almost

sick with the aftershocks, lying sprawled on the ground, looking up at Lindani with her mouth open.

"I'm sorry. But what are you doing?"

"There's an officer in the camp interested in beetles. I used the excuse of finding some for him to get out the camp."

Malusi appeared beside Lindani, and crouched beside her. "From now on, only come when you have something important. It is too dangerous for you and for us this close to the camp."

Elizabeth nodded. "I have something important. Chelmsford intends to attack Sihayo's stronghold tomorrow."

Malusi made a gesture of disgust. "The King already guessed he would. Sihayo is not there. A few of his sons have been left to fight the whitemen, but most of Sihayo's people are with the main army in oNdini already."

"The sons that killed Sihayo's wives?" Elizabeth heard the sharpness in her voice, and she didn't temper it.

Lindani crouched down, too, interceding between her and Malusi. He looked at her with eyes that told her to please not make a fuss. "I know your feelings on women being harmed. The women ran from their husband to be with some men over the border. Sihayo is old, and they wanted young husbands, but he could not allow them to shame him like that. His whole reputation was at stake."

"The only thing that got me out here to tell you about the attack was that the British care as little for those women as the King and Sihayo do. They are only using them as an excuse to do their own murdering."

Lindani clicked his tongue. "Inyoni, you know the ways of our people. The King commands young women to marry men of his choosing, and they have to accept it. You have said many times that your culture is the same. That women are forced to marry men they do not love, sometimes much older than themselves, to please their parents or to increase their family's wealth. What would happen to those women if they ran from their husbands and took up with other, younger men?"

"Nothing good," Elizabeth muttered, "although they certainly wouldn't be dragged back home and murdered."

Lindani lifted his shoulders in a helpless gesture. He hadn't done the killing, and if Nosipho ran from him, she knew he would never kill her. Banish her, perhaps, but never harm her.

She sighed. There were those who used their power wisely, and those who abused it, in Zululand and in England. Everywhere.

She only needed to think back to the opium dens of China to know that.

She looked across at Malusi, but he was staring off towards the camp, and ignored them. He was listening to every word they said, though, she had no doubt.

"The rumour in camp is the column will follow a path from here to oNdini. The next logical stop will be Isandl-wana. Although the officer I work for says the terrain is too boggy. The engineers will have to drain it, or make it pass-able, before we can move forward. That will take time."

"That is good. The *impi* is still gathering at oNdini." Malusi rose up.

"I must go back now." Elizabeth touched Lindani's hand briefly, the adrenalin that had got her out of camp and into the veld draining away. She was exhausted. She started to rise, but Lindani grabbed her arm. He scooped something up from the ground and held it out to her.

"Don't you need this?" On his palm lay a large beetle.

"Thank you. I'm so tired I forgot about it."

Steeling herself, she cupped her hand over his and felt the scritch scratch of spiky legs on her skin. She peered closer at the shiny black insect. Next time she'd bring a small box.

"Take care. Get some rest." They rose up together and she saw Malusi was already gone.

Lindani gave a shrug. He took one last look at her and disappeared into the bush so suddenly, she felt a moment of abandonment, as if things weren't the same between them any longer. As if there was a distance.

What had happened at the river with Burdell had put something between them.

She shook the feeling off. He was within hailing distance of his enemy, he could hardly stand around at his ease, chatting to her.

Carefully cupping the beetle in her hands, Elizabeth headed back to camp, this time singing an English song to warn the guard she was coming.

She chose *All Things Bright and Beautiful*.

CHAPTER EIGHTEEN

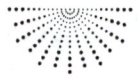

All things bright and beautiful,
   All creatures great and small
   All things wise and wonderful
   The Lord God made them all.

     — CECIL F. ALEXANDER, HYMNS FOR LITTLE
                  CHILDREN, 1848

S o much for being a reserve force.
    Jack lifted off his helmet and wiped sweat from his brow as he marched his men towards the Batshe River. The 1sts had encountered resistance and sent for the reserves early. Sihayo was not letting the British take his stronghold without a fight.

Neither was Zululand itself, it felt to him.

The heat was like a living thing, pressing against him,

resisting his movement through the air. The wet ground was drying in the intense heat, shimmering as the sun sucked up its moisture, so it could dump it back down over them this evening. It felt as if his strength and energy were being sucked up along with it.

His eyes hurt with the brightness of it all.

The primal beauty was almost overwhelming. The green of the grass, the red of the earth, and above it all, the massive, over-arching, eye-watering blue of the sky.

And the sun, branding him with every step. Burning skin and digging searing fingers of heat into his shoulders.

They came over a low ridge and Jack looked in astonishment at the massive sandstone gorge curving in a horse-shoe on the east bank of the river. A rust-red cliff rose up from a base of massive boulders, with Sihayo's stronghold of neat beehive huts nestled to the left.

Chelmsford, Glyn and some of their staff sat astride on the far bank of the river, watching and directing as the NNC and the 1sts came under fire from men hiding in the caves and behind boulders in the gorge.

Jack lifted his rifle above his head and forged across the Batshe, his detachment following behind him like ducklings behind their Mama.

The bottom was treacherously rocky, but the water only came waist-deep.

Wet boots, Jack thought glumly.

He wondered what Jeff Holman was doing about getting him a horse. Although now they were in enemy territory, there was probably nothing he *could* do.

As they assembled on the bank, Manning approached them.

"The general wants you to take the stronghold while the

1sts and the 2/3 NNC keep this lot busy." He waved his hand at the skirmish.

Jack saluted crisply and led his men left, towards the small village set against the hill. The 1/3 NNC was sent with them, and moved ahead at their jogging pace.

His own men turned back periodically to watch the small battle raging in the cliffs, but Jack kept his attention on the Natal Native Contingent ahead of them.

They were further off than they should be. Jack and his men couldn't support them at this distance.

Seeming oblivious to their tactical error, the NNC battalion rushed straight at the village.

If it was defended, and given the resistance in the hills, that was likely, they could come under attack at any minute.

"Move it, lads. We may have a situation on our hands."

The urgency in his tone got the attention of his men, and everyone picked up the pace until they were jogging to the sound of squelching boots.

But when they reached the stronghold, with its circle of thornwood fencing, they found the NNC picking through empty grass-woven huts. There was no one in the village except a few old women.

"What do the women say?" Jack asked Harris, the officer Carr had put in charge of the NNC battalion who had raced ahead of them. He'd been stationed at Pietermaritzburg for a while, and spoke the Zulu language.

"That the whole village left yesterday. Must have seen us crossing the Buffalo and known we'd come straight for them."

"Then why defend against us?" Jack asked, almost to himself. "Why are those Zulus in the gorge risking their lives to defend an empty village?"

"Good point." Harris shrugged. "Natives. Not always logical, you know."

Jack didn't answer, he was watching as one of the NNC officers handed out matches. They were going to burn the village down. Standard practice, but one he'd never liked. Never wanted any part of.

As the first flames licked up the sides of the beehive huts, he turned to look back the way they'd come. There were only two reasons why Sihayo's men would stay behind and fight for an empty village. Either they wanted to delay the British, divert them from something else. Something much bigger. Or their pride refused to let them run from a fight. Even an unnecessary one.

As he walked back towards the river, Jack thought neither reason boded very well.

"WE WERE UNDER FIRE, BULLETS FLYING EVERYWHERE, WHEN Lieutenant Dartmouth, he sort of cries out, and I thought for sure he'd taken a hit."

Elizabeth watched as Harry Stokes paused in his story for effect, looking up from the fire with eyes gleaming.

"But then, the blighter takes a match box from his pocket, empties the matches on the ground, and reaches down to pick up a creepy crawly. Bullets hitting the rocks all around. Gawd! In the heat of battle, he sees this beetle and he stops everything to get it."

Harry looked at his audience with a grin. "Told me afterwards, it's a very rare one. He didn't want to risk letting it get away."

"You said it last night," someone called out, and with a

start, Elizabeth realized they were talking to her. She looked up to see the sentry she'd spun her story to the night before, tin dinner plate balanced in his lap, sitting beside the fire. "Mad as a hatter."

Elizabeth sent up a prayer of thanks for Dartmouth and his peccadilloes, and nodded. "Too right, mate."

"The officers like you, I see, lad," one of the sentry's friends said slyly, wiping up the last of his meal with a hunk of bread. "Pretty boy like you must remind them of their school days." He started laughing, then broke into a hacking cough.

This wasn't the first reference to public schools, young boys and officers. She was tired of it. Tired of not understanding it.

Elizabeth gave the smarmy sod a narrow-eyed look but it was lost on him as he bent double, trying to breathe.

She stood and gave the sentry a friendly nod, turning from the supper fire. Usually, she stayed only long enough to get her meal and eat it, but this evening Harry Stokes's tale had made her linger.

After today's atrocities, 30 Zulus killed, she wanted to get back to her work on the bullets. But she found she couldn't bear to work on anything that might end up being issued to Jack.

So the 2nds ammunition was out, and she needed access to the 1sts ammunition. She'd need to work on that. Find some way to legitimately gain access there. Or else she'd have to sneak in to their munitions stores. Take a chance on being caught.

She arrived at Jack's tent and drew up short. A light already shone there. He was back from dinner early.

"Hello," she called and waited for a moment.

"Come."

She stepped inside. Saw him sitting at his desk, writing. Felt the hum of tension that seemed to grow stronger every time they met.

She needed to diffuse the uncomfortable silence as they stared at each other.

"Were you involved in the fighting?"

He shook his head. "My detachment was sent to the village, but there were only a few women left there. Everyone who could had gone yesterday."

"They are all so pleased with the encounter. The men think it's a sign of things to come." Elizabeth crossed her arms.

"It puzzles me why the Zulus fought at all. There was no one to defend, so why wait for us?"

Elizabeth watched him carefully. Of everything she'd heard tonight, this was the most thoughtful.

"What are your theories?"

"They are proud. They won't let us take something precious to them. Today showed they will stand and fight, even against poor odds."

Perhaps too thoughtful. Elizabeth wondered if he'd shared his views with the staff. Wondered if his superiors would even listen to him.

She moved to her cot, and sat down, her forearms resting on her knees. "What are the men talking about when they make snide comments about officers being interested in a pretty boy like me?"

She watched as shock and embarrassment replaced the contemplative look in his eyes.

"Ah . . ."

"Well?"

"It isn't a fitting subject for a lady to discuss."

Elizabeth smiled wryly. "I'm no lady. You must have realized that by now."

He looked at her a long moment, and she wondered what he was thinking. Then he leant back in his chair. "They are talking about men coming together sexually."

"But how . . ?" Elizabeth frowned.

"I'm afraid I am simply not prepared to explain the mechanics of it." His voice was curt.

She had no choice but to accept that. "However it's done, the enlisted men think you and I do it?"

He shrugged. "Perhaps they take enjoyment in teasing you about it. They may not believe it to be true."

"Still." Elizabeth eyed him. "Have you ever done it?"

"What?" Jack sat straight in his chair. "No."

He looked so indignant, she wanted to laugh.

"You prefer women?"

"I . . ." he looked at her, then away. "I prefer women."

Elizabeth felt her mouth go dry. "I suppose you like ladies. Feminine beauties."

The look he flashed her, jerking his head up from the letter on his desk, pierced her through.

Need. Hunger.

"I'm already deep enough in trouble harboring you without complicating it further." His voice was steady, but his eyes gleamed in the lamp light.

She felt lightheaded. Boneless.

"Jack, I want to thank you for everything you've done for me. I don't know why you have, but please know how grateful I am."

It was the first time she'd used his name to his face, not called him sir.

He breathed in sharply, and his hand clenched.

"If you'll excuse me, I have some duties I need to attend

to." He got up stiffly, shoved his papers and pens into a small box.

Elizabeth said nothing, sat watching him. As he passed her she caught his eye and held it for a moment. And neither of them even tried to hide it this time.

Desire.

CHAPTER NINETEEN

I am in great hopes that news of the storming of Sirayo's stronghold and the capture of so many of his cattle, about 500, may have a salutary effect in Zululand and either bring down a large force to attack us or else produce a revolution in the country.

— LORD CHELMSFORD, 12 JANUARY, 1879

Captain Manning looked ahead, shielding his eyes in the bright midday sun, and contemplated Isand— whatever the hell it was called.

It crouched, sphinx-like, on the horizon, and Manning knew most of the 24th Regiment took its shape as a good sign. The sphinx was their insignia, taken for their regiment's bravery during the Napoleonic Wars in Egypt.

Personally, he thought the looming hill slightly sinister.

But musing about the shapes of hills was not his job.

Snapping his attention back to his duties, he urged his horse forward along the rough road to where the engineers were working.

"How's it coming then?"

Lieutenant Pickford, who'd stopped to watch him approach, squinted up at him in the sunshine. His expression was sour.

"Bloody awful. No sooner do we make some headway, then it rains again. And by God, in this place when it rains, it really hammers down."

"How long until the troops can move, the General wants to know?" Manning slipped down from his saddle to eye the road the engineers were building more closely.

"We're almost there, but it's been a long, hard slog." Pickford shook his head and toed the boggy ground. He looked like a man tried to almost beyond his limits. "Tell the general he can move the column out on the 20th. Whatever it takes, we'll be ready by then."

Manning nodded, and swung back into his saddle. "If you need men, just ask. They're doing nothing but sitting about waiting as it is."

"Send me a hundred more. That should ensure we'll make it."

"I'll arrange it." God, it felt good to say these things and mean it. To have the power. This assignment was the best he'd ever had. He'd lick the General's boots to stay on his staff.

As he turned his mount, Pickford lifted his arm.

"Wait. The patrols, have they seen anything?"

Manning reined in and shook his head. "Nothing. It's the Xhosa all over again. They aren't going to come out and fight."

"It's . . . eerie, out here in the veld. Sometimes when

we're working, it feels like there are eyes on us." Pickford laughed self-consciously, and Manning tried to keep his contempt from showing on his face.

"We have several pickets going out every day, there isn't a Zulu to be found."

"Don't you think that's worse, in a way?"

"Definitely." Manning started moving forward. "I want to engage the buggers, not play hide and seek with them."

"I meant, maybe they're watching us, waiting for their chance."

"Well, I hope their, and our, chance comes soon. The General hoped our victory over Sihayo's stronghold would produce some action, but it's been two days, and so far, nothing." Manning gave Pickford a sloppy salute and urged his horse away in a canter.

Silly old woman.

Pickford was a good engineer, no doubt, but he'd probably never seen much action. He didn't understand the grasp the General had over the mentality of these savages.

Eyes on them while they worked. He snorted, and then laughed as his horse snorted, too.

～

ENTRY WRITTEN JANUARY, 1872

ANOTHER YEAR BEGUN, JACK, AND YOU AND YOUR SISTER ARE growing up so fast. I see the way young Henry from across the way looks at Catherine in church, and wouldn't wonder if he comes calling for her soon.

Not sure I'm prepared for that yet, but I'm trying to hold back time, perhaps.

Sometimes I can't breathe, when the air gets too cold, but I try to hide it from your mother. There is nothing she can do to get these pieces of metal out of my lungs.

I don't want this for you.

I don't want you maimed or disfigured for some stuffed shirt's idea of empire. Of what constitutes glory for England.

It was my experience in the Sikh War that the smallest of advances are hailed as great victories and the most terrible defeats are swept under the carpet. Just crossing the Chenab, after firing all day at empty trenches and a couple of guns, was hailed as a wonderful success. The fact that Sher Singh was long gone and had been for most of the day was taken as a sign the Sikh army had dispersed.

Unfortunately it had done no such thing, as we slowly learned after the crossing, while waiting around interminably for orders from Dalhousie. And when those orders finally came, they were vague in the extreme.

Vague enough for Gough to interpret them as he saw fit. And by now, the General wanted blood.

JACK RAISED HIS EYES FROM THE JOURNAL, STRAIGHT INTO THE clear gaze of Elizabeth Bird. God, her eyes were so green sometimes. Intense and bright with secrets.

For a long moment, they stared at each other. She looked away first, sat down on her cot and began removing her boots.

"You seem very caught up in that journal."

"My father's recollections from his time as a junior officer."

"Oh." She shrugged out of her coat and lay back on her cot, lifting her arms up and folding them under her head. She stretched, arching her back slightly.

He wondered if she understood how suggestive the movement was.

"What does he say?"

"He was disillusioned. His battalion was in a terrible battle, where they lost at least half their men. He was badly injured, and never truly recovered."

"What do you mean, disillusioned?"

Jack shrugged. His father's views could well be considered treasonous. He couldn't, wouldn't besmirch his father's honour now.

"If you mean he saw how the empire is run, how people are crushed and destroyed so England can become a little richer, or a little more important, and hated it, then your father and mine had the same views."

Jack stilled. "I thought your father was a farmer."

He saw her start, then shake her head. "My father was a trader in China. He's been dead six years."

"I'm sorry. I lost my father a little over six years ago myself. Just before I became a soldier. I didn't understand how he felt about the empire when I signed up. Perhaps if my mother had given this journal to me after he died, or if he'd given it to me himself . . ."

"Why didn't she?"

"I think she was ashamed of his views." Jack closed his eyes, suddenly deeply, achingly tired. His mother's letters were always so full of the surface details, never asking too much or probing too deep. He'd been right to think she'd been terrified he'd say something to show he was unhappy with army life. And after his injury last year, she'd been even more jolly, never alighting for more than a moment on a single point, but fluttering madly from topic to topic, petrified if she settled, the conversation would turn serious.

It added to his grief at her passing to realize since his father's death she'd felt guilt, shame and fear.

"My mother agreed with my father, but she was with him in China. She saw firsthand what was done in the name of the empire." Elizabeth turned on her side, resting her head in her hand, her expression serious.

"I think that was it. My mother had no understanding of my father's experiences. Perhaps he didn't want to burden her with what happened . . ."

He needed to look away from where her breasts strained against her cotton shirt. He needed to get his mind out of the gutter.

"You feel the same way as your father, don't you?"

"What?" Jack jerked his gaze up to her eyes.

"You think Frere is making war for his own, mysterious reasons."

"I . . . don't know about mysterious reasons, but my heart is not in this fight. The Zulus have done nothing to provoke this attack by us, and I'm sorry to be under orders in this situation."

"You're sorry, but you'll follow your orders, anyway. You consider it your duty."

"Yes, I do." He looked at her curiously. "You don't approve?"

Elizabeth closed her eyes, her expression blank. "I think it's wrong that the Empire is forcing a war, but I can respect your individual code of honour. I know why you continue."

"And your brother?"

Elizabeth snapped her eyes open.

"My . . . brother?"

"You said he signed up to the 24th. Does he feel like you do, that the war is wrong, or will he be bound by his oath to serve?"

"I don't know what he believes," Elizabeth said quietly.

"A family rift?" Jack lifted a brow. "Is that why he left? Did he take the Queen's shilling as a rebellion?"

Elizabeth nodded. Said nothing.

"I'm sorry you haven't been able to find him, Elizabeth. What will you do when this campaign is over?"

"I don't know."

For a moment he wondered if he should say something, make some kind of offer of protection. But she sat up, hunched away from him, as if trying to make herself insignificant.

"He may be back home already. He may be there waiting for me."

"Yes, of course . . ."

"I'm sure of it," she said forcefully, shoving her feet into her boots, as if trying to hide her distress with bravado. "There will be someone at home for me."

Then she stood and walked out.

CHAPTER TWENTY

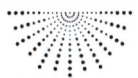

I see no chance of us advancing for 7 days – Road near camp over a swamp must be drained, and supplies must be stored at Rorke's Drift – The rain latterly all over Natal has been incessant and the roads are reported impassable . . .

— LETTER FROM CHELMSFORD TO EVELYN WOOD, 14 JANUARY, 1879

"See anything today, Burdell?"

Jack looked up from his dinner, across the table to Shaw, and shook his head. "A few Zulus in the distance. Could have been warriors, could have been herdsmen. By the time we got to where they'd been standing, there was no trace of them."

"The Natal Mounted Police are better picket scouts, anyway, with their horses. As you say, by the time you arrive anywhere, everyone's gone."

Jack shrugged. "I'd rather be out scouting than sitting around."

"I'd rather be fighting." Jervis leaned across and cut in on the conversation. "I'd rather have your batman, too." He laughed wickedly. "Thought you'd refused a batman in the past?"

Jack kept his face neutral, refusing to get drawn in to Jervis's baiting. He said nothing.

"What is it with you, Burdell? Why so surly all the time?"

"It's the company I'm forced to keep," Jack answered, rising from the table.

Jervis laughed again. "I've been watching little Private Bird. The way he moves, the way he's so skittish around the other men."

Jack stilled, turned back to face Jervis. He would have to play this so very carefully.

"I'd almost say he was a girl, but he sits like a man, strides around like one, too. You can tell a woman in men's clothing by the way she keeps forgetting she isn't wearing long skirts and a corset. Bird has clearly never worn either."

His statement forced a laugh from Jack. "Where on earth do you come up with this poppycock?"

Shaw laughed too. "Had a lot of experience with women who dress up as men, have you, Jervis?"

"As a matter of fact, yes." Jervis smirked. "There was a woman masquerading as a male doctor where I was stationed in Gibraltar. Could tell straight away. She always got out of carriages cautiously, as if she were going to trip on her skirts. And twice I saw her curtsey instead of bow, by mistake."

"And you exposed her, did you?" Jack raised an inquiring eyebrow.

"Well, not in so many words." Jervis cackled. "I let her

know I knew, and . . ." he paused, a lascivious look in his eye. "I'm too much a gentleman to kiss and tell."

Jack turned away in disgust. Not just with Jervis, but with himself.

He'd actually been contemplating making advances on Elizabeth. But knowing she was in his power, that he could expose her at any time, would she think she had a choice in the matter? Like Jervis's doctor, would she feel blackmailed into having sex, just to keep her secret?

He flicked viciously at the canvas flap of the officers' mess entrance as he walked out. He didn't know what was happening to him. What rot was setting in on this dark continent. Because even the thought that she may feel forced to sleep with him did not diminish his wish to try.

ELIZABETH TESTED THE STACK OF AMMUNITION BOXES TO SEE IF it was stable. She had to make sure it could take her weight. All was lost if it came crashing down.

Unscrewing each case of ammunition, pulling back the tin seal, lifting out the bullets and damaging the soft copper shells slightly and then putting it all back together was taking too long. And now that she was sneaking in to the 1sts munitions tent, she was flirting with disaster.

Once the tin seal was removed, it couldn't be replaced, but Elizabeth didn't think the soldiers would worry much about that under fire, when all they wanted was to get at their bullets. With the lids screwed back on, it was impossible to tell which had intact tin seals and which didn't.

But that left the problem of what to do with the seals, where to hide them. If someone found them, there may well be a check of the ammunition. She needed another way to even up the odds between the British and the Zulu and she thought she might have found it.

She heaved herself up onto the top of the stack, and then stood slowly, arms out for balance, the sharp knife she'd taken from Jack's tent blade down in her hand.

She'd heard the men talking about target practice, and how some of the bullets had gotten damp. Damp gunpowder didn't work so well.

And what were they having every single day, sometimes all day, but rain? And what if that rain was somehow falling into the munitions tent?

She felt a slight wobble beneath her, and stilled for a moment, then lifted up her knife and slashed at the canvas roof of the tent. It was so thick, the knife glanced off, and she was forced to grab a handful of canvas and work the tip in, pushing it away from her body.

She held her breath as the heavy fabric ripped loudly, but no shout rang out. She chose another part of the roof, and went to work again.

She had no idea when her handiwork would be discovered, but the low grumbles of thunder were already growing to the east. Soon a storm would blow this way, and give the crates a good soaking. It was the best she could do, in the circumstance.

She carefully lowered herself back to the ground.

She'd felt guilty, almost sick at what she was doing, before Sihayo's stronghold, but now, as long as Jack wasn't getting bum bullets, she felt nothing.

Or rather, she felt something, but it wasn't regret.

It was satisfaction.

~

"You're out late."

Elizabeth froze in the darkness of the tent. Spun slowly to Jack's bed, where he sat, fully clothed, completely in shadow.

"You're in early. Can't you find a match?"

"I didn't try. I wanted to think, and I don't need a light for that."

She took a step back to the entrance. "Shall I leave you in peace? I could go . . ." She wondered herself where she could go.

"No." He spoke sharply, and she felt her heart somersault in her chest, then start up an erratic beat.

"All right. Thank you." Unsure whether to light the lamp or not, she went to her cot and sat down, facing him. It was nice like this. She didn't have to avoid looking him in the eye in the dark. She didn't have to worry about her face betraying her.

"That day at the river . . ." His voice was low, an octave deeper than usual, and Elizabeth froze, lifted her head like a springbok scenting a leopard.

"Why didn't you cover yourself? Every other woman I know would have done."

"How many women do you know who dress as men and pose as soldiers?"

She had forgotten how women reacted in her old world. And saw at last the reason for his confusion. He had thought her willing, perhaps, until he'd seen the fear and anger on her face. Had pulled her up the bank expecting an embrace, not a narrow-eyed, cornered cat. He hadn't understood the deadly consequences of her answering the fire in his eyes with a heat of her own.

Too jumbled up inside, too edgy to sit with him like this,

strangely cut off from the rest of the camp, she stood, and he stood with her.

"Wait." There was a rawness to his voice, a desperation in the way he stepped forward to grip her arm.

Elizabeth stilled, her attention on his lips, on the way he was drawing her closer to him.

She bumped into his chest. The feeling of their bodies pressed together made the hair stand up on her arms, the back of her neck. She wanted to be closer still. She tentatively slid her arms around his waist, tipping her head up to him.

She saw all she needed in his face.

"I don't want you to think—", he started to say, and she stopped him, rising up on her toes, brushing her lips over his.

He made a sound, like a bridge giving beneath a terrible weight, or the final creak of a tree before it crashes. He held her head in place, kept her lips on his, and then his hands lifted up to her cheeks, traced the curve of her neck and moved to the front of her jacket. She felt him fumble with her buttons, and in a mirror of his actions, she began unbuttoning his coat.

He pushed her jacket off her shoulders, and started on the buttons of her shirt, giving her small, light kisses on her mouth, on the side of her neck.

By the time he reached the final button, just above her navel, they were both trembling. He angled his hands into the gaping shirt, loosening the ends of her breast bindings and pulling the whole length of it out. She shivered at the sensation of her breasts being free and then jerked as his fingers brushed across them.

She saw the flash of his smile in the dark, and smiled back as he bent her slightly over his arm. For a moment, she clutched at his shoulders but he murmured something soothing, kissing her on the curve where her neck and shoulder met as she relaxed into his strength.

Then he bent his head to her breast, drew the tip into his mouth, and Elizabeth screamed.

CHAPTER TWENTY-ONE

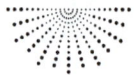

The heart of a man to the heart of a maid – Light of my tents, be fleet.

Morning waits at the end of the world, And the world is all at our feet!

— RUDYARD KIPLING, THE GIPSY TRAIL

"Shhhh."

Jack held her tight against his chest, the buttons of his open coat digging into her bared breasts, and Elizabeth startled to giggle.

"Quiet, you sound like—"

"Sorry." She tried to breathe deeply, burying into his chest. "What do I sound like?"

"A girl." There was laughter in his voice.

She finally felt calm enough to lean back and look at him. It was almost too dark to see, but there was something in his expression, something tender, that melted her bones.

"If I promise not to scream, will you do that again?" she whispered.

He started, stared down at her.

"What am I doing with you?" He sounded lost. "I feel like a lecher and a bully. You understand you can tell me to go to hell? That I'm only pushing my luck because you're letting me."

She strained to make out his face in the darkness. "I'm not going to tell you to go to hell."

"I . . ." He made a sound like a man in pain. "I'm pleased to hear it." There was an edge of laughter to his voice again, a playfulness which Elizabeth had not seen in him before. He pulled her unbuttoned shirt over her head and slipped off her coat, maneuvering her backwards, his big body a solid wall.

A mild sense of panic gripped her and she bit back a shriek as her knees hit the back of his cot and she bounced down onto it, naked from the waist up. And unlike at the river, this time, she felt vulnerable. Exposed.

"Jack . . ." She swallowed.

"Shhhh, sweet girl," he whispered in her ear as he bent over her and tugged off her boots. Slowly pulled off the rest of her uniform, one piece at a time.

Looking down on her, Jack started on his own clothes, and she could swear his hands were shaking as they fumbled with his buttons. A tension built between them, and when Jack kicked his drawers off and stood naked before her, he waited one last, long moment, as if expecting her to change her mind.

When she said nothing, he gave a sigh and sank beside her on the narrow bed, his body heat enveloping her.

He started stroking her softly, lulling her, calming her, until she began moving restlessly against him, exploring the width and strength of him with trembling hands.

"This is good." She didn't mean to sound so surprised, but she was.

"Believe me, it gets even better."

She did believe him.

As his mouth worked its way down her body, and his hands stroked her like he could not get enough of her, she put all her trust in him.

And when he entered her, when her body clenched hot and tight around him, burning with the pain of her first time, and she looked into his face and saw his eyes closed, his head flung back as he fought to control himself, fought to keep it gentle for her, she felt that trust honoured.

She was falling over the edge, carried over by him, her pleasure bittersweet – tainted by the searing pain of knowing he couldn't, shouldn't, put his trust in her.

～

WHAT WAS HE GOING TO DO WITH HER? JACK LAY, HEAD propped up, looking down on Elizabeth as she slept.

She lay fully against him, her fists curled like a baby's, resting against his chest.

That the longing, the sheer wanting, of the last two weeks had been requited, brought no peace. He wanted her beneath him again right now. He wanted her safe, away from here. He wanted her too much.

And what were the rules? What did she expect from him?

She wasn't some labourer's daughter, giving him the come-on from behind a haystack, or a hard-eyed whore from the taverns in Pietermartizburg. Yet she wasn't a conventional miss, either.

He had an uncomfortable feeling she would laugh if she could read his mind.

He had a terrible suspicion she was living in the moment, and cared nothing for whether he'd marry her or not.

She was a mystery. A curious dichotomy of impatience and shyness, demanding, and yet, he would swear to it, a virgin until last night.

Why she had chosen him, why he should be the lucky bastard she gave herself too, he almost didn't want to know.

He realized how truly little he did know of her. He had no idea where she came from. Only that the loss of her farm to her uncle must mean complete destitution for her to risk so much by coming here to find her brother.

There was a wildness to her. A spark of temper in her eye. She may have done this in part for the adventure of it. With no parents or brother to hold her back, she could have taken her chance and run with it.

He had only to think of her by the river to understand how possible that was.

She'd risen to every challenge she'd encountered in the camp. Throwing herself wholeheartedly into the work Chambers gave her, taking pride in a job well done for the job's sake. She contradicted every trite view on womanhood his fellow Englishmen held.

Considering social mores and rules, Elizabeth Bird was either a hoyden or the bravest woman he'd ever known.

The clatter of a bucket nearby startled him out of his reverie.

The camp was stirring around them, and Jack knew he needed to get them both up and dressed, before someone came with a message for him, or Chambers sought Elizabeth out.

The soft, muted light of the early sun through the white canvas of his tent illuminated her skin, golden with a smattering of freckles.

He frowned, peered closer. He'd always thought her face was tanned because of the sun, but her shoulders, her chest, her breasts all had the same, smooth glow.

He thought back to the river, and realized even then, her skin had been more golden than white, as if she'd spent many hours without a shirt on.

He ran a hand down her back, pressed a kiss to her forehead, and she stirred.

"We must get up. We're late already."

"Mmm." She half-opened her eyes, and peered up at him through her eyelashes, satisfaction in her smile.

He felt the desire roar to life again, and groaned as he eased himself off the bed.

"None of that. Up." He tossed her her uniform, and her smile widened.

"Up, you say?"

He shook his head, grinning, and pulled his drawers over his erection, but made no effort to turn away as she sat up herself and began winding the strip of cloth around her breasts.

"God, if I had a week and a room in a hotel." He heard the strain and longing in his voice.

"We could." She stood, pulling her rumpled shirt over her head. There was something about the way she said it, intense and fearful.

"You know I can't."

She pulled her trousers on slowly, as if she had no

strength. "I know." She lifted her face to his as she buttoned them, and he saw the worry in her eyes.

"We'll be free soon. With our gun power and rocket batteries, this campaign is likely to be over shortly."

She nodded, biting her lip, and a tear fell onto her cheek.

He put out a finger, brushed the tiny drop away, at a loss to understand how his words could make her cry.

CHAPTER TWENTY-TWO

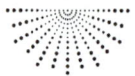

Mounted patrols went out every day sometimes capturing cattle, never meeting opposition. The general feeling of the natives seems to indicate that those in this particular part of the country do not care about fighting and wish to 'come in' with their families and cattle . . .

— AN ENTRY IN THE DIARY OF LT. COGHILL,
COL. GLYN'S ORDERLY OFFICER

Lindani shaded his eyes, and stood with the sky to his back on the rocky outcrop, making sure the men of the Natal Mounted Police had caught sight of him.

"Let's go," he called to Malusi, and all ten of them, in full battle dress, ran across open ground and over the crest of the hill, cutting immediately right and around the side of the outcrop, out of sight.

They crawled on their bellies, circling around almost to

their original starting point, and hid in the rocks, watching as the NMP men thundered up the hill on their horses.

"They went straight over the hill." The whiteman who spoke lifted something to his eye, and looked out over the narrow valley.

"Where the hell have they got to?" The man who snapped out the question was undoubtedly the captain of this company, and he led his horse right to the edge of the drop, lifting a similar object to his own eye.

"They've legged it. There's no sign of them."

"Were they a scouting party or warriors out scavenging provisions for a larger force?"

"Impossible to tell." The man who spoke now caused Lindani a moment's pause. His eyes did not just travel over the valley, in the direction the NMP thought they had gone, he looked everywhere, with the stillness of a hunter.

"Well, we'll go back and report it. Either way, the horses won't make it down that slope. Not exactly horse country, is it?" The captain snapped the little tube he'd been looking through shut.

"And they know that only too well," the dangerous one said.

The men turned their horses back, and the hunter gazed thoughtfully at the boulders where they hid.

Lindani could hear his heart beating in time with the horses' hooves on the stones as they rode away.

That had been a close call.

"Did we fool them?" Malusi asked when the horsemen were out of sight.

Lindani, the only one among them who understood English, nodded slowly. "They think we may be warriors, part of a larger group. They've gone back to report it."

"Good. It will keep their eyes in this direction."

"The one man. He looks hard as the head of an *iwisa*." Lindani tapped the round, polished head of his own stick. "Mean as one, too. A hunter, maybe, or a trader. Someone who speaks Zulu, who knows us."

Malusi clicked his tongue. "That one, I know who you mean. He looked at the rocks as if he knew we were here."

"If he thought for a moment we were, we'd be dead or captured." Lindani's hands twitched.

"We're meeting with Inyoni tonight. She can tell us if these tricks are working."

Lindani nodded, but could not force any excitement over the thought. Every time Inyoni met with them, she risked death or discovery. Every secret she stole put her in danger.

And yet, she had done so well, learned so much, the general now had some specific questions he wanted her to answer.

Lindani almost hoped she did not come tonight to meet them, although as it had been two nights already, he knew in his heart she would. And he was honour-bound to give her the questions, just as she was honour-bound to find the answers.

"I cannot believe no one has realized she is a woman," he said, more to himself than to Malusi. "How can they not see it? She is in danger every time she moves or speaks, down there."

"I told you, the eye sees what it wants to see, not what is really there." Malusi started after the other scouts, back towards their camp.

"I hope you're right." Lindani caught up to him, slashing at the long grass with his *iwisa*.

"I am," Malusi said. "That is why these whitemen see savages instead of equals, boys instead of men. To see us any other way would be uncomfortable for them because they could not justify what they are doing."

Lindani swung his *iwisa* again. "What I would like to know is the reason for this attack on us. If Inyoni discovers nothing more from them than why, I will be in her debt."

"The general has wanted to know that from the start," Malusi agreed. "But now the matter is urgent. Inyoni must do whatever is necessary to find out."

Lindani turned and looked one last time in the direction of the whitemen's camp. Whatever was necessary could be the death of her.

MANNING LEANED BACK IN HIS CHAIR AND READ THE NMP's picket report for Lord Chelmsford. The NMP had seen the warriors running in the direction of oNdini, Cetshwayo's stronghold, exactly where the general thought they'd come from.

He finished the brief entry and added a summary of it beneath the earlier picket reports. The NMP were the only ones to have seen anything.

It was as if Zululand was deserted.

Damn and blast these bloody Zulus. Fight-shy, every last one of them. The general probably had far more men in Central Column than he needed, although Manning was sure there'd be a heated exchange when they got to oNdini.

Cetshwayo wouldn't give up his kingdom without a fight, even if it looked like he was prepared to let the burning of Sihayo's stronghold pass without retaliation.

Manning could feel the mood in the camp was one of dangerous boredom and complacency. With nothing to do for days on end, and no sign of the enemy, Manning knew the men's minds were turning to mischief. There'd be a few floggings before Pickford's road was ready to travel on, of that he was sure.

He decided to call the officers in this evening and ensure they kept the discipline of their men. Anyone stepping out of line, starting now, would feel the whip.

He gathered his papers together and rose, rearing back in surprise to find a young soldier at the entrance to his tent.

"How long have you been there?" he snapped, angry at being startled.

"Less than a minute, sir." The little private saluted him, his eyes on his boots. "I've come with a message from Lieutenant Chambers, sir."

"Well?"

"He would like to see you about men to move the wagons, sir. When we go to Isandlwana."

"Say that again, private."

"I beg your pardon, sir?"

"Say that accursed, unpronounceable name again."

"Isandlwana."

"I-sund-lwana. Is that how it's pronounced?"

"That's how the Zulu speakers in the NNC say it, sir." The boy's eyes seem to dart around the tent. Probably nervous at being questioned by one of Chelmsford's staff, although his edginess was irritating.

"Ah, good. Very well, tell Chambers I'll be with him in an hour, after I've debrief the general on the picket reports."

"Yes, sir."

Manning moved forward, forcing the private to back out his tent, and then strode swiftly towards the general's accommodations. Just as he turned into the main camp, he had the sense the private hadn't moved away from his tent, but carried on loitering there.

Skiving off, no doubt.

He'd definitely call the officers together this evening. The rot was already setting in.

~

"I'M CONSIDERING RESIGNING MY COMMISSION." JACK PICKED UP his tea and hunched his body around it.

Shaw nearly choked on his. "You're what?"

"My mother died recently, and its made me think of home. I inherited the family farm when my father died and I think I'll go back to it. I'm tired of this life."

"You, a farmer, Jack? I don't see it."

Jack buttered a piece of toast. "Oh, I'm a farmer, all right. I ran that farm towards the end of my father's life almost single-handedly."

"And ran screaming to the army as soon as you could."

Jack nodded, swallowed his toast. "When my sister married Henry, and I had someone capable of running the place, I did join up." He took another gulp of tea. "But I've seen both sides of the coin now, and farming wins."

"Well, deciding has obviously eased your mind, you look in good spirits today," Shaw commented. "Not so glum as usual."

Jack grinned back at him. "I am in good spirits. The time has come to settle down."

"The young ladies of wherever you live will be delighted to hear it. As will their Mamas."

Jack laughed.

"Burdell?"

Manning spoke so sharply, Jack's laughter died in his throat.

"Yes?"

"I hear that little redheaded lad is your batman."

Jack nodded tightly.

"Well, tell him if I catch him loitering instead of doing his duty again, I'll personally be the one to flog him."

"What are you talking about, Manning?"

"Chambers sent him with a message for me as I was on my way out, but halfway to the general I realized I'd forgotten something, came back, and there he was, just inside my tent, skulking, trying to shirk his duty."

"I know for a fact that lad works all the hours God gives him for Chambers, Manning, and I have no complaints either. Are you certain of your story?" Jack spoke pleasantly, but he saw Manning blanch at the underlying edge to his words.

"Are you accusing me of making it up?" Manning's lips were white with anger.

"Not at all. Just that it is out of character for the lad. He works like a dog in this camp, and Chambers will be the first to tell you that. What was his excuse?"

"Said he thought he'd dropped something in my tent when he was there to deliver his message, and came back to look for it."

"There you go." Jack shrugged, dismissing the incident.

"Now see here, Burdell. I didn't believe him. He was shaking like a leaf, guilty as the day is long."

"Even if you're right, all he's guilty of is taking a few moments of respite from his work and the heat in the shade of your tent, while the rest of the camp sits around on their arses."

"Well," Manning's shoulders relaxed slightly. "I expect that's true. But I'll announce this now." He raised his voice, and most of the officers in the mess lifted their heads in his direction.

"I'm calling all the officers to order this evening. The men are getting too lax. Some discipline needs to be injected into this camp before the Zulus waltz in here and murder us all in our beds while we sleep."

"That's us privates safe, then," the porter clearing away Jack's plate muttered under his breath. "We don't have the luxury of beds."

The comment bordered on insubordination but Jack let it go. He was in too good a mood to make an issue out of it and pretended he hadn't heard. He kept a blank face as Manning saluted and strode out of the mess.

"I used to like Manning, when he was a plain old officer of the 24th." Shaw watched him go. "Now, I understand more clearly the impact of power on personality."

"What impact is that?" Jack leaned forward, mug raised to his lips.

"The more power you have, the more of an arse you become."

Funny, Jack thought. That could apply to the Empire, as well.

CHAPTER TWENTY-THREE

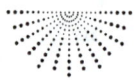

We have done with Hope and Honour. We are lost to Love and Truth, We are dropping down the ladder rung by rung;

— RUDYARD KIPLING; GENTLEMEN-RANKERS,
BARRACK-ROOM BALLADS

E lizabeth skirted the mess tent, and her stomach gave a regretful rumble.

She had to see Lindani and be back in the camp before Jack came out from dinner, and something told her he'd be out of there this evening as early as propriety allowed.

She grinned. Her heart skipped a beat at the thought of what they had done together last night. The possibility of doing it again gave her a hot, restless feeling in the pit of her stomach.

Her steps slowed as she reached the sentry. It wasn't the

one she'd spoken to last time, and she steeled herself for spinning her insect story again.

"Evening," she called out before she lost her nerve.

"Evening." The sentry slid her a curious look.

"I'm on insect duty again tonight. See you in a bit." She walked past him, making her steps carefree and confident.

"Wot? Insect duty?"

"For Dartmouth," she called.

"Oh, 'im." The sentry gave a snort. "Blimey, I ask you."

Despite what they inferred about Dartmouth's mental health, Elizabeth could hear the men were proud of him. A prime specimen of English eccentricity and the pursuit of science.

She moved quickly through the bush, aware she did not have much time, her eyes and ears alert for any sign of life.

The cack, cack of a guineau fowl came from her left, and she stilled. Both Lindani and Malusi could impersonate the birds and animals of the veld so well, she had no idea whether it was them or not.

"Lindani?" she whispered softly. She crouched down to see if she could spy the guineau fowl under the bush and looked straight into Lindani's eyes. Even though she was half-expecting it, she recoiled back in shock.

"It's us, little bird." Lindani called softly, and heart slamming in her chest, she lowered herself back onto the ground, and saw Malusi lay beside Lindani in the undergrowth.

"You keep stopping my heart." She reached out her hand and Lindani gripped it, like he would a fellow warrior.

"I'm one of the boys now, am I?" She gave him a cheeky grin. The irreverence of the enlisted men was affecting her.

He nodded slowly, as if realizing what he'd done.

"You deserve the accolades of a brave warrior, Inyoni. But you will always be the sister of my heart."

Malusi said nothing, giving no praise. He was too hard. He didn't have it in him.

"I'm not brave. I tremble with fear half the time, and shake with anger the other half." Elizabeth folded her hands on the ground and rested her chin on them. "I found a way to look through the papers of an officer on Chelmsford's staff today." Unexpectedly, involuntarily, her whole body shivered as she remembered Manning's fury when he'd discovered her in his tent. She'd had nowhere to hide, no other way out.

"You were caught?" Lindani pulled himself forward to see her better in the darkness and Malusi leaned forward as well, but not with concern, with the eagerness of a lion scenting a kill.

"Not in the act, thank goodness. I heard him coming and got to the entrance just in time, spun him a story about looking for something."

"He didn't suspect you?"

Elizabeth shook her head, gave a humourless laugh. "Even if I confessed, they probably wouldn't believe me. They cannot conceive of an Englishman

. . . or woman, betraying her own for an African nation. It is beyond their imagination."

"What did you discover?" Malusi cut through their conversation and Elizabeth shot him an angry look.

Lindani ignored him. "You were lucky to get away with it, you never could lie well."

But Elizabeth shook her head. "Things have changed. I have changed. Everything I do in that camp is a lie. I'm very good at it now."

She closed her eyes. It was a loss of innocence she hadn't bargained on. The price of honouring her agreement with the general.

The loss of her sexual innocence she did not regret at all.

Somewhere in the bush a kieviet called and she realized time was slipping away from them. She needed to get back. At last she looked at Malusi.

"The officer's papers show they think the main force will come on a direct path from oNdini, if they come at all."

Malusi lost his sulky look. "Good."

"And the other thing I managed to see was the commander of a much smaller column to the north-west, Durnford, has been reprimanded by Chelmsford. He's considering making Durnford join with Central Column to keep an eye on him. Seems Durnford's a bit too eager to engage."

"I will pass this on. The general is very pleased with what you've given me so far."

It was the closest to praise she would ever get from him.

"From the beginning, he wanted to know the whiteman's reason behind this attack. Now, it is vital you find out. By any means possible."

There was silence between them for a moment, as Elizabeth absorbed the implications of the order.

"If the King can understand what it is they really want, it would help him with his strategy." Even Malusi must feel the tension, that he'd offered an explanation.

"I understand." Elizabeth gripped her fingers together.

"Also, he wants to know when the column plans to move again."

Lindani shot a fierce look at Malusi, as if enough was enough, but Elizabeth nodded, uncertain. "I've heard we move on the 20th of January. The road is almost ready, and we're moving to Isandlwana, setting up a temporary camp there while the general decides which way to proceed."

"So in two days. That should be plenty of time. The warriors have left oNdini already."

Elizabeth rose to a crouch. "When do we meet again?"

Malusi considered it. "At Isandlwana. It is too dangerous to come out every night."

Lindani nodded. "Agreed. And find the answer for the general very quickly, so you can leave this column."

His words made Elizabeth's stomach lurch. Was the end so near? Why did the thought of that strike panic within her? "Leave the column?"

Lindani frowned at her question. "When the *impi* gathers to sweep the whiteman from our land, they will not stop to ask if you are a Zulu spy, little bird. They will kill every man in a red coat they see."

HE SAW HER SLIP INTO THE TENT AHEAD OF HIM AND HIS HEART slammed in his chest. He was already a fool for her. He knew it, and he didn't care.

She didn't light the lamp, and he smiled as he took the last few steps to the entrance.

He stood still just inside, letting his eyes become accustomed to the darkness. She was removing her jacket, flicking at the front as if it were dirty.

"Rolling around on the ground, were you?" he teased softly, and then frowned as she jerked in surprise.

But she drew herself up and nodded. "You could say that. Checking under a wagon for Chambers."

She turned her back on him, laying the jacket over a chair, and he couldn't stay away from her any longer.

He caught her from behind, enveloping her in his arms,

and was gratified to feel her lean back into him, snuggle in as close as she could.

"Manning didn't hound you again today, did he?" He nuzzled her neck.

She stilled beneath him. "No, although he was very angry with me. Did he say something to you?"

"Shouted, more like it. He's got a bee in his bonnet about lax discipline, and you chose the wrong moment to hang around in his tent."

"Hang around?" she said indignantly, easing something inside him. "I work harder than most of the men."

"That's what I told him."

"Good. Despicable toady."

He chuckled at her vehemence. "Why do you call him that?"

But she didn't answer, because he'd swirled his tongue in her ear, and her arms came up and back to hook around his neck.

She twisted her head to kiss him, and he slipped his tongue into her mouth, pulled her back harder against his erection.

She spun to face him, panting, and the look of desire, of haste, in her eyes was the most beautiful sight Jack had seen in his life.

He lifted her up, cradled his hands under her arse, and if there'd been a wall handy, he'd have had her up against it.

She made a sound in her throat, a sort of purr, burrowing her hands under his open jacket, and sliding them around his sides, up his back.

She murmured something in his ear, and for a moment he thought she'd said something in Zulu, but then she bit down on his earlobe, and he realized he must have misheard.

She was a heady mixture of virgin and siren, eager and curious.

"Could you be any more perfect than you are?" he whispered as he lowered his lips to hers. She jerked her head back.

"I'm not perfect." Her hands came up to cup his face. "I'm true to what I believe in. I'm honourable. But your view of honour may not be the same as mine."

He kissed her, and thought how wrong she was.

She was his dream woman.

CHAPTER TWENTY-FOUR

Road at present quite unfit for convoys to pass – Our first move must therefore be to the Isanblana hill where there is wood and water –

> — CHELMSFORD IN A LETTER TO COL.
> EVELYN WOOD

Elizabeth lay deep in Jack's arms, listening to his heart beat, and realized how steep the price of loyalty was. She would not change her decision, but that she had to choose was a bitter taste on her tongue.

She had known from the start he would consider her an abomination when he discovered the truth. At the very least, he would feel betrayed by her even if he never found out what she was – if she simply disappeared.

Knowing that had helped her keep a small part of her heart from him.

But after their lovemaking tonight, she had torn down the wall. Broached the distance. Smashed it with her bare hands.

She was his, and she had to give him up.

Jack wasn't the enemy of the Zulus. Most of the men in this column were not their enemies. And yet, some day soon, they would face each other in battle and kill and maim each other. And for what?

Lindani was right. The reason behind this was important.

Discovering why Frere was pointing his war machine in the direction of Zululand was the most vital piece of information she could uncover.

"Do you know why we are here?" she whispered to Jack.

"Why we are here?" His voice was a soft touch on her ear. "You mean, are we fulfilling God's purpose?"

"No." She laughed softly. "Why has Frere sent us here? Why are we fighting the Zulus?"

She saw him smile. "I thought you were having an attack of conscience after our lovemaking."

"No. I have no regrets."

"I am glad of that." He brushed a kiss on her forehead.

"*Do* you know why Chelmsford and Frere have us out here?"

"Tenacious, aren't you? I was hoping to answer more important questions." He shifted, and she felt his arousal against her belly

"Like?"

"Like, can I make us forget where we are?"

"We both know the answer to that is yes." She trailed a hand down his chest, and touched him lightly with the tips of her fingers. "But if we are facing death, I'd like to know why."

Shifting to his side, he began to explore her body, his hand stroking and kneading her skin.

"I heard, and this was only by accident, that Frere is worried the Empire will go to war with Russia over the Balkans. If we do, he wants to have the whole of Southern Africa under British control, rather than risk the Russians making a deal with the Zulus over harbour rights along the east coast. If the Russians are able to get supplies and dock safely in Southern Africa, it would be an immense blow to British naval supremacy."

"Where did you hear that?" Elizabeth looked up at him, her mind spinning.

"In the officers' mess one evening at Helpmekaar. Chelmsford was discussing it with some of his aides, and didn't realize I was within earshot."

"And if the Empire doesn't go to war with Russia?"

"They'll conquer the Zulus anyway. They are too afraid of losing their trade advantage on the route to India not to secure it."

Elizabeth closed her eyes. One tiny part of her heart had held out hope there could be a solution, a way out if only they knew why. But it turned out knowing the reason made no difference to the outcome. "It seems there is nothing else for it but war, then."

"You hoped there was a possibility we would turn back?" Jack spoke gently, as if to a delicate lady.

"Of course I did. Who would want to shed blood and take lives?" She said it fiercely, and was horrified at the tears in her eyes.

"Hush." He smoothed back her short hair. "Your peace-loving heart does you credit, but most of these officers cannot wait for a chance at action. It is the one sure way to move their careers forward."

"It isn't right, Jack. The Zulus didn't ask for this. If what you say is true, they're being attacked because Zululand is strategically important in a game they aren't playing."

"I know. But it's Frere's job to think of the Empire, and what is best for it. He doesn't care about the fairness of it. Or if he does, he squares it with himself as a necessary evil."

"Well, if he wants a war, he'll get one." She spoke bitterly, then realized she'd said too much, with too much feeling.

Jack looked thoughtful. "Maybe he will, maybe he won't. The Zulus have yet to show themselves."

"And if they do?"

"Then Chelmsford and Frere will throw everything they can at them."

LINDANI WAITED WITH MALUSI JUST LONG ENOUGH TO SEE THE tents of the camp being struck, the ox-wagons loaded. As soon as they were sure the column was moving towards Isandlwana, they could make their way to the main *impi*.

When the first wagon set off, so did they, angling north east to the column's north.

The sun was just rising, its sharp, hot fingers turning the cool dew clinging to the long grass into a carpet of diamonds. A carpet that left a dark green trail behind them as they ran.

A perfect path for the pickets to follow, only this time they did not want them to. They were not laying a decoy.

Their instructions were to join the main *impi* in the Ngwebeni valley, which lay hidden behind the escarpment opposite Isandlwana. The Inyoni escarpment. The irony that it shared its name with his adopted sister did not escape Lindani.

Every step he took away from her felt like a step too far. He knew she was vulnerable. The secret that she was not a boy was already out. Known by an officer.

And . . . there had been something more in the way Inyoni looked away from him. Something in the stubborn set of her jaw.

A thought struck, and he missed his step over the treacherous path, his knee buckling before he righted himself.

If this man was being improper with her, blackmailing her for sexual favours to keep quiet, he would make it a point of honour to be the one to kill him on the battlefield.

"It seems we will need to take the long route to the general," Malusi called behind him, and Lindani turned his head. Saw a flash of metal in the bright sun behind them.

A picket. They heard the hooves a moment later, and knew they were in trouble. Foot soldiers they could outrun and outwit any time. But a horse? On relatively clear ground like this? The odds weren't in their favour.

"I don't think they've seen us yet." Lindani looked at the clear trail they'd made behind them and willed the sun to hurry with sipping up the dew.

As one, they veered east, leaping on the rocks and picking a trail through the driest grasses. When they came to some hard-packed ground, they followed it, and Lindani pointed to a *donga*, a deep erosion trench.

"In there." The hooves were louder behind them, and any moment they would be spotted.

Malusi jumped in with him, but he was shaking his head. "We will be trapped here like a sick buck by hyenas."

"We can't outrun the horses, and they've picked up our trail," Lindani whispered, pressing himself up against the *donga* wall. The overhang would shield them from the view of anyone looking down into the deep slash in the ground.

The thunder of hooves dislodged a few pieces of red earth from the overhang and they fell to the floor of the *donga*, exploding into a thousand grains of sand.

The soft blow and snort of horses being reined in made Lindani squat down, curl in on himself. Malusi did the same.

"The trail disappears where the grass gives way to rock and hard-packed earth."

It was the man again. The wily one from before.

"How long do you reckon they passed by here, Fields? And can you tell how many there were?"

"More than one. But not too many. Two to four, I'd say. The tracks are fresh. We must be right behind them."

"If it's only a few of them, they're either scouts or foragers, and we could waste the whole day looking for them. I'd like to know where all these Zulus are. There's supposed to be 40,000 warriors at Cetshwayo's disposal. If that's the case, where the bloody hell are they?"

"Waiting for us closer to oNdini, maybe." Fields said. "Drawing us deeper into their country, maybe thinking to cut us off from our supplies from behind."

"Ouch. That's a nice thought."

"It's a possibility." Fields made no apology for his scenario.

"Chelmsford thinks they'll be like the Xhosa. They'll use ambush tactics."

"You know my feelings on that. I think Chelmsford is mistaken. I've lived in Natal for fifteen years. There's nothing prouder than a Zulu warrior. They face their enemies head on, and see glory in the battle."

"You sound like you admire them."

"I respect them," Fields answered. Lindani heard him click his tongue at his horse, and then the whole company moved out.

"That's the second time we have nearly been caught by that man," Malusi said softly when they couldn't hear the hooves any more.

"He is a clever one. He knows what Chelmsford has yet to find out." Lindani scrambled up the wall of the *donga*, and held out his hand for Malusi, who scorned it, climbing up easily on his own.

Without discussing it, they continued east, unwilling to take the chance the picket wouldn't come back and try to pick up their trail. They could turn north later, in the blue-grey hills up ahead.

"What is it that the wily one knows?" Malusi kept pace with him.

"That the Zulus are a force to be reckoned with."

CHAPTER TWENTY-FIVE

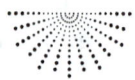

Do the staff think we are going to meet an army of school-girls? Why in the name of all that is holy do we not laager? *(Captain Duncombe to Hamilton-Browne at the Isandlwana camp.)*

— HAMILTON-BROWNE, A LOST LEGIONARY
IN SOUTH AFRICA, 1911

Jack looked around his tent in amazement. Everything had been unpacked.

Elizabeth, either playing efficient batman or gifting her lover with a wonderful surprise.

That he didn't know which annoyed him, although given Elizabeth's habit of turning things topsy-turvy, it could be a bit of both.

There, on the table beside his cot, was his father's journal, and Jack moved forward to pick it up. He had no further duties today, and the letter he'd half-written to his sister, telling her of his decision to return to the farm, lay like a coiled snake at the bottom of his writing box.

The weight of his guilt irritated him; the farm was his, after all. But he knew he would want to run it himself, and that meant Henry would leave, taking his sister and niece and nephew with him.

He sighed. He would think of something, some way around it, but not now. Now, he wanted to be pulled back into his father's past.

He eyed the hard wooden chair next to his folding table, but couldn't face the discomfort.

He took up the book and lay on his cot, folding the pillow double. It smelled of Elizabeth, the fresh, clean scent of her, and he inhaled deeply as he opened the journal.

ENTRY WRITTEN JANUARY, 1872

ON THE 12TH OF JANUARY 1849 WE ADVANCED ABOUT TEN miles north to Dinga, and Gough's plan was to leave the baggage there the following day and advance on Sher Singh at Rasul, where intelligence had placed him.

The idea of finally seeing some real action perked the whole blood-thirsty lot of us up no end. The lessons of Ramnagar had faded from memory and we were eager to give the natives a well-deserved drubbing.

At lights out that night, most of us found it difficult to sleep. My stomach was turning somersaults.

I would finally engage the enemy in the name of the Empire. At last I was a hero. More than boring John Burdell, farmer-to-be and all round stick-in-the-mud.

My father was a man who was loose with his fists. You toed the line or you got knocked over it. So I toed the line, and had the reputation of a good boy around the village.

I didn't want to be a good boy. Or a cowed boy. I wanted to be a devil-may-care lad who could make a girl smile with no more than a wink of his eye. And not just because I was the heir-apparent.

So I signed up and here I was, about to face the enemy for the first time, and with no clue what I was in for.

Gritty-eyed and jumpy, we set off the next day, the 13th, and if you'd asked me that morning how things were, I'd have said it was the best day of my life.

JACK CLOSED HIS EYES AND PICTURED HIS FATHER, TALL, LOOSE-limbed, leaning against the fence, his head thrown back in a laugh.

How little he'd known him.

He'd never said much about his days as an officer, and because of it, his time in India had taken on a mysterious glamour for Jack. He'd imagined a dark, intense time filled with adventure and danger, and he'd wanted the haunted look in his father's eyes for himself. There was honour in pain and loss.

He wondered what ghosts his father had faced to write this journal, how much he must have feared for his son to finally talk frankly about a time he'd spent half his life trying to forget.

And how that sacrifice had been wasted, hidden in a drawer by his mother, too afraid of what it said, too afraid of facing the dark heart of her husband's pain, even if it meant watching her son go off to war.

He came to a decision, and it eased something within

him. He'd already told Shaw he was going to resign his commission, but now he made firm plans about it.

He'd have to see out this campaign, there was no possible way he could get out of it, but Elizabeth needed to leave the column as soon as he could arrange it. He'd have to think of some way to officially send her to Pietermaritzburg, or Helpmekaar at the very least.

He wanted her. Not just now but forever. And he needed to tell her that.

Jack had faced the Xhosa, been deafened by the boom of the rocket battery and had felt the sting of a bullet. But never had he felt so fearful. Because he honestly had no idea if Elizabeth would agree to be his.

∿

"What does Inyoni mean?"

Elizabeth felt her heart stop in her chest. "S . . . sir?"

"Inyoni. Those NNC boys keep saying the word when they talk about the hills opposite us." Chambers gestured to the Inyoni Heights directly in front of them.

"I . . . I don't know what it means, sir."

"Really? I thought you did know something of the local tongue. You always seem to be listening to the black fellows as if you know what they're saying."

"No. I just like the rhythm of their speech."

"You can hear rhythm in their speech? I just hear a mixture of words and clicks."

Elizabeth shrugged casually, taking a breath to keep her temper. "You could ask one of the NNC officers, sir. Some of them speak the language of their men."

"No. Always asking for things, those lot. Wanting more provisions."

"Well, they aren't well equipped."

"That's not our problem, Bird. Our duty is to look after the stores assigned to our battalion. We safeguard them at all costs. Everyone else must sort themselves out."

"Yes, sir." Elizabeth looked up from the neat line of wagons to the massive hill behind them.

Isandlwana.

They'd been allowed to pitch their tents as they pleased, and the 1sts had set up on one side of the track, the 2nds and the NNC on the other, all on the lower slopes. In front of the camp was a shallow dip, full of *dongas*, rising up gradually at first and then steeply, to the Inyoni Heights.

"Are we going to laager in, sir?" she asked Chambers, turning back to him. If they were going to surround the camp with the wagons for protection, she'd rather do it now, and get it over with.

"I've received no orders to that effect, but I admit, it is strange." Chambers looked up from his lists. "I'll let you know when we receive the orders, Bird, but perhaps the general doesn't think it's necessary in this instance."

"Because we won't be here long enough?"

"That, and really, I get the feeling the general doesn't think the Zulus capable of an attack on us. It would probably be a waste of time to laager in."

She should have been glad they were so complacent, but she couldn't find it in her. She wished no one dead.

DARKNESS FELL SWIFTLY, AS IT ALWAYS DID IN ZULULAND. No golden sunlight late into the evening like Elizabeth remembered vaguely from her few English summers. Here the sun went down as if it were in a hurry to leave.

Despite the gloom of early evening, she picked her way easily through the tents towards the general's private mess.

What she was going to do when she got there, she had no idea.

Chelmsford had ridden out almost as soon as they'd reached Isandlwana on a reconnaissance mission. Elizabeth wanted, needed, to know what he planned to do, otherwise she feared any meeting with Lindani would be a dangerous waste of time. She had nothing new for him except the reason for the invasion, and that couldn't help them.

She'd thought of offering her services as a waiter, but she worried the general and his men would stay up too late, and she had to meet with Lindani, as well as keep things as normal as possible with Jack.

Her web was becoming more and more tangled.

The mess tent was in front of her, and she heard the clink of real crystal and the scrape of silverware on china. The conversation was muted.

Coming to a quick decision, she strolled casually around the back and dropped to the ground, lying right up against the canvas in the deep shadows.

She lay there for so long, listening to banalities, she missed the beginning of the first interesting sentence.

". . . it ends in the most spectacular gorge and waterfall."

"And we think the most likely threat lies in that direction?"

The aide asking the question sounded like Manning.

"Well, even if the *impi* isn't going to meet us on the battle-field, our scouts say the two chiefs in that area are loyal supporters of the king. They could well harass us as we move forward to oNdini."

"The general is sending Dartnell east tomorrow with his men to search the hills and the Hlazakazi ridge. We can't advance further without taking the chance of being attacked from the rear unless we clear those hills."

There was a pause in conversation, and more scraping of silverware.

"A few of the 24th officers are angry we haven't laagered in." Manning again.

There was a snort. "Waste of time. Honestly, some of Glyn's men are real old grandmothers."

There was a general snickering, and the talk turned to other things.

Elizabeth stood and walked off, exhilarated with her success. She had some interesting news for Lindani.

Deciding not to delay her rendezvous, she kept walking, taking the track back towards Rorke's Drift as Malusi had told her to.

At least no laager of wagons meant she could slip out easily tonight to find them. No more lies about insects. That excuse was wearing thin, and she lived in fear of someone asking Dartmouth about the little trips he was sending her on.

She was glad, too, of the road, although it was already rutted and damaged from the wear and tear of today's move. The moon had nearly waned, and there was no light to see by. Ruts and all, the road was a far easier path than the bush tonight.

As soon as the camp was far enough behind her, she whistled softly, and felt extraordinarily relieved when it was answered.

She stood still on the track, waiting, and Lindani whistled again, just off in the bush.

She made her way between the aloes, and found both men crouched beneath a thorn tree.

"I see there are no wagons around the camp. It was not

so dangerous for you, after all?" Lindani patted the ground beside him, and she squatted down on her haunches, careful not to get the knees of her uniform wet and muddy.

"No. They see the camp as temporary at best, and the threat from the *impi* as negligible."

Lindani clicked his tongue. "If they were but to look over the top of the Inyoni Heights, they would see the most terrifying sight. There are already five thousand warriors in the Ngwebeni valley."

Elizabeth gasped. "That's directly in front of the camp. How have they managed it?"

"The generals are breaking the *impi* into small groups, and they have been making their way slowly from oNdini." Malusi chuckled. "If any of the whitemen's spies from the Natal chiefs see them, they see only a group of two or three hundred men."

"Are more men coming?"

"Many, many more are coming." Lindani gestured with his arms. "I have heard another twenty thousand are coming. The biggest *impi* ever assembled." There was unmistakable pride and awe in his voice.

"When do they attack?" Elizabeth felt a chill on her skin, despite the close, humid heat of the evening.

Malusi shrugged. "We are too junior to know these things. But I have heard not for three or four days. The new moon is nearly upon us, and the evil spirits are close to the ground. The *inyangas* have cautioned the generals against an attack until the moon begins to wax."

She still had time then. Time to get Jack out of the camp. Out of danger.

"Have you discovered the reason for this war?" Lindani asked her.

"I have learned there is nothing the King can do to stop

it. Frere wants to safeguard the east coast to keep a tight hold on the route to India. If Zululand remains an independent state, the King can negotiate with the Russians, or anyone he chooses, for harbour rights, and Frere can't risk that. Nothing King Cetshwayo says or does will change this."

She crouched silent for a moment, terribly, terribly saddened, but Malusi moved impatiently.

"So we cannot avert this war." He seemed to accept it with relish. He wanted this, Elizabeth realized. Wanted to prove himself on the battlefield.

"Chelmsford is looking east, towards oNdini and the Mangeni Falls for the *impi*. He is sending some of the NNC that way tomorrow to see if it is safe for the column to proceed."

"The general will be pleased with this." Malusi grinned in the dark and they all rose.

Lindani reached out and grasped her arm. "Come away with us now. You have done everything you can here."

Surprised, panicked, Elizabeth jerked her arm free. "No." She stopped, horrified at her own reaction. "Lindani, I can't." Her voice was quiet. "There is no danger for three or four days. That is plenty of time. I have things I must do."

"What can be so important? Anything can happen. What if Chelmsford does send a picket over the Heights? The *impi* will be forced into action, new moon or not." He reached out his hand again, impatiently. "Come now."

Elizabeth took a deep breath. "I cannot."

"Why?" His eyes narrowed and hardened. "You have realized you would rather be an Englishwoman after all?"

Anger flared within her, white hot.

"How can you even think that?" She tried to clear the tremble from her voice. "Here I stand before you, at risk to my life, giving you information that will help you kill the men behind me." She gestured back towards the camp. "Men I eat with, and share tents with. Men I work with and talk to every day." Tears burnt her eyes and slid down her cheeks. "Men I have come to like."

"Inyoni—"

"Putting you ahead of them is a choice I make because I love you like a brother, and I love Zululand, which is my home, but it is the hardest thing I have ever had to do."

"I am sorry." Lindani dropped his hand, and she saw sadness in his eyes. The same sadness she'd seen when she first pledged her services to the general.

Somehow, he'd known better than she how heavy a price she'd pay.

"I know." She brushed the tears away with the back of her hand. "Come for me in two nights time, on the 22nd. I'll be ready then."

"Even though it is hard for you to betray them, how will going back there help you?" The tension in Lindani was palpable, and Elizabeth shook her head. How could she explain she wanted to say goodbye to Jack? Convince him to leave the camp?

"Please understand," she whispered, even though she didn't understand it herself. She saw Malusi looking at her, the old distrust back in his eyes, but she ignored him.

Lindani nodded, but it was an angry movement. "I'll come in two nights' time." He took a step away, then turned back. "I only hope it won't be too late."

CHAPTER TWENTY-SIX

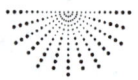

No sign of Zulus or cattle could be discovered. We mounted up onto the Malakatha range which is fairly level and open, and from the distant spurs we could see a long distance into the main valley. A few kraals were visible and from some we saw a few women running away with bundles on their heads, but otherwise the country was deserted. Some natives say that the inhabitants have gone to the King, others say they are in the Indeni bush . . .

— LETTER FROM LORD CHELMSFORD TO SIR
BARTLE FRERE

"Knock, knock," Elizabeth called softly, hesitating at the tent flap.

"Come." Jack's voice sounded raw. He cleared his throat

as she stepped in to the warm glow of lamplight. "You don't need to announce yourself, we're beyond that."

She nodded. Yes, they were way beyond that.

"You're soaking wet. It isn't raining again is it?" He stood, reaching out to brush damp hair from her face. "Your skin is cold."

"I went for a dip in the stream at the back of the camp." She spoke lightly, as if it were quite normal to jump, clothes and all, into a stream late at night.

"Why on earth did you do that?" Jack unbuttoned her jacket and set it to dry on the back of her chair. Water dripped from it in a steady rhythm. Like the ticking of a clock.

"I wanted to be clean." She felt no cleaner, though.

"You need warming up." His voice deepened, his hand slid beneath her clinging, wet shirt, and she shivered.

So many secrets. So much at stake.

She stepped back. "You know you once wished for a week and a hotel room? Please, let us do that. As soon as possible."

"Oh, we will." He grinned.

"I mean, tomorrow. Or the next day, at the very latest."

"We can't do that. Or, I can't. I think it's a very good idea for you. I've been thinking how to get you to Pietermaritzburg."

"No." She shook her head. "I won't go. Not unless you come too."

His eyebrows lifted. "It's not safe here. I want you away."

Elizabeth choked back a laugh. "I agree. It 's not safe. And I'll only leave with you."

She saw a considering look in his eyes, could almost see his thoughts at work.

"Don't even think about playing the superior officer card, Jack. You could force me to go, but if you do, I swear, you'll never see me again." She held his gaze.

"Why would you do that?"

She slumped onto her chair, leant back against the wet coat, and shook her head.

He breathed out, an explosive sigh. "All right, I won't force you. But why won't you go?"

The second man to ask her that tonight.

"Why won't *you*? What if I told you I knew something was going to happen? Something terrible. That if you stayed, you'd die."

"I can't go because I am part of a battalion that is counting on me to stay and do my duty." He braced his legs apart, bafflement and anger in the lines on his face.

"Something terrible, as you put it, could happen at any moment, I agree. We're at war. I very much hope that if we see action, it won't result in my death, but there is always that chance. That's why I want you as far from this column as I can get you."

Despite his words, she saw he'd been lulled into the same dangerous complacency she'd found throughout the camp. He thought there was a strong chance the Zulus wouldn't attack. No matter what he thought about the potential danger to her, he had almost no fear for himself.

Elizabeth gritted her teeth in frustration. "I won't leave unless you do. Sitting around somewhere worrying is not how I choose to pass my time."

They stared at each other for a long moment, at an impasse. Then Jack raised an eyebrow.

"I know how I choose to pass mine." His leer was designed to soften her, and it worked. The anger she'd felt a minute ago dissolved.

She let him pull her up from the chair into his arms, only holding back when he tried to kiss her.

"Under what circumstances would you leave with me?" she whispered against his mouth.

"If they call off the war, or once we've reached oNdini and taken over the country."

His tone was so casual.

Elizabeth dropped her head, resting her forehead against his chest.

Never, then.

THERE WAS NOTHING LIKE MARCHING IN THE PITCH DARK TO shake loose your thoughts.

Leading his men through the black night, with its chirps and rustles, its warm breezes, Jack let his mind run free. Except it wasn't free. It was chained to a slender private who was not what she seemed.

The thought of her, dressed in her soldier's uniform, so quiet and hardworking, made him smile. He'd caught himself a rare and curious bird.

Why hadn't he declared himself yesterday?

Jack did not think he was a coward, but he knew if he'd asked Elizabeth to marry him last night, she would not have said yes. Or she would have only said yes if he agreed to leave camp with her.

He wanted a condition-free, joyous acceptance.

Something was worrying her. There had been shadows in her eyes last night, and for once, she had not looked at him as they rocked together on the cot, but instead tucked her head under his chin, pressing as close to him as she could.

"Bloody hell– Sir!"

Jolted to the present, Jack was just in time to glimpse the white-and-brown flash of a cow-hide shield up ahead.

"Weapons ready," he called softly.

What were they up against? A single straggler? A group of scouts?

They were near the top of the Inyoni Heights, on a routine sweep of the ground to the north east of the camp. The chances of it being anything more than a scout or scouting party were slim.

Shouts erupted to their right, the Zulus were heading east, and they were calling to each other in the dark, their cries foreign and unnerving. It brought home how far from England he truly was.

He led his company in the direction of the noise, running as fast as possible over the rough ground on a hill in the dark. He heard swearing behind him as some of the men fell foul of the rocks that seemed ever-present in this landscape.

They were gaining, though. Perhaps the scouts had not thought their pursuers could make much progress in the dark, but he and his men were used to the rough ground by now, and Jack could see movement just up ahead.

Suddenly, they found themselves among the enemy, as surprised as the Zulu warriors to have caught up so quickly.

There was a crack of a shot and the ground exploded at Jack's feet, forcing him to leap back. He fell amongst the rocks as the night suddenly crackled around them, wild shots flying everywhere.

A Zulu ran past him, and Jack grabbed his ankle, bringing him down next him and lifting his rifle in one smooth move.

He froze, his mouth open, as he stared into a familiar face illuminated by the gunfire all around them. The cowherd from the river. The one who'd spoken to Elizabeth.

And suddenly, from a far corner of his mind, he recalled the servant who'd been with Elizabeth when she'd first come into the camp as a trader.

He'd never asked her about that. About who her servant had been, where she'd gotten that cart, horse and those two cows to sell.

The warrior stared straight back at him, the shock no less evident on his face. Shock and worry.

With a cry, he rolled away from Jack and scrambled to his feet, and Jack could do nothing but watch him go.

Then one of the Zulus called out an order, and like a well-oiled machine, the warriors ceased fire and ran east, disappearing in seconds in the dark.

"We follow them, sir?" A private asked eagerly as Jack pulled himself up.

"Anyone hurt?" Jack called out.

There was silence, and Jack could barely believe their luck.

"Then we follow them." He needed to find that scout, now that he was thinking, moving again.

Jack started forward, his rifle at chest height, ready.

They kept going in silence for another minute until the ridge ended abruptly. Jack peered down the hill, then left and right.

Nothing.

The Zulus were gone.

LINDANI PATTED THE BARREL OF THE GUN, FEELING THE HEAT OF it from the recent firing. It was the first time he'd ever used one, and he'd had to admit the noise and the flash of gunpowder in the dark was impressive.

It had done the job of drawing the picket away, stopping them from cresting the hill and stumbling upon the Valley of Shields, as they had started calling it.

The Ngwebeni valley, just over the lip of the escarpment, was packed with nearly 25,000 Zulu warriors.

Malusi joined him. "I know that group," he murmured. "They are a dangerous lot. They like scouting in the bush; not like some of the whitemen. We're lucky we saw them before they reached the top of the Heights."

Lindani remembered the hand on his ankle, the smooth movement of a gun being leveled at him. They were more dangerous than Malusi realized. The man who had him on the ground was Inyoni's officer. And Lindani knew he'd been recognized.

"We'd better follow them, make sure they go back to camp." Malusi beckoned two other scouts, and they started back the way they'd come, taking a path higher up the hill than the whitemen had returned by.

Lindani looked after them as they disappeared into the darkness, furiously thinking through his options, of the wisdom of telling Malusi what had just happened. Still unsure, he jogged forward until he caught them.

" . . .just like the Xhosa," the voice of a redcoat drifted up. "Quick attack and then run. Bush warfare."

"Those scouts were headed due east, going back to their main camp most likely."

Malusi elbowed him to get a translation, but Lindani shook his head, needing to hear everything. To hear if the officer said anything about Inyoni.

Her time as a spy was over now.

"We need to have scouts here at all times, especially if the *inyangas* don't want us to attack for a few days. This won't be only group they send this way." Malusi spoke quietly.

They'd reached the lip of the escarpment, and Malusi lay on his stomach and leopard-crawled forward. Lindani did the same, and they lay, looking down on the British camp, lit by lanterns and small fires.

Somewhere, an owl called.

They exchanged uneasy glances.

"Does the owl call their name, or ours?" Malusi asked in the dark silence and Lindani couldn't answer. The call of the owl meant death to someone, and they were poised for battle, after all. Perhaps it called all their names.

"The one officer in that picket, he recognized me from the river. He is the one who came to find Inyoni the day she was bathing."

Malusi sucked in his breath. "You are sure?"

"There is no doubt."

"Then Inyoni is finished. She should have come away with us yesterday." Malusi spoke as if she were already dead.

"No. I will get her out of the camp tonight."

"You will have to seek permission first. Even the sight of one warrior might alert the whitemen to the army that sits directly above them."

Lindani knew it was true. He owed it to his family, to his unborn child, to follow the protocol in this matter. He was in the general's power as much as Inyoni.

"Then let me get permission."

They scrambled up and ran, bent low, away from the winking lights of the Isandlwana camp and headed back up the hill, following the plateau and then stopping as the ground fell steeply away into the valley.

To keep from discovery there were no camp fires lit, and it was a strange sight, so many warriors talking quietly among themselves in the dark.

Lindani knew that fires were being lit to the east to confuse the large scouting party the whitemen had sent out this morning, to make them think they were looking at the main Zulu army in the distance.

If the small group of scouts they'd just chased off had come over the Heights and stumbled upon them . . . he shivered. Everything would have been for nothing.

Malusi disappeared into the darkness, but returned almost immediately. "I have spoken to someone." He rested a friendly hand on Lindani's shoulder. "The general is officiating at the war ceremony for one of the *ibutho* under his command. Down through the valley."

"I'll go find him."

"Wait. There is someone here who wishes to speak with you. Your father's brother."

Lindani frowned and peered into the darkness. Bangizwe swaggered out of the gloom in full battle dress, his accolades and tokens of bravery from the King and his *indunas* hanging from him.

"My nephew."

They embraced, but always with his uncle, Lindani sensed the anger and hostility just below the surface. It wasn't just since Lindani had taken his father's place as chief. He remembered it had always been so.

Bangizwe was only a few months younger than Lindani's father, the first son of Lindani's grandfather's second wife. Whereas Lindani's father had been the first son of his first wife. So fell the difference between chief and not.

"I hear it whispered you have impressed the general. That the little white girl is spying for us below."

Lindani recoiled at the poison in his uncle's words, even though they were spoken evenly. Why would this make

Bangizwe so angry? It brought honour to their family name and village.

"We have done our duty." He stepped away from his uncle, and a prickle of awareness made him shiver. The same prickle he got when hunting and suddenly knew somewhere in the darkness, a lion was watching him.

"Just as I have always done my duty," Banizwe said, but his voice was low and only Lindani could hear him. "I have done my duty and spent my whole life in my *ibutho*, working for the King. And never in all that time have I been given permission to marry, or given cattle to compensate me for my services.

So you must tell me, my nephew, the secret of doing duty the way you do it. For I would very much like to understand how a faithful, experienced warrior such as myself can be so much less fortunate than you. Who has done *nothing*." Spittle flew as Bangizwe hissed out the last sentence, and Lindani felt the slow beat of fear within that any sensible man felt when looking at a rabid animal.

"There is no secret. Perhaps my success is due to my honest dealings, uncle. For I have always dealt openly and fairly, like my father before me, and my people respect me for it."

"I will be chief yet, you insolent child." Bangizwe stared at him, and the fear in Lindani intensified. His uncle's eyes were like those of a warrior who has taken *muti* and danced around the fire for many hours. Wild and dangerous. Unfocused.

Before Lindani could respond, his uncle whirled around and in a moment was lost in the dark.

"Not a happy family meeting?"

Malusi must have been waiting to one side for him, and Lindani started towards him, happy to see a friendly face.

He tried to shake off the feeling of cold fear Bangizwe had inspired in him.

"My uncle's poison looks are nothing to me." He did not need to talk about his family's problems now, he needed to get to the general, get the permission he needed for a rescue mission. The two of them started down the hill, to where the battle initiation ceremonies were being held.

"Beware jealous uncles." Malusi shook his head. "They have to sit by and watch their family home go to their young nephews, while they have nothing. And for a loyal warrior like your uncle, who thinks the King has cheated him because the cattle sickness means he cannot pay his men their due . . ." Malusi shrugged. "Watch your back, my friend."

A shiver ran down Lindani's spine. "I will."

And from above them on the escarpment, they heard the owl call again.

CHAPTER TWENTY-SEVEN

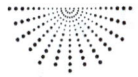

About 1.30 am on 22nd, a messenger brought me a note from Major Dartnell to say the enemy was in greater numbers than when he last reported, and that he did not think it prudent to attack them unless reinforced by two or three companies of the 24th Regiment.

— MAJ. CLERY, COLONEL GLYN'S STAFF
OFFICER

"Wake up, Bird."

Elizabeth came out of unconsciousness with a shout as hands grabbed her shoulders and shook.

"Up. My God, it's taken me over fifteen minutes to find you. Cushy set up for a private, Private."

Elizabeth looked at Chambers blankly, her mind scrambling to catch up.

Instinctively, panicked, her hand slapped at her chest.

But for once, she'd fallen asleep in her uniform, only her boots lay beside her cot.

The chances she and Jack had been taking came home to her in retrospective horror. That she was in her own cot and in uniform was only because Jack was on late night picket duty.

"Get those boots on and get to the store wagons, now. Dartnell has sent word – he thinks he's found the main Zulu army out at the Mangeni gorge. Chelmsford has told the 2nds to prepare to march out. If we're lucky, we can catch them and force them to engage."

That wasn't right, was it?

"What time is it?" she asked, her voice cracking.

"Nearly 2am. Move your bloody arse, Bird."

Elizabeth tugged on her boots as Chambers left. Lindani had said the main army was gathering just over the escarpment. Could they have been drawn east for some reason? Or could the generals have changed their minds?

She had no way to tell. Perhaps Dartnell was mistaken, perhaps not.

She stumbled out the tent, dodging amongst the 2nds as they donned their jackets and belts.

Chelmsford had ordered quiet, lest they alert any scouts to their movements, and the talk was hushed and excited.

A few 1sts stood watching from tent entrances, undisguised envy on their faces.

"Every soldier is to take his full ammunition quota, Bird, start handing it out," Chambers barked as she joined him at the wagons.

"And the reserve ammunition?" Elizabeth began unscrewing the lid off a box of ammunition and ripping off its tin seal.

"To be kept ready in case someone is sent back for it. The

wagon won't make it across those *dongas* to the east. I've already told the colonel's aide."

"Colonel Glyn is going with the general?" Elizabeth felt a frisson of shock. They must really believe they had found the Zulu army then.

"Yes. Lt. Col. Pulleine is to take command of the camp."

Chambers sounded pleased. Pulliene was an administrative officer, and he had close dealings with the quartermasters.

"And Captain Burdell?"

"What of him?" Chambers gave her a considering look. No doubt recalling that she had her own cot in Jack's tent.

Elizabeth felt the hot sweep of temper and looked down to hide it. Breathed deeply. "Nothing sir, just wondered if he was back from picket duty or not?" Under control again, she looked up, looked him in the eye.

Chambers nodded. "Got in just before I woke you, but it looks like he has something to report, so he's in with the colonel and the general. I heard his company won't be going. They've been out for nearly six hours and they won't be fresh for the fight."

Could it be as simple as that? A twist of fate that spared Jack and herself? Kept them far from the action. She paused a moment, looked across to the Inyoni Heights, a solid black obstacle against a starry sky. Was Lindani still up there, or had the army moved on?

He'd been right.

Anything could happen, and she may have given up her chance to return home with him.

The thought froze her. Had she given up Zululand for an extra night with Jack? She felt like a traitor to both that she didn't know if it was worth it.

"What do you think this is, Bird?"

Chambers' shout made her jump.

"Keep that bloody ammo coming."

～

LINDANI SLIPPED THROUGH THE CROWD, MAKING A PLACE FOR himself near the front. The place of initiation was deep within the valley, where they'd risked lighting a single, roaring fire.

With the ceremony already underway, there was no possible way to speak with the general until it was over. He'd been initiated already, yesterday, when he and Malusi arrived in the valley, and with every new wave of men coming in, the ceremony began anew. The warriors shuffled forward, in full war dress. Shields, spears and *isagila* polished and cleaned, hides tied below their knees.

Even though the sun had long set, the weather was close and hot. Storm weather. The smell of rain filled his senses.

The sound of the drums crept up on him gradually, so softly did the drummers start playing. One moment, he thought there was silence, and then he realized the drums had been beating softly all the while, getting louder and louder until with a crescendo they cut off.

For a moment, aside from the crickets, there was no sound.

Then the *inyangas*, the herbal healers, began circling the massive fire, half crouching, throwing handfuls of *muti* into it.

The general stepped into the middle of the arena, the white and scarlet plumes in his head dress swaying as he moved in all his finery. He had a copper bracelet on his arm, the sign of an award of great courage from the King.

"We prepare for war."

The warriors lifted their voices, shouting their battle cry. Lindani felt the noise deep within, vibrating in his bones.

"We did not ask for this war, but we will not shirk it. We fight to kill."

The drums began again, a cacophony, wild and out of rhythm. An orgy of violence in sound. Then they calmed, beating in time and weaving a complicated music, holding Lindani in their throbbing arms.

The warriors danced, each one holding the shield of the man beside him, becoming a single, unified line, leaping in the firelight.

The inyangas sprinkled them with *muti* and gave them snuffs, and their movements became more jerky and frenzied as the effects of the powerful drugs and medicines took hold.

The general appeared again.

"This day, I put the enemy in the hands of this *ibutho*. Do not disgrace us. Conquer them for your king. Let your battle wounds be to your front. Let there be no wounds to your back, to show you have run like cowards. For if so, you will find I become your enemy, too. Let us be brave as lions."

Another shout went up and the stamp of feet and bass of the drums seemed to rise from the ground like a heart beat and become a thing of its own, making Lindani want to throw himself into the circle of dancers and run through the fire, even though he'd been given no *muti* himself.

His scalp prickled, and his body shook, his chest tight with suppressed emotion.

The sky overhead rumbled, the thunder booming in a slow roll, ending in a growl. Lightning flickered to the east, and fat drops of rain hit his face.

"The ancestors have blessed us," Malusi said, his words

shaking Lindani out of his trance. He shook his head to clear it.

"May it be so."

~

JACK KICKED OFF HIS BOOTS AND LISTENED TO THE RAIN, LIKE the taps of a hundred demented woodpeckers, on the canvas roof of his tent. Thank God they'd got back to camp before the storm broke.

He should be tired but his mind was still spinning from his encounter with the Zulu scouts. That no one had been hit in the wild shootout was nothing short of miraculous.

He ripped off his jacket at the inanity of the thought.

He didn't care that no one had been hurt. He thought only of the scout, the herdsman from the river and the trader's servant at the Helpmekaar camp. All one person. Always connected to Elizabeth.

What the hell was going on?

Elizabeth was nowhere in sight, her bed unmade and ruffled, as if she'd just risen from it. He imagined Chambers had her equipping the 2nds before they marched out to support Dartnell, and resisted his sudden urge to touch her sheets, to feel if her body heat still lingered there.

The Elizabeth of a few hours ago. Not the Elizabeth he thought of now. Thought of with a suspicion that shredded his insides.

He could not, would not, confront her with his questions in front of Chambers and the men of his own battalion. She'd be back soon enough.

He tossed his jacket over his chair, lay down and picked up his father's journal. There were only a few pages of writing left, although only half the book had been used. He felt a quick flash of loss, as if his father had been visiting and now suddenly the time was up.

He'd never felt so close to him.

ENTRY WRITTEN JANUARY, 1872

IT WAS 13 JANUARY 1849 AND WE WERE ON THE MOVE TO Rasul. After marching five miles, we received word that there was a strong Sikh presence to our left at the village of Chillianwallah. Gough sent out a reconnaissance team, later joining them, and through the thick jungle behind the village to the west, they saw Sikhs amassed in strength.

Unable to continue on to Rasul without exposing our left flank and rear to attack, it looked like we'd have to deal with the threat before we moved on.

As it was 2pm by this time, Gough decided to settle in, and attack on the morrow, but when a few of the Sikh light guns opened fire on us, Gough instructed some of the heavy guns to return fire.

Suddenly we were being attacked from thirty different points through the jungle. Gough had entrenched us too close to the Sikh position, and we were forced into battle.

The senior officer over our whole Division was Brigadier General Campbell. Like Gough, he was a great believer in hand to hand combat, his address to us before we were sent off to storm the enemy's guns was the admonition that we must not fire our muskets, that all the work must be done with the bayonet.

You will probably laugh at this, Jack, but we were so fresh-faced and green, so enthusiastic to do our commander's bidding, that we set off, hot for action, without even loading our muskets.

And so keen for a taste of blood were we, we jogged forward to engage far too quickly, leaving the two supporting native units behind us. Afterwards it would also be found that due to some confusion, our supporting artillery went left while we went right.

So there we were, all but running, muskets unloaded, straight into thick jungle towards entrenched guns with no supporting infantry and no supporting artillery.

A nightmare in the making.

Soldiers were cut down to the left and right of me. It was wholesale slaughter, and yet, still we ran forward. We were too shocked to do anything but continue.

Near the Sikh's guns there was a shallow pool, and we branched left and right around it, some even risked trying to run straight through. Within moments there were bodies floating in plumes of their own blood on its surface, and I remember the noise and the sudden burning agony of taking a hit.

The bullet cut through my lung and I fell, unable to do anything but watch as my friends fell around me.

Amazingly, some of the 24th did reach the guns, and hand to hand combat, exactly what Campbell asked of us, did commence. But we were outgunned and outnumbered. And in the end we had no choice but to retreat, with hundreds upon hundreds either dead or wounded.

From starting out as the best day of my life, it became the darkest.

Question, Jack. If you do still want to go in to the 24ths, question everything. There are ways to appear to be following orders where you can follow your own initiative. Stay alive. Keep your men alive if you can.

Question, question, question.

THE LAST LINE WAS WRITTEN WITH A PEN PRESSED SO HARD, IT had torn the page. Jack shut the book gently and lay it on his chest, closing his eyes and trying to imagine that level of carnage.

While he'd seen action, it was the quick ambush tactics of the Xhosa, a few dead here, a few there. It blunted the effect.

What it must be like to see body after body fall around you, he wouldn't like to know.

Slowly, incrementally, the silence crept up on him. It must have been this quiet for some time; the rain had stopped, the 2nds must have left, and still Elizabeth was not back.

He hesitated a moment, then heaved himself up on the low cot and reached for his boots.

There was nothing for it. He'd have to go looking for her.

CHAPTER TWENTY-EIGHT

The General ordered the 2nd Battalion, 24th Regiment, the Mounted Infantry, and four guns, to be ready under arms at once to march.

— MAJ. CLERY, COL. GLYN'S STAFF OFFICER

Chambers had gone at least ten minutes ago, and Elizabeth felt confident he wasn't coming back. She stood before the reserve ammunition wagon for the 2nds and looked around. With the excitement over, everyone was back in their tents and asleep.

She wondered if Jack was waiting for her, but couldn't risk going to check. If he saw her, there would be no way she could come back, and now was her only chance alone with the wagon.

Climbing into it, she crawled to the back, out of sight under the canvas cover, and pulled the small screwdriver she needed to remove the wooden lids from her belt pouch.

It was pitch dark, with no moon at all, and she had to work mostly by feel, too afraid to light a lamp. But she'd been opening the boxes without thought for Chambers earlier, and her hands knew what to do.

It was her head that was reluctant. For every bullet she took out and damaged with the screwdriver, she thought of the person who might get it. The faces of men who had passed her with a friendly word, kind to a soldier they thought too young to be here.

She was killing them as surely as if she were running at them with an *iwisa* in one hand and an *assegai* in the other.

With only one box open, the bullets all around her on the rough, splintered wagon floor, she stopped, pulling her legs up and wrapping her arms around them. She closed her eyes and rested her head on her knees.

What to do? What to do?

Every bullet damaged meant one less warrior sacrificed to British Imperial games. One British soldier left on the battlefield with a jammed rifle.

If not for Jack, the scale would definitely weigh in the Zulus favour, but any chance he could be the one standing weaponless on the field was one too many.

Inaction was as powerful in this instance as action.

"What to do?"

She didn't realize she'd said it aloud until light spilled over her and she jerked her head up.

Jack stood at the open end of the wagon, lamp in hand, his face lit from below, just like the first night he'd taken her into his tent.

Only this time she knew him, could read the expression on his face.

Horror.

~

"WHAT ARE YOU DOING?" HE SPOKE CAREFULLY, BECAUSE HE wanted so very much to be mistaken.

Her face, so stricken a moment ago, went blank.

"What does it look like I'm doing?"

"Damaging bullets." He hadn't wanted to say it, and he knew if he were mistaken, she may never forgive him. But how could he be mistaken? The scout's face, wide-eyed and shocked, came back to him.

"I could be checking them," she answered, but there was no heat in her tone.

"Hiding at the back of the wagon in the dark?"

"No. You're right." She curled up even tighter on herself, as if she were in real pain.

"There is no brother, is there?" His voice was hoarse.

"Not in the sense I told you about, no. In my defense, I didn't know you then, when I lied."

He ignored that. "And your name?"

"My name is Elizabeth." Her head rose up, and she looked indignant, as if accusing her of lying about her name was worse than finding her sabotaging bullets. "And Bird ... well, Bird is my name too, although not the one I was christened with."

"So who are you, then?" He was trying so hard to keep his voice even, but it was coming undone at the edges.

"Elizabeth Bird Jones."

"And are you mad?" He leaned forward, losing the struggle to keep his temper, keep his voice down. "Your parents are dead, and you've decided to take on the British Empire in the name of your father's philosophies?"

She looked genuinely taken aback at the suggestion, and Jack felt the world skew away from him, felt himself sliding down a hole. If this wasn't it, what was it about, then?

"You still don't have any idea, do you?" She spoke slowly, bemused. "I told Lindani the British wouldn't believe me even if I confessed, and I was right." She paused, and looked straight at him.

"I'm a Zulu spy."

~

HE WAS STILL REELING FROM HER STRANGE CONFESSION AS HE watched her fidget on her cot. He'd hauled her out of the wagon and she'd come quietly with him to the tent, saying nothing. Looking away from him.

He felt as if he'd swallowed glass. Felt his insides shred with every breath he took. He'd been harbouring a spy. Loving a spy.

Still loved her.

"Why would you spy for the Zulu?"

"Because I am a Zulu. Why wouldn't I try to help my people any way I can?"

He looked at her, and honestly thought for a moment she must be addled. "A Zulu?"

She laughed, but bitterly. "You don't believe me, do you?" She shook her head. "Even you, Jack, the most intelligent man in this camp, cannot conceive that I'd align myself with them. But I lost any loyalty to England long ago. I'd be mad to turn my back on the people who saved me from the sea, who took me in, over the people who have never done anything but kill those I love."

"You've been living amongst the Zulu?" Something ugly reared its head within him, and he clenched his fists.

She nodded. "For the last six years."

"Doing what?" His feelings, his jealously and his horror, were unworthy, and he fought them.

"Making beer in the beer hut, mainly, so I don't have to go out in the sun, because of my skin. Teaching Lindani to read and speak English—"

"The scout!" He shouted it out, and saw her lift her head in horror. Look him in the eye for the first time, and the knife in his gut twisted deeper.

"You saw Lindani? When?"

He didn't remember grabbing her, but suddenly she was hauled up against him, her eyes wide with shock.

"First tell me who the hell he is to you? Your lover? Did you go from my bed to his, carrying my secrets with you?"

She recoiled, and her eyes glistened with tears. "How could you ask that?"

She spoke as if he had betrayed her, not the other way around.

"Then what?" He let go of her coat, and she stumbled back, her arms crossed in front of her, as if she were afraid.

"He is my brother. He saved me from drowning and his mother and father took me in. He has been my protector since the moment he pulled me out of the sea." She straightened up.

"You think I betrayed you, Jack, but that isn't so. I'm being loyal to my own, and you should respect that. I have always respected your loyalty to your men, even though they want to kill my people."

"And us?" He could barely get the words out.

"I treasure our time together." She lifted her hands in front of her body, one palm cupped into the other, facing upward, like he'd seen some of the old Zulu women they'd come across do. A gesture of thanks.

"You were never going to love me: someone who would sleep with you without promises of marriage, someone who dressed as a man. I knew that, and I didn't care. I loved every minute I spent with you, even though it has made everything I've done so much harder."

He had no answer to that. He'd never told her he loved her.

"When did you see Lindani?" Her hands dropped to her sides, and she asked softly, almost pleading.

"A few hours ago. My company ran into him and a few others, running east, towards the Mangeni gorge."

"He wasn't harmed? You didn't hurt him?"

Part of him, mauled by her betrayal, ripped up by the knowledge her loyalties lay elsewhere, wanted to punish her, hurt her with a lie, but he forced himself to shake his head, and watched as she drooped with relief.

"They went to Mangeni? The same direction as Dartnell says the main army is camped." She spoke slowly, considering something.

"What do you know of it?"

He thought she would tell him to go to hell, but she shrugged.

"Lindani told me something else, but he also said things can change. If Dartnell can see the army, and you saw Lindani headed in that direction, perhaps things have changed."

She was telling the truth, he'd bet his life on it.

"So what do we do now?"

He saw the moment she started weighing up her options. Saw her eyes dart from the tent entrance to him, and try to gauge whether she could dodge past him.

As if he would let her go.

Perhaps sensing his thoughts, she spun and bolted for

the back of the tent, throwing herself on the ground to roll under the canvas, but he was bigger and quicker than she was.

He lifted her up, an arm around her waist, while she flayed and kicked out, as silent as he so as not to attract attention neither of them wanted. A bizarre struggle, with not a sound uttered.

He hauled her to his kit, struggling to hold her one-handed while he grabbed up some rope.

"You're going to tie me up?" Her voice was a squeak of indignation and anger.

He was forced to wrestle her to the floor face down and use his knees to hold her there while he tied her hands. She fought him all the way.

By the time he had her secure and propped up against the centre tent pole, looping a final piece of rope around her waist to secure her to it, they were both panting.

"I'm sorry. I can't let you go." He lifted his hands up in apology as she shot daggers at him with her eyes.

"Yes, you can," she hissed back.

"No, I can't." God knows how much havoc she could wreak before she left camp. She may have a right to her loyalties, but he had loyalties of his own. "I can't let you go and I can't bring myself to hand you over, either."

He shook his head. "Elizabeth, my love, what the hell am I going to do with you?"

CHAPTER TWENTY-NINE

Report just come in that the Zulus are advancing in force from left front of camp. – 8.5 am

— NOTE FROM LT. COL. PULLEINE TO
GENERAL CHELMSFORD, 22 JANUARY, 1879

The picket came in at 8am, just as Jack was leaving the mess tent, hot with the news of Zulu activity in the north east.

Jack felt a cold tickle at his nape that had nothing to do with the grey, misty weather. He'd been in the north east last night when he'd run into those scouts.

What were the Zulu still doing up there?

He followed the picket leader to Pulleine. It seemed the picket had seen sufficient Zulus through the mist to warrant real concern.

The newly-appointed camp commander looked up at the hills, worry and indecision etching deep lines on his face. "Let's have the men form a column in front of the camp, facing the Heights."

Jack went to give his men the order, glad Pulleine was being prudent. He hesitated at his tent, wondering if he should go in, then cursed himself for a coward. He needed to tell Elizabeth what was happening.

She lifted her head and stared accusingly at him.

"A body of Zulus were spotted up on the Heights, in the north east. Pulleine has ordered the troops to stand in formation in front of the camp. So I'll be gone a while."

Her eyes widened and she strained against her ropes. "Jack—"

"I have to go now, I'll be back as soon as I can."

"Wait, Jack. Damn it, come back."

She didn't shout, but he could hear the urgency in her voice. He nearly did turn back, but his men were waiting for him. He'd have to hear what she had to say later.

WHAT WOULD SHE HAVE SAID TO HIM? THAT IF THERE WERE Zulus up on the Heights, then maybe Dartnell had been fooled last night. Maybe Jack had been fooled too, by Lindani and, no doubt, Malusi.

Would she have said it?

How could she not know?

All she did know was that she didn't want him going out there with that confident, devil-may-care attitude, that belief that he was impervious.

He needed to let her go.

His anger at being tricked, his honour as an officer and his feelings for her were warring inside him, she could see it in his eyes. But he couldn't keep her tied up in his tent for much longer, and he must know it.

He had to choose.

The minutes ticked by and she could hear the calls and orders of the officers as they formed up, and then quiet.

Perhaps it was nothing. After all, today was the day of the new moon. The dark time. The Zulus wouldn't want to attack.

She sat still as she could, trying to hear what was happening, and her eyes were fixed on the tent entrance when a shout of laughter and the murmur of talking signaled the men standing down and going back about their business.

"Nothing?" she asked as Jack came in, but she already knew. He looked curiously relieved.

"Nothing. Or nothing we can do anything about. Pulleine has orders to defend the camp, so we can hardly go chasing after them and leave the camp vulnerable, and it looks like they aren't coming to us."

"Good."

"You don't want them to come down on us now, with half our men gone and only two guns?"

She made a sound of frustration, clenching her fists. "Of course I don't. I don't want anyone to have to attack anyone. But you picked this fight, after all. You can't be annoyed if you get what you asked for."

"Now I'm 'you', part of the hated Empire?"

"That is how you're behaving." Elizabeth leant back and closed her eyes, at a loss what to do. "Let me go, Jack. What is keeping me here going to help?"

"Do you want to go?"

She lifted her head. "Yes, I want to go. I have no future with you, and I have no life at all in England. The only thing is, I'm afraid . . ."

She trailed off at his closed expression.

"What are you afraid of?" He crossed his arms in front of him.

"It doesn't matter. Let me go."

"I can't do that. Let you go where, exactly? Back into the bush? Alone? You said yourself you have no idea where the Zulu army is, do you think they'd let you within 100 yards of them anyway dressed as you are?"

She laughed. "I wouldn't be dressed as I am. I'd have these clothes off in a moment."

She'd finally broken through his wall. He actually gaped.

"What do you expect? I live with the Zulus. This uniform is the most clothes I've worn in six years. And getting used to these boots has been murder."

"You walk around half-naked . . ."

"Yes, I walk around half-naked. And funny, but I only lost my virginity when I started walking around fully clothed and dressed as a man."

It was a cheap shot, but she was at her limit of patience.

She saw her barb had hit its mark. His face flushed.

"Deflowered by my uncontrolled lustful advances, is that it?" He dropped his arms to his sides and stood stiffly in front of her.

"You know I was as willing as you. My point is that it isn't the clothes, or lack thereof, it's the– "

"I understand your point." For the first time he seemed reflective, the wound of her betrayal not as raw.

"Earlier, what were you going to say? What are you afraid of?" His voice had lost its harsh edge.

She rested her chin on her knees. "I'm afraid after this war, there won't be a Zululand left."

~

"Have you seen Bird, Burdell? Damned if the lad hasn't disappeared." Chambers hailed Jack as soon as he stepped from the mess tent.

Jack blinked. These blind men still thought his beautiful little spy was a boy.

"Just having him do a few things for me, if you don't mind."

He held the mug of tea he was taking to Elizabeth in his hands, wanting to get on so it would still be hot for her.

"My God— are those warriors up there?" Chambers was looking due north, to the escarpment that lay next to the Inyoni Heights in the north east. The grey, misty weather of earlier had been burned away by the sun, and the sky was almost too bright to look at.

Jack squinted. "You're right. We'll need to get out a watch glass."

"They're just standing there. Watching us," Chambers said, shading his eyes.

"The Xhosa did that too. We'd see a group in the distance, just looking, then they'd disappear. We never saw them again. Or not that we knew."

"Bit unnerving, eh?" Chambers kept his eyes on the Zulus. "I'll let someone know." He took a step towards Pulleine's tent, then stopped. "When you're finished with Bird, have him report to me, will you?"

"Of course." Jack nodded and moved off, his eyes, like Chambers, unable to keep from looking at the north hills.

He lifted his tent flap quietly, and saw Elizabeth trying to undo the ropes on her feet with her teeth.

God, he loved her.

"Chambers is looking for you."

She gave a startled cry, spat out some sisal. Then glared at him.

He knelt beside to her, and lifted the hot cup of tea to her lips. "I brought some biscuits, as well."

She said nothing, but she drank the tea.

"I have a farm in England. Up near the border with Wales." He tipped the mug higher. "It's a fair size. We farm sheep, mainly, but there is an apple orchard, and vegetables. A few dairy cows."

He leant back on his heels. "I'm resigning my commission as soon as this war is over."

He watched her throat work as she swallowed, and felt an inconvenient heat blossom low in his gut.

"Why are you telling me this?"

"I'm a soldier. And before that, I was a farmer. A gentleman farmer, maybe, but a farmer, nevertheless." He reached out and touched her arm. "Neither profession has taught me a romantic way with words."

She looked up at him, and he could see she didn't have the first clue what he was on about.

"I'm asking you to marry me."

"Marry you?" She choked on her last swallow of tea. "Why would you– ?"

The bugle sounded a call, cutting her off.

Chelmsford back already?

"Burdell." One of the officers from the 1st Battalion called from outside the tent. "Pulleine wants us at his tent."

"Coming right away." Jack moved to the entrance, in case

anyone tried to look in. He turned to her and lifted his shoulders. "I'm sorry. I'll be back as soon as I can."

"Untie me first," she whispered.

He shook his head. He couldn't let her go yet. Not without hearing an answer.

"You have to tie up all the girls you propose to, Jack?"

She called it softly as he stepped out, and he almost missed his footing. He had to hold back his laughter all the way to Pulleine.

CHAPTER THIRTY

Now here was the fat in the fire with a vengeance. The big Zulu army within four miles of the left flank of the camp, Colonel Pulleine without mounted men, or only a few, only two guns, not more than 900 white men in all, the camp not laagered and the General away on a wild-goose chase, at least thirteen miles from him.

> — HAMILTON-BROWNE, A LOST LEGIONARY
> IN SOUTH AFRICA, 1911

J ack watched the power play as Pulleine read the note Durnford handed him.

Durnford had just arrived from Rorke's Drift with 500 Natal Native Contingent men, pulling ahead of his wagons in his haste to answer the summons from Chelmsford telling him he was needed for support. The general's wording on the slip of paper was vague in the extreme, and Jack could see Durnford had hoped to find fresh orders in camp.

There were none.

As the senior officer, Durnford was theoretically now in command of the camp, but Jack could see he did not want to be bound by Pulleine's orders to defend it. He wanted action.

"If you saw Zulus this morning and then again just before I arrived, there could well be a move on the part of a small section of the Zulu army to cut between this camp and Chelmsford. Attack his left flank and rear."

A few officers shifted on their feet. Durnford made a good point; one perhaps Pulleine, and by extension his staff, should have considered.

"You have command, sir. What do you suggest?" Pulleine tugged at his moustache and looked down again at the hastily scrawled note Durnford had handed him, the mottled light coming through the canvas shading his eyes so Jack could not read his expression.

"Pincer movement. I'll send two of my officers with their men up into the Heights, and I'll take the foothills. We can head east towards General Chelmsford and see what we catch between us, eh?"

There was a murmur of agreement.

"I'll want two companies from you, Pulleine." Durnford half-turned, as if acquiescence to his request was a foregone conclusion.

Jack wondered what was going through Pulleine's mind as he rocked back on his heels.

"With regret, I can't do it, sir. I have my orders from the general as well. My duty is to defend the camp. The general took more than half the men and four of the six guns with him. I need all the men I have."

Durnford turned back, gave Pulleine a long look. "At least extend your picket line up the Inyoni Heights. Give me some support."

Pulleine nodded decisively. Jack knew it was because the pickets had been going up there anyway. It would be more than within the bounds of his orders.

"I'll instruct one of the companies to support your officers for some of the way."

Durnford nodded his thanks, uncaring of the details, and eager to get moving.

Jack stood in the aftermath of the meeting, watching Durnford's troops mount up again to ride out. They were lean, hard-looking men, native forces from Natal serving under equally tough-looking white officers.

At ease on their horses, they looked around at the sprawling camp with interest. The morning sun had long since burned through the clouds and mist, and he tried to see the neat rows of white tents through their eyes.

Jack wondered what they must think of the British. The Natal Zulus had very specific reasons for going to war against Cetshwayo. Did they wonder at Frere's?

As Durnford led them out of the camp, one of the men at the back gave Jack a cheeky wave, and he raised his hand in response.

"Burdell, the commander wants us back inside for a few minutes, to sort out the picket roster." A 1st Battalion officer poked his head from Pulleine's tent.

Jack looked back in the direction of his quarters and sighed. Elizabeth would have to wait a little longer.

WHY DID HE WANT TO MARRY HER?

It could be the sex, but Jack didn't strike her as a man ruled by passion. No, she had a sinking feeling it was his more honourable instincts at play.

His sense of what was right would certainly include getting her out of Zululand, out of the grasp of the savage natives.

He truly didn't understand, and how could he? Would she have understood before she came to live in her quiet village?

They both came from such an arrogant culture, so sure of its superiority.

The thought of her in traditional Zulu dress had rendered him speechless. He would consider getting her away from Zululand worth any sacrifice.

It had crossed her mind, before she told Jack her secret, that she would not be easily received after her years away, but his reaction, his jealousy, had brought it home hard and true. Even he, her first lover, a man who knew she'd been a virgin, had still wondered if every Zulu man she'd come into contact with, unprotected and half-naked, had raped her.

She'd be the object of titillated, scandalized gossip.

Only the respectability cure-all of marriage would silence the tongues.

That the Zulus hadn't touched her, where Jack had, that they had never behaved with anything but the utmost respect to her, was what had finally humbled him. Yet he still could not let her go back to them. He'd rather have her tied up than free in the bush, doing what no proper English-woman should.

His actions should make her hate him, but she knew his motivation came from respect and affection for her, and a deep-seated English sense of right and wrong.

That same sense of right and wrong meant she was sure she would not be tied up much longer, and then she'd have to make a choice.

And it was a choice, because although she'd been trying to avoid thinking about it, she had to face that when Jack asked her to marry him, in that exasperating, ridiculous way, her heart had leapt with joy for a moment, before reality intervened.

"Oh, Jack," she whispered, trying to wriggle her hands free once again. "What am I going to do about you?"

LINDANI CLOSED HIS EYES, FACING INTO THE HOT LATE-MORNING sun, his heart heavy in his chest while he waited for a word with the general. Worry and fear lay like stones in his stomach.

He'd been refused an audience with the general the night before. Hard-eyed *izindunas* had told him the general had left the battle ceremony for an important meeting with the other generals, and was not available to the likes of him.

But he'd begged them to pass on a message, and at last, he'd received his summons.

Despite the *inyangas'* warnings about the time of darkness, the generals were military men, and having a divided enemy force was too good an opportunity to pass up. They must be discussing their options, weighing up the threat of the spirits to the threat of the whiteman.

Lindani understood that they could not hope to hide twenty-five thousand men from the British much longer, and he understood the tactical advantage of dealing with this camp now; holding, as it did, all of the column's supplies, yet only half the men and a mere third of the big guns. The

King wanted them to eat up the enemy columns one by one, and this division of the main force was a fortuitous occurrence.

But—Inyoni.

She was down there, possibly — no, definitely — exposed. Perhaps in chains already.

If only she'd come with him the night the whitemen had set up camp.

"You have something to tell me?" The general finished with the scout he'd been giving orders to, looked up, and Lindani felt as if his gaze pierced right through him.

"My sister, *isiKhulu*. She is spying for you below, disguised as a soldier."

"Yes, her information has been most useful."

"I think she has been discovered as a spy."

The general inclined his head, waiting for more.

"I would like to go down there with a small group of scouts and rescue her." Lindani didn't make it a question. His stomach lurched with nerves.

The general shook his head. "We have decided to attack the camp later today. Before those who left last night return."

Lindani felt his world fall away. "I could rescue her right now. By myself."

"No. We want them to be completely unsuspecting, as they are now. One warrior inside their camp will put them on alert. We want them complacent."

"She will be killed by the *impi* if we attack. She is white and in uniform. No one will realize she is one of our own." His voice seemed to come from someone else.

"One person's sacrifice, for the opportunity we have." The general shrugged, but his eyes were not as hard.

"She is a woman. Not a warrior."

"A woman who offered to do a warrior's work." The general lifted his hands, regretful but undeterred.

"Then, please. Let me fight with the *ibutho* most likely to be first into the camp. Give me a chance to find her."

The general turned his face to the warm wind blowing off the mountains and shielded his eyes, as if he could see over the escarpment and down to the British camp.

"You are a young man, with no war experience. You would ask for the honour of being the first into the camp, amongst men at least ten years older than you, men who have spent their whole lives in the service of the King?"

Lindani kept silent. They both knew Inyoni's sacrifice earned him the privilege he asked.

Minutes ticked by, as if the general had all the time in the world. As if this was a matter over which he could deliberate. At last, he turned to look at Lindani. "I grant you permission. I will speak with the general who commands the left side of the chest. Report to him when the time comes to gather for the attack."

Then, with nothing more, no smile, or even a nod, the general moved off.

Lindani stood for a moment looking over the valley filled with men. From what the general said, they were going to implement the attacking formation of the horns of the bull. A right and left horn, made up of the young, fleet-footed men, would flank the enemy, and when they had almost encircled their foe, the chest of the bull, the older, experienced warriors, would move forward, engaging their enemy front on.

His age and experience should have put him in one of the horns, but because of Inyoni, he would have the honour of being in the chest. Being one of the first to attack the camp.

He heard a noise, a shouting, behind him, and turned to

see a small group of warriors running along the lip of the valley, overtaking the herd of cattle they were driving before them, and running between the panic-stricken animals.

For a moment, he wondered what the excitement was, and then froze as a group of mounted NNC men reined in just behind the running men.

Even from this distance, he could see their stunned, horror-filled faces as they took in the enormity of the Valley of the Shields. Twenty-five thousand armed warriors, sitting quietly, waiting their turn with the *inyangas* for the final rituals of battle.

He watched as a few of the men dismounted, almost fell from their horses, and then lifted their guns to fire a volley into the massive *impi*.

Just as the smallest movement will attract the eye of a lion, this tiny piece of defiance in the face of the might arrayed before them was all it took.

The young *amabutho* closest to the NNC men rose up with a shout, and as one man raced up the steep slope towards the enemy, their war cry filling the valley with its power.

Lindani felt a prickle of awe along his arms and the back of his neck.

The battle had begun.

CHAPTER THIRTY-ONE

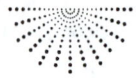

When an army is being led out to war no one speaks even a little; it is an evil day, for men are going to die; and they eat nothing.

— FROM THE RELIGIOUS SYSTEM OF THE AMAZULU BY REV. CANON HENRY CALLAWAY, M.D., 1870

J ack stepped out of Pulleine's tent and turned straight for his own. Working through the new picket duties and camp defense strategies had taken over half an hour, broken only by the arrival of a messenger from Chelmsford, telling Pulleine to pack up camp and move east to join him, thus making waste of their time spent arranging shifts.

The humidity was beginning to lift in waves from the

damp earth, and the hills in the distance shimmered like insubstantial air castles.

He should have let Elizabeth go.

If she were found tied up in his tent, there would be trouble for both of them, but especially for her. An official eye would immediately discover there was no Bird enlisted, and sooner or later they'd discover her secret.

He should have let her go.

He only hoped to God she was safe and undiscovered.

At the sound of galloping hooves he checked his step and frowned as Shepstone, Durnford's political officer, came flying into camp.

There was something in the way he rode, in his wild eyes. Jack turned back and ran towards Pulleine's tent, arriving there just as Shepstone threw himself from his horse.

"Attack!" He took a deep breath. "The pickets on the Heights are under attack."

"How many Zulus?" Pulleine had stepped out of the tent at the sound of Shepstone's arrival, his voice clipped, calm.

"Thousands, sir. Thousands of them."

Jack turned and looked back at the Heights. Somewhere out in the bush, the shrike he'd heard every now and then since they'd set up camp warbled its tune, *piet my vrou, piet my vrou*, and the crickets chirped in the long summer grass. Oxen lowed near the wagons behind the camp.

The echo of gunfire reached him just as he was about to ask Shepstone if he'd actually seen the Zulus, or whether it was an exaggerated second-hand story.

No doubt about it, there was fighting just out of sight in the hills.

Pulleine's gaze flicked in the direction of the Heights,

jumped back. "Lord Chelmsford has ordered me to pack up camp . . ."

"Sir, please understand the gravity of the situation. Without a doubt, Lt. Raw's unit has found the main Zulu army. They rushed us the moment they realized they'd been discovered." Shepstone reached out a hand to grab Pulleine's sleeve, recovered himself just in time and lowered it. "You cannot believe . . ." He wiped his forehead.

"Raw and Roberts are retreating, firing every few hundred yards. The company you sent up to support them are firing as well. You need to get men out there. Secure the camp."

They all heard more crackle and pop of gunfire, and Pulleine gave a short, sharp nod. "That is precisely what I intend to do."

LINDANI FELT ONLY PRIDE FOR THE *IMPI*. AFTER THE INITIAL rush of the young *amabutho*, the rest of the *impi* rose up to join them, realizing the element of surprise was slipping away. But what could have descended into chaos was tamed by the *izinduna*.

In the three miles it took to run from the Ngwebeni Valley to the lip of the escarpment, order had been established. Ice balled in Lindani's stomach as he realized the generals must have anticipated the possibility of this outcome well in advance. Each leader took up his position, calling orders to his men as he ran.

They were a fearsome force to be reckoned with.

He ran left, to where he thought the left side of the chest would form up. The men were jostling in the crush but silent, as befits an army about to do battle, and Lindani was suddenly shoved from behind.

"What are you doing here, little boy? Your place is on one of the horns with the other youngsters, not here with the men."

"Bangizwe." Lindani recovered his footing and carried on running forward, turning his head to see if his uncle was following.

He was.

"I said, what are you doing here? Among the senior men of the *uMbonambi ibutho*?"

"I am doing the general's bidding, my uncle. You can ask him, if you feel important enough to bother him, as we go to war, about the placement of one warrior in the *impi*."

"The general's bidding?" Bangizwe tried to shove him again, but Lindani swerved out of his reach.

"What could you do for the general here?" He lunged at Lindani, his eyes wild with rage, and grabbed him, pulling them out of the maelstrom and to one side of the regiment. Lindani could feel his uncle's fingers trembling as they dug into his arm.

"That is between the general and I." This was no time for a fight, and he kept his tone neutral.

"You have not served more than two years in your *ibutho*, and already you are given special favours?" Bangizwe's face was contorted, uncontrolled, and Lindani felt unease slide like an adder through his stomach. It was a hard-won honour for the prestigious older *amabutho* to strike the first battle blow, and it was not easily shared, but for Bangizwe to feel this strongly . . .

His uncle seemed out of his mind with anger. Perhaps he had taken war *muti* early. There was a glassy look to his eyes.

"I have worked for the King all these years. And still I have nothing, and you have everything. Even this last honour."

Lindani relented. Did he not have everything, as his uncle said? "I have special permission to go forward only because Inyoni is spying for the general in the camp. I need to find her before a warrior kills her by mistake."

Bangizwe's eyes narrowed. "That one? The white witch?" He spat. "The general should let her die."

"The general is a better, more loyal man than you." Lindani's patience was at an end. "When this war is over, you will not gain entrance at the village gate. I am the rightful chief, and, along with Inyoni, I have given valuable service to the King. Your claims of my youth making me a poor leader will fall on deaf ears. You and your trouble-making are not welcome."

Bangizwe struck out, mamba-quick, and Lindani lifted his shield just as the heavy head of his uncle's stick came down. The blow on the shield's hide sent a shock of vibration through Lindani's hand, and dumbstruck, he lowered it. There was foam and spittle around Bangizwe's mouth and he worked his lips, as if struggling to speak.

A cold dread bloomed inside Lindani. This jealousy and rage of his uncle went far deeper than he'd ever suspected. But the *ibutho* was running headlong past them for the escarpment, and he needed to be near the front, needed to get in a position to help Inyoni. This other, more personal battle, would have to wait.

A gap appeared in the mass of bodies just in front of him, and Lindani made a dash for it, slipping between the men and burrowing deep into the crowd. Out of sight of his uncle.

"Slow down, slow down. We wait," an *induna* bellowed

from the side, and Lindani felt the mass of men check their pace, but he did not. He began weaving his way forward to the front.

"The horns must get into place," the *induna* shouted. "We don't show ourselves at the edge of the escarpment yet."

The whole mass of men stopped, and spread out so everyone could sit down.

Lindani tried to find a sense of calm as silence settled on them. But the tension was too thick, Bangizwe's attack too shocking.

He tried to picture Nosipho, with her smooth taut belly filled with their unborn child. His mother, with her beautiful, serene face as she stirred the cooking pot. And Inyoni, trapped down below, dressed in the uniform of the enemy. But his thoughts only built the tension higher.

So many people relying on him.

Warriors were not supposed to think of their families before battle, lest they not fully commit to the fray. But as Lindani looked around at the men surrounding him, he saw some had the soft, sad faces of men thinking of their loved ones, of how they may never see them again.

And yet, if they did not go to war, their families would suffer English rule. They had no choice but to fight with their whole hearts.

And so they waited. The horns of the bull needed time to encircle the camp and the final rituals of battle needed to be given before they could take the whitemen on face to face.

And as the sound of gunfire to the right intensified, Lindani felt his mind slipping from sad thoughts of home and hearth, and filling with the hard, cold thoughts of a warrior going to do what he must.

~

Manning was both sorry to be returning to camp, to hurry Pulleine along, and pleased to be entrusted with such a task.

He was exhausted. They'd been on the move, in tense circumstances, for nearly ten hours, and there would be no rest for him when he got to the camp. At least not straight away.

The distant glowing red light of the camp fires in the dark hours of morning, evidence of the Zulu army, was burnt into his mind's eye, and he felt jumpy with excitement at the thought they were at last chasing the Zulus down and forcing them into pitched battle.

As he neared the *dongas* at the foot of the Inyoni Heights to his right, he heard the distinctive sound of gunfire coming from the north.

A skirmish?

Too curious to let it go, Manning urged his mount forward into a canter, and looking ahead and left towards the camp, saw the N Battery pulling the camp's two guns into a position facing north east, directly in front of the Inyoni Heights.

A company of the 1sts was leaving camp and heading north in the same direction as himself, no doubt to support whoever was firing in the hills lying to the left of the Heights.

Action at last.

Delighted with his fortune, Manning waved at the artillery men setting up the guns and carried on north. At the very least he could bring back word of the exchange of fire to the general, at best he could exchange some gunfire himself.

He had to slow his horse on the rocky ground of the

foothills, but he'd already almost caught the company he'd seen leaving camp and hailed them.

"Found some Zulus?"

"Not just some," one of the junior officers called back to him. "Quite a few, by all accounts."

Manning doubted it, but he'd take a look, all the same. Perhaps this was an attempt by the local chiefs of the area to cause mischief, and worry the army while the main Zulu force got into place in the east.

The hill flattened out slightly half way up the left side of the Heights, and Manning drew his horse up short, leant forward to be sure of what he was seeing.

A company of the 24th, along with two smaller companies of the NNC, stood in an extended line, firing at a stream of Zulus in the distance.

The strangest part of it was the Zulus were not responding to the fire at all, they made no sound, just ran, in a narrow column, off to the left, disappearing around the back of Mkwene hill.

"What in God's name are they doing?" Manning felt a chill at the sight, and could see from the wide eyes and backward glances of the other men, they felt the same. There was a deadly purpose in the way the warriors ran past, undeterred by the gunfire, almost uncaring of it. Where were they going?

"There are too many of them. If they decided to turn on us and advance, we'll be overrun." The officer who spoke, a man Manning knew to be a hardened veteran, was sweating, and he wiped a kerchief across his brow. "Make an orderly retreat, lads. No breaking ranks, just nice and easy down the hill."

Manning raised his rifle and shot off a round.

He'd been hot for action, and by Jingo, he'd found it.

CHAPTER THIRTY-TWO

I observed that the enemy made little progress as regards his advance, but appeared to be moving at a rapid pace towards our left. The right extremity of the enemy's line was very thin, but increased in depth towards and beyond our right as far as I could see, a hill interfering with extended view.

— BATTLE ACCOUNT OF CAPTAIN ESSEX,
DURNFORD'S TRANSPORT OFFICER.

Excitement gripped Harry Stokes as his company officer ordered them forward in battle formation to support the two guns. Excitement and relief.

The sound of gunfire to the left was evidence that at last something was happening. It was worse waiting for it, better when you were in the thick of things. Otherwise you could find yourself imagining things were much worse than they were.

They moved forward to where the ground sloped gently down towards the *dongas*. The Zulus would have to come down the Heights, over the *dongas* and then up the gentle incline to get to the camp, and with the two 7 pounder guns and the line of men standing before the camp in an extended arc, they would be mown down.

Suddenly the boom of a gun rocket sounded to the east, the way Durnford had gone with his troops earlier.

Durnford's rocket battery was firing?

For the first time since the orders came down, Harry felt a touch of nerves.

It was impossible to see very far to the east, the way was blocked by the hilly terrain, but for the rocket battery to fire — Harry swallowed hard. There must be sufficient numbers of Zulus to warrant that. You didn't loose a rocket battery on a few men.

He waited expectantly for a second boom, but the battery was silent. He almost wondered if he'd imagined the first sound.

"Hang about." Jenkins called out, and Harry saw him pointing up.

He lifted his gaze and saw the first few Zulus appearing on the top of the Heights.

And then more.

And then more still.

"God preserve us." Harry hadn't thought a lot about God recently, but he thought about Him now.

The Zulu line extended the length of the ridge and Harry could just make out their officers or generals. Dressed in plumes and tails, they were running up and down the line, shouting and screaming at their troops.

Then as one the whole line began to shout, stamping

their feet and hitting the wooden shafts of their spears against the wooden supports of their shields.

"Sheeeeeeeee. Sheeeeeeee. Sheeeeeeee. Sheeee. Shee. Shee. Shee. Shee. Shee."

Above the chant, Harry heard one of the generals scream an order, and with a cry that seemed to echo across the valley, the Zulus poured over the rim, shouting as they went.

The slopes of the Inyoni Heights became a seething mass of warriors, headed straight for the Isandlwana camp.

"Steady, lads, steady," his commander called out, and Harry drew in a decidedly unsteady breath, looked down the line and saw a mirror of his own fear on the faces stretched to his right and left.

He watched the big guns being loaded, but in the face of the numbers coming at them, two suddenly looked hopelessly inadequate. Chelmsford had gone hightailing it off with the other four.

Harry couldn't help the bitter anger that rose up in him. What did the high-ups think they were doing? Chelmsford had either been tricked or had seriously miscalculated.

Those Zulus must be laughing their arses off at them.

He shifted, every nerve in his body screaming at him to run for his life.

"Hold the line, boys, we've got the advantage." The commander's was so certain, so calm, but it didn't look like they had the advantage to Harry. There were thousands of Zulus running down the slope. Thousands of them.

Harry clutched his Martini-Henry to his chest and sent up his first genuine prayer in years.

He felt bad about it, but Jack was glad now Elizabeth

was tied up. Before the Zulus were sighted, he wished he'd let her go, but not anymore. She was safe in his tent and couldn't get up to any more sabotage where she was.

She couldn't go anywhere anyway.

Joining her Zulu brother in the middle of a battle was simply not possible. She'd be killed by her own – if the Zulus were her own – simply because of the colour of her skin.

As he advanced to the far right of the camp with his men, to take up their ordered position, his heart stuttered in his chest at the thought of what would have happened if he'd left the meeting with Pulleine a little earlier and untied her.

She'd have been running up the Heights in her uniform into the line of fire. He shivered.

A single boom of a battery rocket came from the east, and he cocked his head in that direction.

Durnford had taken that route, part of his pincer move-ment, and he'd taken his gun with him, but who could he have encountered so far to the right? Shepstone claimed the main army was to the left and directly in front of them. Jack frowned.

The gun did not fire again, and rather than reassuring him, it made Jack even more uneasy.

A shout from one of the men by the two guns in the line caught his attention and he looked up to see the Zulus ranged up along the Heights.

This had to be the main Zulu army. Jack blinked, unsure whether to believe his eyes. There were thousands of men up there, standing shoulder to shoulder, and not in a thin, extended line, either; at least two or three men deep. At least.

"Sir?"

One of his junior officers called his attention from the

terrifying sight, an unspoken request for reassurance and guidance. His men looked shocked, their eyes wide with fear.

Jack shaded his eyes against the morning sun. "Battle formations, lads," he called, and his calmness seemed to help them collect themselves as they formed their battle line.

"We've done this a time or two. We all know what to do." Jack hoped they didn't think too much about it, because although they'd fought the Xhosa many times, they'd never come up against so large, or so organized, a force.

That they were organized could not be doubted. Jack could see the way they formed together in companies, heard the yells of the officers, and it came home to him that this was a trained army, not a bunch of savages with sharp sticks.

He'd thought the staff had misinterpreted the Zulu action at Sihayo's stronghold, but the sheer depth, the staggering blindness of their misconceptions hit him like the boom of the rocket battery that had fired just once and no more beyond the hills to the east.

What if I told you I knew something was going to happen? Something terrible.

Elizabeth's words the night she'd tried to persuade him to leave the camp came back to him, slamming into him like a hammer blow. Had she known of this? Had she given up her chance to leave in order to persuade him to go with her?

God Almighty.

Suddenly the unnerving chant of the Zulus up on the horizon was replaced by a massive shout, and Jack watched as the warriors streamed over the summit, down the slopes of the Heights directly at them.

He wrenched his attention away from the waterfall of men, hard though it was, and looked behind him at the camp.

To where Elizabeth sat tied fast in his tent, out of his reach for the moment.

His arrogance and confidence in British military superiority might just be the death of her.

~

LINDANI STOOD WITH THE SENIOR MEN, AND TOOK THE SNUFF the medicine man handed him; *muti* to make him brave as a lion, and impervious to the whiteman's bullets.

He heard the men in the line discuss the progress of the Zulu right horn, running past the two companies that had discovered them. How could the whitemen not be curious about where they were going? Did they not realize their enemies were going around the back of Isandlwana, to encircle the camp?

The left horn had poured down the east slope of the Heights, out of sight of the camp, and from the single boom of a large gun, he heard the generals surmise they had encountered the NNC troops that had gone east along the bottom of the Heights earlier, and overcome them.

The generals made them wait for both horns to make good progress as they ran on either side of the camp.

When they were satisfied the whitemen could not stop them, even if they finally worked out what was happening, they called the chest forward to the top of the Heights, the better to focus the Englishmen's attention straight ahead, instead of to their flanks and rear.

Lindani stood slightly back, not wanting to push himself forward disrespectfully. There would be time later, in the rush down the hill, for him to find the front of the line.

The generals rallied the troops, screaming out the praise

songs of their battalions. Shouting war songs. Reminding them their honour and their courage were at stake.

And they all began to chant as they stamped their feet and hit their shields: Shee. Shee. Shee. Faster and faster. Lindani felt the vibration run through his arm with each blow of his *assegai* on the wooden frame of his shield, his every sense heightened by the *muti*.

And over the torrent of noise, the most senior general suddenly screamed, "Kill them."

Lindani was swept over the hill in the wave of warriors, his heart almost bursting with excitement and blood lust. The *muti* made his vision jump, and he concentrated only on not falling as he ran down the steep slope, on the line of the enemy below them.

He felt separate from the world. An observer.

They shouted as they ran, calling their chiefs' praises, and praises to the King.

"The wind!" a warrior called out in warning, and the older men threw themselves down, one of them grabbing Lindani's shoulder and pulling him down with them.

The rocket shell exploded with an ear-splitting crack just below them, throwing earth and shards of rock into the air. Lindani staggered to his feet, his ears ringing.

He had never heard such a loud noise. It had been beyond his imagination until today.

They carried on forward, towards the foot of the Heights, and suddenly the crack and whiz of bullets was among them.

"Nothing but hailstones," one of the warriors called out proudly, and his call was taken up by the others.

"Catch stones." The jeering chant carried in the warm midday air, but Lindani saw a warrior catch a bullet with his chest and it went through him and out the other side, spraying the ground behind him red with blood. With barely a grunt, the man fell face first.

And then the warriors were falling, left and right, and calling the warning, "The wind", whenever the men at the big guns stood away from them, as it meant a shell was about to be fired.

Lindani tried desperately to rekindle the urgency of getting to Inyoni he'd had earlier, but he could not. All he could think of was killing.

Killing as many whitemen, interlopers and thieves, as he could.

Killing the men coming to destroy Zululand.

CHAPTER THIRTY-THREE

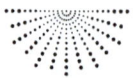

When 'arf your bullets fly wide in the ditch,
  Don't call your Martini a cross-eyed old bitch;
  She's human as you are – you treat her as sich
  An' she'll fight for the young British soldier

— RUDYARD KIPLING, THE YOUNG BRITISH
SOLDIER

From inside the tent, Elizabeth sat frozen, listening to the sounds of the *impi* chanting on the Heights.

Lindani had begged her to leave but she would not. And now she was trapped down here, with Jack in the field anyway.

She'd heard the thunder of hooves, the excited shouting about Zulus, and had not been surprised when Jack took so long to return, but with the Zulu battle calls ringing out from the hills, she realized now he wasn't cloistered away in a meeting, but out forming a defensive line with his men.

The chanting changed to a hoarse cry, and she shivered. The guns boomed, the rifles cracked. The *impi* was spilling over the Heights.

The line of fire sounded far out, extended towards the *dongas*.

How could she be so helpless?

She jerked at the rope, but Jack had done a thorough job. There was no way she could get free of this without him untying her. And she had failed miserably to convince him to do that.

She weighed up the chances of release if she called out. Chambers was issuing orders not that far from the tent. She opened her mouth to shout.

Closed it again.

What could she say?

There was no way he'd untie her without talking with Jack first, and Jack would be in the field. Killing Zulus.

Her lover trying to kill her brother.

Elizabeth began to struggle against her ropes again.

IT WAS PAST MIDDAY AND THEY WERE PINNED DOWN BY THE gunfire. Lindani felt calmer now, the effects of the *muti* not as strong. He remembered the day Inyoni shot the old rifle Malusi had given her, and how it had blasted through the shield.

She'd tried to warn them, but they thought they knew better. They hadn't wanted to hear it.

These whitemen had even better rifles than the one she'd

used. Rifles that shot bullets strong enough to go through a warrior and kill the warrior behind him, as well.

For the moment, though, he was safe. Gone to ground in the network of *dongas* at the bottom of the Heights with whoever else had made it down the slope.

They were safe, but they were trapped. Every time a warrior tried to climb out of the natural trench and advance on the line, they came under a hail of fire.

The onslaught of noise, smoke and blood was a hell Lindani had not found in his darkest nightmares.

There was a murmur of interest among the men, and Lindani looked left, almost reeling back when he saw Bangizwe staring at him, raw hatred in his eyes. His uncle was following him still. Dogging him through this battle as best he could.

But even his uncle could not resist the pull of the action coming up from the east, and he too turned his head left.

A group of NNC men were retreating back to the camp, the troops that had gone east earlier that morning with the big gun, now fleeing in the face of the Zulu's left horn. The big gun they'd taken with them was missing, and Lindani felt a flare of pride in the warriors of the horn, to have over-come such a powerful weapon. That single boom from earlier was the only shot the whitemen had managed to get off.

The retreating NNC troops were firing behind them as they went, harassed by the left horn, although Lindani was sure it was only a breakaway group of warriors. The others would still be racing to get beyond the camp and meet up with the right horn to form a neat circle.

The mounted NNC men reached the line of *dongas* in which Lindani and the rest of the *ibutho* lay and plunged their mounts into the far left trenches for cover. They kept up their fire on the warriors chasing them for only a few minutes, then they rose up over the ditches and ran, without their horses, to form an extension of the camp line.

More and more men from the *uMbonambi ibutho* made it down the hill and joined him and the others in the *donga*, and a general started shouting there was a gap, that between the NNC men who'd taken up a position on the far left of the camp line and the redcoats, there was open ground. That in the moment before the smoke cleared from a round of fire, they could sneak through.

Spurred on by this, some of the men leapt out of the *donga* and ran forward, and Lindani watched in horror as they were cut down by fire from both the NNC and the redcoats.

"Bring me some cattle," the general shouted, and a few of the warriors scrambled off to carry out his order.

Lindani saw with shock one of the big *indunas*, the general of the *uKhandempemvu ibutho*, run down the slope to join his men, and urge them on.

He ran back and forth in front of them, as if unconcerned by the bullets flying all around, castigating his men for hiding in the *dongas*.

Lindani heard him start to sing a praise song to the King just as a small herd of cattle, terrified to the point of collapse by the noise, was forced into the deep gulley where he lay.

"Who will run with the cattle towards the line?" their *induna* called, and before Lindani could even think to move, ten men rushed forward, eager for the honour.

They forced the small herd up and over the *donga*, driving it straight at the British line, hiding amongst the petrified beasts.

The guns were very powerful, because their bullets felled the cattle, exposing the men hiding behind them. But still, three warriors moved far enough forward and were suddenly behind the enemy line.

With a whoop of victory, the *uMbonambi* began to leap over the *donga*.

Lindani heard another cry of victory to the right, and saw the great general had finally convinced the *uKhandempemvu* to run straight into the teeth of the guns.

As he watched, the great man ran forward one step, two steps, with his men, then fell, stopped by a bullet straight through his forehead.

His heart lurched. If so mighty a warrior could be struck down, what chance had he? And yet, his sense of purpose was back. He watched the British line falter, unhinged by the rush of thousands of warriors in the face of their cruel fire. Watched them start to step back, and then turn and run.

Now was his chance to find Inyoni, and get her off the battlefield.

And he would take pleasure in killing every whiteman who got in his way.

FIRE AND LOAD, FIRE AND LOAD. JACK COULDN'T REMEMBER when he'd been doing anything else. And still the warriors kept coming down the slopes, going down into the *dongas* out of range.

Those who made it.

The slaughter was horrific. The warriors had to jump over the bodies of the fallen to get to safety, and Jack could see the horror on their faces at their losses.

Yet it did not stop them coming. They had an edge in this fight. The British soldiers were following orders, but the Zulus were fighting for their country. For their sovereignty.

And it showed.

As he called the load and fire commands to his men, 'Ready' and 'Present', he wondered how much longer they could keep this up.

The ammunition was coming. Ten minutes ago Chambers himself ran up with boxes of it, but the cart drivers were also making themselves useful, running up to the line in a steady stream.

Jack used the butt of his Martini-Henry to smash the lid of a box open, and loaded up on more bullets.

If they stopped firing for even a moment, if there was even the slightest pause, one or two of the warriors trying to breach the line would succeed, and then God help them.

God help Elizabeth.

He certainly hadn't, even when he had the chance. His inability to let her go meant she was caught in a trap.

If the line broke, and Jack didn't see how it couldn't, his first duty was to free Elizabeth, protect her.

He saw a company of the NNC had taken up the line to the right of him, but the men were not armed with Martini-Henrys and only the few white officers among them had pistols. The short-sightedness of the staff in failing to train and arm their Native Contingent came home to him in a very personal way.

The sound of gunfire to his right made him focus east, and he saw Durnford retreating with his men before an advancing party of Zulu warriors. Like a long arm extended in a column to the right of the camp, they pushed forward, driving Durnford before them.

There was no sign of the rocket battery.

Remembering the single boom of fire, Jack realized it must have been overcome.

These Zulus could fight.

Durnford was already in line with the Zulu force that had gone to ground in the *dongas* at the bottom of the Heights, and he and his men leapt into one of them, using it to return fire at the wall of men coming at them.

But despite their massive losses the warriors were not deterred, and Jack saw Durnford's company abandon their horses and run up the slope towards the far right.

"Burdell, support Durnford," one of the senior officers shouted to him, and Jack was forced to extended his line even more, moving his company, strung out like wide-spaced pearls on a necklace, across to the far right, passing behind the NNC men.

They had just taken up position, covering Durnford's flank and stopping the Zulu's advance, when a herd of cattle was chased over the *dongas*, straight at them, and at the same moment, Durnford's men fell back.

"Durnford! Why are you pulling back?" Jack watched in horror as he and his men were suddenly left swinging in the proverbial breeze. Their position over-exposed and vulnerable.

"We have no more ammo," Durnford yelled back. "I'm going to confer with Pulleine. Retreat. Everyone retreat."

Jack looked at the three unopened boxes of ammunition at his feet and shook his head. What in God's name was going on?

He raised his Martini again but as he did, he saw the middle-aged Zulu general who had been running up and down, encouraging his troops, had succeeded.

In the face of firing so hot, his ears were ringing with it, the warriors leapt over the *dongas*, straight for the line. As if they were immortal.

It was the most incredible thing he'd ever seen.

Their bravery seemed to sting the rest of the *impi* into

action, and all along the Zulu line, the warriors poured out of their trenches and rushed the camp.

"God and the Saints preserve us," a junior officer wailed, and Jack knew they had lost.

From the camp, the bugler sounded 'The Retire'.

"Retreat. Form together," Jack called out.

His men moved into a box formation, and started back, keeping the fire rate up.

"Sir." A private grabbed Jack's sleeve, and Jack looked up to where he pointed.

The Royal Artillery guns had answered the bugle's call and were moving back, and as the gunners ran beside the cannons, a wave of Zulu warriors engulfed them. Jack saw the first man fall. Stabbed through with an *assegai*, screaming as he died.

From now on, the fighting would be hand to hand. And the Zulus would have their revenge for the many thousands of their brothers, slaughtered on the slopes of the Inyoni Heights.

Like the battlefields of old, bayonet against *assegai*, cold steel on steel.

CHAPTER THIRTY-FOUR

In a moment, all was disorder, and few of the men of the 1st Battalion 24th Regiment had time to fix their bayonets before the enemy was among them using their assegais with fearful effect.

— BATTLE ACCOUNT OF CAPTAIN ESSEX,
DURNFORD'S TRANSPORT OFFICER.

The box formation broke.

"To me, to me," Jack called, but it was too late. The men were too panicked, too terrified to listen. Their eyes wild and their movements jerky.

They began to run for the camp — that open, unlaagered huddle of tents in enemy territory — and again the depth of British arrogance hit Jack full force.

Giving up on trying to rally his company, Jack drew his pistol and ran.

A Zulu leapt out of nowhere, screaming, his eyes almost blank with battle frenzy, his *assegai* arm drawn back. Jack shot him in the chest, through his cowhide shield, carried on running as fast as he could for his tent. For Elizabeth.

He had to get there first.

He started assessing their escape route, and looking through the camp to the Rorke's Drift track he almost stumbled when he saw a column of Zulus come around the back of Isandlwana, cutting off the road.

They'd neatly encircled the camp, and there was no way out.

Jack reached the line of tents, and turned to see how the rest of the men were faring. Saw them rally in a line, fighting with their bayonets and pistols.

Then one of the Zulus called out, fear in his voice, and a hush descended as the massive sea of warriors, poised to break over them in a deluge, stopped and looked up.

Unable to help himself, Jack followed their gaze and saw the moon edging across the sun.

An eclipse.

The moment of silence ended and the noise, the screams and the crack of pistols, hammered his senses again. The tiny humans going about their bloody work under an uncaring heaven, busy with its own mysterious business.

The sun going dark seemed full of portent to him. The mark of an evil day.

It made him even more desperate to reach Elizabeth.

THE ZULUS HAD BROKEN THROUGH. SHE COULD HEAR IT IN THE victorious tone of their calls, and the screams and shouts of the British.

The light in the tent dimmed, and she wondered if there was another storm brewing, if the massive, heavy clouds of a Zululand summer downpour were blocking the sun. She shivered.

Outside there was a thud of feet, the sound of someone running straight for the tent, and she bit her lip to stop herself screaming as Jack ran in.

He had his dagger out, and for a moment, she wondered if he were going to stab her.

"You bastard." Her voice shook with reaction as he grabbed the rope around her and began sawing into it.

"I'm sorry, Elizabeth. If I had known they would attack . . ."

"Sorry isn't enough," she cried. "You're going to die, you bloody idiot." She blinked away the tears that were suddenly blinding her.

"You think of me?" He stilled, and reached out a hand to touch her cheek. "I will get you out, I promise you. There must be some weakness in the Zulu line, some place we can break through."

"There will be no weakness in their line," she told him, couldn't help the pride in her voice as she said it.

At that, he dropped his hand and hacked at the ropes again.

They had just begun to give when with a snap of canvas, a Zulu warrior ran into the tent. For a single thump of her heart there was silence, as they all froze, watching each other.

"Bangizwe," Elizabeth breathed.

"I knew I'd find you, white witch. I've seen my nephew racing around looking as well. Lucky for me, I found you first."

Elizabeth sensed Jack rising to his feet to her right, saw

his hand edge to his waistband, where he'd stuck his pistol. Saw him grip his dagger more firmly.

He suddenly stepped in front of her, blocking her from Bangizwe's sight.

"Does he know you're a spy? Or have you cast a spell on him, that he is so willing to protect you?"

Jack paused when Bangizwe addressed her directly, unsure, perhaps, if this was someone she knew. Unable to understand what he said.

"Shoot him, Jack. Now."

But as she called out, Bangizwe feinted left, deeper into the tent, his *assegai* in his right hand, an old muzzle-loader in his left.

Jack spun with him, pistol raised, but Bangizwe had already lunged forward with the *assegai*, striking Jack in the right shoulder.

Jack's pistol dropped to the floor, and he stumbled with a cry, his arm useless, his face white with shock and pain. His blue field jacket turned dark with blood as he lifted his dagger in his left hand, small and outclassed by the *assegai*.

She fought against her ropes, overcome with fury at how helpless she was.

"First you, and then Lindani," Bangizwe said, lifting his old rifle. "I will be chief."

She never thought the end would be so senseless. Tied to a post, absolutely at his mercy.

"Let the whiteman go, at least," she begged.

"You have no bargaining power," Bangizwe laughed, trying to aim the rifle at her, while still holding his *assegai*.

Jack staggered in front of her again. "Who is this fellow?" He spoke through gritted teeth.

Elizabeth opened her mouth to answer, but Bangizwe threw down the *assegai*, steadied the rifle and shot.

With a cry, Jack stepped back, and then stopped, surprised.

"Inyoni." The words were almost whispered, and Elizabeth turned to see Lindani in the entrance of the tent, his chest a pulpy mess of blood and flesh. He fell to his knees, and it seemed Jack did too.

"Lindani." His name ripped from her throat, and she strained her arms towards him, then jerked as a pistol cracked right in her ear.

Bangizwe gave a cry, and she saw Jack had gotten on hands and knees to find his gun and had fired it left-handed at Bangizwe, nicking his side with the shot.

"Don't come back to the village, witch. There will be no welcome for you there." Bangizwe looked down at where his *assegai* lay, then back to the pistol in Jack's hand, and Elizabeth saw him realize the odds were against him.

Clutching his side, he dodged around Jack and ran past Lindani, striking Lindani's head with his elbow as he leapt out the tent, toppling her kneeling brother to the floor.

"Untie me, quickly." Elizabeth heard the sob in her voice. Jack dragged himself to the pole and lifted his dagger again, hacking a few more times until the ropes were free.

Numb from sitting in one place for so long, Elizabeth crawled to where Lindani lay, a strange keening coming from his throat.

"Lindani." She cradled his head, keeping her eyes away from the terrible damage to his body.

He couldn't answer, but his eyes focused on her when she lifted his head, and there was a flicker of recognition in them.

He made a sound, ending in a terrible gurgle, and she saw the life force drain out of him.

"No!" She clutched him tighter to her, as if that could

somehow bring him back, but his eyes stared up at her, blank and empty. Not Lindani anymore.

"Elizabeth, we have to go."

She felt Jack's hand on her shoulder, and the outside world intruded. She could hear the screams and shouts of a battle raging at its height outside the thin canvas walls, but she did not move. She knelt before her brother, and then lifted her face to the sky, where he now was, and ululated her sorrow.

COLIN HARRISON WATCHED IN HORROR AS THE ZULUS BRAVED the guns and the rifles, pouring out of the *dongas* and rushing the line. The Retire sounded and the call went up to retreat. He looked back at the camp.

Retreat to where?

The camp was open, indefensible, and then he cried out, because through the tents, he could see more Zulus coming from behind the camp, from around the back of Isandlwana and to his left. They'd been encircled.

"To me," an officer called, and unsure what else to do in the face of the overwhelming force stacked against them, Colin ran to him.

At least twenty other 24ths converged on the officer, who Colin recognized as Captain Greene, and they formed a circle, back to back, rifles raised.

"How much ammo have you got on you?" Greene called out.

"Not enough," someone answered, and amazingly, there was a ripple of laughter.

"Well, do your best lads, that's the spirit."

Colin could hear the approval in Greene's voice, and he

wanted not to let him down, wanted to be thought a cool customer in the face of danger.

He would go out doing his duty. Take as many of Her Majesty's enemies with him as he could.

The thought settled him, made him feel less jumpy. He was going to die, it just came down to how honorably he went.

One of the men let out an incoherent cry, pointing at the line, and Colin saw the gunners, pulling the guns back to camp, dragged under by a wave of warriors.

"They're disemboweling them," the man next to him whispered in horror.

Colin's hands started to shake.

My darling Cecilia. I love you.

Then the warriors were on them, around them, screaming, their eyes frenzied with battle lust, with rage at their dead littering the slopes of the Inyoni Heights.

Colin let off a round, watched one of the warriors running at him fall. Heard the deafening blast of rounds being fired all around their little circle of redcoated men. The gunfire cleared a space around them, littered with dead warriors.

A bullet came whizzing in, and Colin looked around wildly, swung his Martini in the direction of an armed Zulu and took aim, watched the man duck.

A Zulu near him cried out and fell, and Colin realized it was almost impossible to miss hitting someone in the current crush of men, in the chaotic, scrappy battlefield the camp had become.

The Zulus started throwing *assegais* at them, and the soldier two down from where Colin stood fell.

"Close ranks," Greene screamed, and they edged in to fill the gap in the line, shuffling back so as not to step on the fallen man, gasping like a fish with a blade through his throat.

"I'm out of ammo, sir." The man who called out was sobbing.

"Fix your bayonets. Everyone who runs out of ammo, fix your bayonets." Greene's crisp, clear commands seemed to help them pull themselves together.

A cry suddenly went up amongst the Zulus, and they stilled for a moment, looking to the sky.

Colin jerked his head up quickly, too afraid of taking his eyes off their attackers to look for long. He gaped.

The sun was going black.

"My God, what evil is this?" the soldier beside him whispered.

A strange light spilled over them and Colin wanted to kneel and pray. Beg God to be with him in this dark hour.

But the Zulus, after their moment of silence, began shouting even more wildly, attacking more ferociously, and Colin shot off his Martini again. He felt in his pouch for the next bullet and discovered he'd just shot his last one.

It was time for the bayonet.

Time to make peace with death.

CHAPTER THIRTY-FIVE

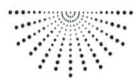

I can't understand it. I left a thousand men here.

— LORD CHELMSFORD ON HIS RETURN TO
ISANDLWANA THAT EVENING.

There was only her and her heavy heart in the world.
Lindani was gone, and Jack had run out of the tent
as well, cursing, unable to pull her to her feet with only
one arm.

Around her the battle raged. Twice a warrior had come to
the tent, drawn by her cries of mourning, and then hurried
away. She hardly noticed them.

Another movement at the tent entrance caught her eye,
and then Jack was back.

"If you want me to die, Elizabeth, stay where you are,
because I won't leave without you." His eyes were glazed,
feverish, and Elizabeth noticed the whole right sleeve of his

jacket was caked in blood. He swayed on his feet. "I've found a horse. I have to keep hold of it or it will run, it is so panicked, which means I have no spare hands. So, please, my darling, lovely Elizabeth. For both of us. Get up and come to me."

The desperation of his words penetrated the thick haze of helplessness and despair she'd drawn around herself like a blanket.

Slowly, still stiff, she rose to her feet, and walked across to him.

"Thank God." He looked about to pass out, but shook his head in a little jerk and breathed deeply. "Can you ride?"

She saw he was holding onto reins with his left hand, and the horse was trembling as it stood. She turned back to look at Lindani.

"Now, Elizabeth. We have to go now." His voice was a whip crack, and at last the full horror of the camp invasion became clear to her.

Much was obscured by the tents, but through the rows she could see groups of redcoats fighting back to back, surrounded by Zulus. If they stayed even one moment more, they would be found.

She looked up at the sky, expecting the dark thunder clouds, and instead saw the moon passing in front of the sun. The sight was so strange, it blew away the last traces of her fugue.

Leaving with Jack now meant leaving for good.

There would be no going back to Zululand after this.

A strange sound of pain rose in her throat, and then she looked at Jack, glassy-eyed and grim, and swallowed down hard on her sorrow.

"You get on first. I'll help you up." She took the reins from him, and gave him a push as he hauled himself into the saddle, and for a moment she thought he'd pass out with the pain. "Move back, I'll take the reins."

Without waiting for him, she scrambled in the saddle and forced the horse around, needing to get clear of the tents to find the best way out. It had been six years since she'd ridden.

"Head for the track to Rorke's Drift," Jack said, his left arm coming around her waist to anchor them both together.

"Won't everyone be trying to get through there?" Elizabeth urged the horse, a lovely chestnut, forward.

"Perhaps."

Jack's voice was fading.

"Hold on to me, Jack. That's all you have to do. Hold on."

A small group of Zulus rounded some tents just in front of them, and with a cry, rushed towards her.

"Wait, my brothers, I am a spy for the King. I have important news for him."

The warriors stopped, surprised at her call in Zulu, and not waiting to see if they believed her, she turned her mount left, away from them. Not towards the track, but still in the direction of the river. A gun cracked, the bullet whining past her ear like an enraged bee, and in panic the horse began to gallop.

If only she were armed. Perhaps Jack – she felt back with her hand, looking for Jack's pistol holster, and her hand found the small leather pouch on his belt. She pulled the gun from it. She had no idea how many bullets were left, but gripped it tightly as they raced through the camp.

Small vignettes of horror and bravery were all around her. Warriors ritually disemboweling their slain enemies to release their spirits to the sky, pockets of British troops standing back to back, slashing their attackers with their bayonets, and falling one by one to throwing spears or bullets.

The noise, the smell of blood and gun smoke, the terrible atmosphere of doom suffocated her, and she turned her eyes ahead, and refused to look anymore.

"Help! Please help," a soldier, his chest cut open to the bone, screamed as she galloped by, and she had to close her eyes for a moment to shut him out of her heart.

An *assegai* flew at her, and she instinctively threw her arm up before her face, but it past harmlessly to the left.

She gave the chestnut its head and made for a gap in the Zulu line created by some mounted NNC men trying to break through. They had bunched together in a concerted move to ram their way to freedom, and for a moment the attention of the warriors was drawn in their direction.

She passed the desperate battle, but it was surely a matter of time before some gave chase, and the ground was so broken and rough here, Elizabeth wondered if the warriors would not make better time over the rocks than the horse.

Jack's hold was getting weaker and weaker around her waist, and as they lurched across the veld, she knew he would soon pull them both off.

"Hold on, please hold on." She was sobbing, realized there were tears streaming down her face.

Out of the corner of her eye, she saw a warrior running parallel to the chestnut, saw him start to angle towards them.

"Usutu!" He screamed King Cetshwayo's battle cry, and leapt at them.

Elizabeth lifted the pistol and shot him in the face, and he dropped like a stone, his head hitting the rocks with a crack that would stay with her for the rest of her days.

God help her, she'd killed one of her own.

At the sound of the pistol, Jack murmured something in her ear, tightened his grip a little.

"Just a little longer, my love. A tiny bit more."

She could see the river before them, a raging, pounding torrent of brown water and debris below the high, rocky bank. She ducked her head down and looked back past Jack, saw her pistol shot had drawn three warriors to them, running swiftly over the rough ground, *assegais* raised. She pointed the pistol under her left arm and shot at them, but the bullet flew wide and they were not deterred.

The ground was a bit smoother closer to the banks, and the chestnut had picked up speed, hurtling them at the river. Elizabeth did not rein it in, but urged it faster, and cried out as they plunged over the side into the water.

The current plucked at her, grabbed her, as they tumbled through the foaming water, and Elizabeth hung on with her thighs, clutching Jack's arm around her waist with all her strength.

The chestnut broke the surface, screaming and thrashing, as the river swept them downstream.

They had to make the other side.

Elizabeth felt as if her arms would snap as she clung to Jack with one hand, the horse's mane with the other. They hadn't come this far to—

With a shake of its head, the chestnut found its footing and scrambled up the opposite bank.

Panting, gasping for air, Elizabeth turned and saw the three warriors standing on the far bank, *assegais* at their side.

Perhaps the King had commanded them not to cross the river into Natal.

"Go well, my brothers," she called to them in Zulu, giving a salute, and she saw the surprise on their faces.

It was her final goodbye.

She turned the horse in the direction of Helpmekaar. Rorke's Drift was too close to Isandlwana, and she was afraid the fighting might have spilled over there.

Behind her, Jack coughed water from his lungs.

"Where are we going?" His voice was so faint, she barely heard him. She could feel the heat of his fever through layers of cold wet clothes.

She took a deep breath, and wiped tears and river water from her cheeks. There would be time for weeping later.

"We are going home," she answered.

Wherever home was.

CHAPTER THIRTY-SIX

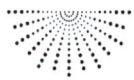

We speak of disaster and failure and inglorious warfare only as regards those who made the war and undertook its management. Our brave soldiers acted as bravely as ever men acted in any war; implicitly obeying orders which they knew must end in failure, marching calmly into the jaws of death, enduring hardships innumerable without complaint and entering into the conflict of battle with genuine enthusiasm, notwithstanding the fact that the sympathies of the many were not in the cause.

— EDWIN HODDER, HEROES OF BRITAIN, 1880

It was much easier pretending to be a boy in Helpmekaar and then later, Pietermaritzburg, than the big port of Durban. Everyone in the smaller towns, much closer to the action, were too shocked, too frightened by what had happened, to notice a young batman who was prepared to look after his master tirelessly.

Durban, though.

The sense of fear was less here, in the wide, open streets, and red brick buildings, although still present in the too jocular laughter of the men and the nervous, watchful eyes of the women. The rumour was that the Zulus would press their advantage, take revenge on the invasion of their land and the slaughter of their men, and wipe the English out of Natal as well as Zululand.

Being on edge, and afraid, made the men jumpy and ill-tempered, looking for an easy mark to prove they were still in control. Still strong.

Elizabeth clenched the thin sheet she'd pulled over Jack in her hands as she thought of the hard-edged, filthy rudeness of the shipping clerk when she'd requested adjoining cabins on board the ship they were taking to London.

She had twice thought of leaving. Of making Jack as comfortable as possible, and then sending a note to his doctor and the local army liaison. Slipping away.

The press of the crowds, the petty fights and victories, the sneering arrogance of the administrators – all of this would be waiting for her at the other end of the journey, only a hundred, a thousand times worse.

And she would have to come forward. Let her grandmother know she was alive.

She would be with Jack, at least.

She didn't doubt he loved her. Didn't doubt he would marry her as soon as he was well enough, but she wondered if he realized what their life would be like, what people would think of her, if it came out where she'd been living these last six years.

She looked out the window, into streets wet and muddy

from a summer shower, and longed for the feel of the earth beneath her bare feet and the cool mist of rain on her bare shoulders. On her face.

"What are you thinking?"

The whisper jerked her out of her reverie, and she turned her head, was caught in the intense blue of Jack's eyes. There was confusion there, and a thread of fear.

"About travelling." She tried to smile, but failed.

He lifted his left hand and awkwardly touched her arm, letting his thumb stroke her skin. "It will be all right."

"Yes." She managed the smile this time. "Of course it will."

∾

20 February, 1879

Dear Mrs. Colin Harrison,

I am sorry to inform you that your husband, Sgt. Colin Harrison, died on 22nd January last. I regret I cannot give further or fuller information.

Yours

Col. ---

∾

She was in the apple orchard again.

Jack could see her from where he stood, high on the hill, sitting on the fence watching the wind blow the leaves.

He knew Catherine thought her a strange one, and there was a haunted look in her eyes that made even his niece Maddie, usually a chatterbox, leave her alone.

For propriety's sake, she slept in the little room next to Maddie's, in the eaves, and the villagers looked with curious eyes at the serious, withdrawn girl he'd brought home to be his bride.

He moved his arm in its sling, impatient with it. Another month, the doctor said, and it should be back to normal.

And in another month, they'd be married.

He was nervous enough, unsure enough, to wonder if that wasn't too long.

He saw her start to swing her legs on the fence, and wondered if she would ever really be his as he was hers.

He'd helped her contact her grandmother, and discovered she'd passed away only six weeks before, as they were leaving Cape Town on the ship home.

From the suspicious and surprised tone of her lawyers' letters, he realized they had given Elizabeth up for dead long ago. And who could blame them?

There would be a bit of a battle over her inheritance, but it looked as if she would be well-off, something she seemed not to care about in the slightest.

She missed Zululand.

He could see it in the way she tugged restlessly at her clothes, and stomped in her shoes. The way she sat at the window and watched the rain blow in gusts against the panes. The way she sat shivering by the fire.

And the way he sometimes came upon her, walking through the fields, singing Zulu lullabies to herself.

His heart ached. She had left a piece of herself there, back in that tent, with Lindani. Or in the African sky. She was always looking up at the dull grey English sky, her face set and still. Grieving for that wide, impossible blue and the hot sting of the sun.

She was doing it now, bracing back on her arms, staring

straight up at the sky, and he wanted to call to her, distract her. Make her remember for even one moment that she had him. That he was there.

He took a step forward to shout to her, and at that moment she looked straight up at him.

Jack half-raised his hand, lowered it again.

She watched him, cocking her head to one side as if seeing him in a different way. Then she hopped down from the fence and started through the trees towards him.

She disappeared from view, and he waited, heart tight, constricted in his chest by pressures he didn't know if he could bear.

But when she emerged from the orchard, he could see she was running. And heart suddenly free, soaring, he ran to meet her.

AFTERMATH

There is nothing except mournful glory in the behaviour of the many officers and men who have fallen, however seriously the affair may reflect upon the military dispositions of their leaders; for that some one has blundered in this deplorable affair is, in truth, obvious. Yet, so far from being a blot upon the British annals, the conduct of these men and officers in their desperate straits casts new lustre upon our arms. They were not conquered, but overwhelmed; and the 24th Foot may inscribe the story of that cruel day in January upon their record not only without shame, but with a sorrowful pride and satisfaction. Meanwhile, there is but one word to write as to what must be done. At any cost, with whatever necessary strength, the reverse must be effaced, the savage victors chastised, conquered and disarmed, and these daring Zulus made as harmless as the Hottentots.

— BATTLE OF ISANDLWANA, AS REPORTED IN
THE DAILY TELEGRAPH, LONDON, 1879

CASUALTIES OF THE BATTLE OF ISANDLWANA

Zulu army:

Total force: estimated 23,000 – 25,000 men
Losses: estimated 1,500 – 3,000 men

British army:

Total force: 67 officers, 1,707 men
Losses: 52 officers, 1,308 men

AUTHOR'S NOTE

This book has been a very personal one for me. I grew up in KwaZulu-Natal, attended the University of KwaZulu-Natal for my undergraduate degree (at the Pietermartizburg campus), and took History with some of the experts in the Anglo-Zulu War as my lecturers. I have been to the battle-fields since I was a child, and my sense of place in this story was very strong.

I think my fascination with the Anglo-Zulu War must have begun as a small child with my grandfather's Zulu *assegai*. He claimed he'd found it on one of the battlefields, and I'm not sure if he was pulling my leg or not (he also claimed to have been a pirate) but I believed him when it counted most.

Not everything that happened on January 22nd (for example the British camp at Rorke's Drift's defense against the Zulu reserve force, which happened the same day) is mentioned in this book. None of my characters could have known about Rorke's Drift in the time frame in which the story is set.

Readers who are interested to learn more can use the reference works I give at the end as a starting point.

As in all historical fiction which centres on an actual event, I've had a difficult time with names.

When to use the names of the actual men involved, and when to make names up?

Because the senior officers involved, in particular Lord Chelmsford, Colonel Glyn, Lieutenant Colonel Durnford and Lieutenant Colonel Pulleine, were not point of view characters, I felt comfortable using their real names, and because of their roles, their names are synonymous with the battle in any event. Any dialogue I've attributed to them, though, is purely my own invention.

All other names are fictitious, although I almost used the real name of the officer who did, in fact, stop at the height of the shoot out with Sihayo's followers to collect a rare beetle, although he probably didn't send a private out into the dark African night to find any for him.

Lindani's general, the head of the scouts, did exist and he did in fact preside over the region I set Lindani's village. He was considered the most progressive and brilliant general of the Zulu army and was a great believer in moving with the times. By all accounts he was a crack shot and could speak English, but I didn't use his real name, because facts about most of the Zulu army's movements and thoughts are extremely scarce and I had to make up so much, within the framework of what I could discover, that I felt it safest to give all the Zulus, except King Cetshwayo, fictitious names.

I have only knowingly twisted the facts of the Central Column (or Number 3 Column, it went by both names) to suit my story in two places.

The first is that, because of the poor conditions of the track, wagons were still arriving at Isandlwana late into the night of 20 January. But I needed Elizabeth to eavesdrop at General Chelmsford's mess tent and meet Lindani that night, as well as not get in too late to make Jack suspicious, or worse, come looking for her, so I had them all safely in camp hours before they really were.

The other fact is that, while a company of the 2nd 24th was on picket duty on the evening of 21 January, which meant they were the only company of the 2nd battalion not to leave with Chelmsford in the early hours of 22 January, they were not the ones to almost run into the main Zulu *impi* hiding in the Ngwebeni Valley. A company did almost stumble on to the *impi*, but earlier in the day of 21 January, not the evening.

In reality, G Company, the 2nd 24th company left behind at Isandlwana, was led by Lieutenant Charles Pope, who was killed, along with all his men, on the battlefield.

Tragically, while a great Zulu victory, the Battle of Isandlwana was too resounding a success for the Victorian ego to bear. There was no way the Zulus could ever be seen to get away with humiliating the greatest power in the world, and after regrouping, the British invaded again later that year and crushed the Zulus, taking no prisoners.

The strange coincidence of the 24th Foot only ever having its 1st and 2nd Battalions fighting together twice, and both times being involved in a massive defeat is true, and the 1st 24th officers did organize a luncheon while marching to the Zululand border to commemorate those who fell together at Chillianwallah. The events I describe in Jack's father's diary of the events leading up to and including Chillianwallah are as accurate as I could get them.

And as for Elizabeth, well, there is at least one known case of a young white girl surviving a shipwreck on the east coast of South Africa and being adopted by the local community. The wreck occurred much further south than where I made Elizabeth's ship go down, and the community that took the young girl in (she was probably only 5 or 6 years old, much younger than Elizabeth) were Xhosa, and they loved her like their own. She grew up to marry a chief, had many children, and was much respected until the end of her days. If you're interested in learning more about this real-life survivor, pick up *The Sunburnt Queen* by Hazel Crampton.

There *was* a partial eclipse the day of the battle, casting an eerie light over the battlefield. I can only image what effect it must have had on the combatants of both sides.

And finally, only once I'd embarked on writing this book did I discover that a few of the British survivors of Isandl-wana were officially questioned after the battle as to whether they'd seen a woman on the battlefield.

There were no female camp followers on this campaign, and the question is quite extraordinarily. I would love to know what motivated the officers in the inquiry to ask it.

Michelle Diener

BIBLIOGRAPHY

Some of the most useful primary sources and reference works I used in researching this book:

Allinson, Helen, Private Ashley Goatham. Letters from the Zulu War, The Journal of the Anglo-Zulu War Society: Journal Eight – December 2000

Amin, Maj. A.H., Chillianwala January 13, 1849, Orbat.com, May 19th, 2002

Callaway, M.D., The Religious System of the AmaZulu, 1870

Creswicke, Louis, South Africa and the Transvaal War, Vol. 1 (of 6) From the Foundation of Cape Colony to the Boer Ultimatum of 9th Oct. 1899, Edinburgh, 1900

Duminy, Andrew & Ballard, Charles (eds), The Anglo-Zulu War: New perspectives, Pietermaritzburg, 1981

Fortescue , J.W., A History of the British Army, Volume Twelve, London 1927

Hamilton-Browne, A Lost Legionary in South Africa, 1911

Knight, Ian, British Forces in Zululand 1879, London, 1990

Knight, Ian, The National Army Museum Book of the Zulu War, London, 2004

Knight, Ian, Isandlwana 1879: The Great Zulu Victory, Oxford, 2002

Laband, John & Thompson, Paul, Kingdom and Colony at War, Pietermartizburg, 1990

Montague, W.E., Campaigning in South Africa: Reminiscences of an Officer in 1879, Edinburgh, 1880

Moodie, D.C.F. & the Leonaur Editors, Zulu 1879, 2006

O'Connor, Damian P., Imperial strategy and the Anglo-Zulu War of 1879, The Historian, 22/06/2006

Rattray, David, Guidebook to the Anglo-Zulu War Battlefields, Cape Town, 2003

Smith, Keith (prepared by), Anglo-Zulu War 1879, Documents in the National Archive (PRO), Kew, 2003

Trollope, Anthony, South Africa, 1878

GLOSSARY OF TERMS

Some of the Zulu words used in the book:

amaZulu – People of the sky

assegai – short stabbing spear

donga – a deep erosion ditch

ibutho – army division or battalion

impi – army

induna – headman

inkhosi – chief

inyanga – healer / medicine man

iwisa – club (also known as a knobkerrie)

mealie – corn

oNdini – Capital of Zululand

sangoma – diviner / spiritual leader

umuTsha – traditional clothing of Zulu men, made from a flap of leather and decorated with civet tails.

unwabo – chameleon

EXCERPT: A DANGEROUS MADNESS

Here are the first three chapters of Michelle Diener's best-selling historical suspense novel A Dangerous Madness:

The Duke of Wittaker has been living a lie...
He's been spying on the dissolute, discontented noblemen of the ton, pretending to share their views. Now he's ready to step out of the shadows and start living a real life...but when the prime minister of England is assassinated, he's asked to go back to being the rake-hell duke everyone believes he still is to find out more.

Miss Phoebe Hillier has been living a lie, too...
All her life she's played by society's rules, hiding her fierce intelligence and love of life behind a docile and decorous mask. All it's gotten her is jilted by her betrothed, a man she thought a fool, though a harmless one. But when she discovers her former fiancé was involved in the plot against the prime minister, and that he's been murdered, she realizes he wasn't so harmless after all.

And now the killers have set their sights on her...

The only man who can help her is the Duke of Wittaker--a man she knows she shouldn't trust. And she soon realizes he's hiding behind a mask as careful as her own. As the clock ticks down to the assassin's trial, the pair scramble to uncover the real conspiracy behind the prime minister's death. And as the pressure and the danger mounts, Phoebe and Wittaker shed their disguises, layer by layer, to discover something more precious than either imagined–something that could last forever. Unless the conspirators desperate to hide their tracks get to them first.

A DANGEROUS MADNESS: CHAPTER 1

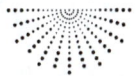

S unday, 10 May, 1812

PHOEBE STOOD NEXT TO THE PORTRAIT OF SIR HAROLD Fitzpatrick as instructed, the note the footman had given her crumpled in her fist.

She hadn't seen Sheldrake all evening, had had to endure hours on her own of being either snubbed or fawned over, but he must have seen her—the note was evidence of that. Just one more odd instance in a string of them.

A waving motion caught her eye and she turned slightly to see a hand reach out from behind aquamarine velvet curtains. A man's hand.

He grabbed her sleeve and pulled her into an enclosed nook that by day was a perfectly innocent bay window. Phoebe blinked, trying to adjust to the sudden dark after the well-lit gallery.

"Sheldrake?" She peered at the man taking up most of the small space.

"Good grief, keep it down, would you?"

Phoebe's betrothed's forceful whisper was as loud as her soft-spoken question, but she bit her tongue.

She wondered what her tongue would look like after they'd spent a lifetime together. Maybe one day she'd bite it in half.

"Look, dear thing, I needed to speak to you in private, without anyone seeing me here." Even in the dark, Phoebe could see Sheldrake plucking at his lapels.

"Well, this is very private." She waited patiently for him to enlighten her, and there was an uncomfortable silence. For the first time since she'd been jerked into the dark, into what would be considered a scandalous rendezvous, Phoebe felt the gentle hand of trepidation caress the back of her neck.

"My dear, dear thing. I . . . that is to say . . ." She saw the shadowy outline of his hand coming up to his head and realized he was mopping his brow with his kerchief, even though the Halliford's house was made of such thick stone, it never truly got warm.

A buzzing started in her ears.

"I can't marry you, Pheebs. I know that's going to make things difficult for you and I want to go through with it, of course I do, it would solve a number of problems, but I don't have the time for it, you understand?"

"You don't . . . have the *time* for it?" Her words seemed to be coming from far, far away.

"No. I'm . . . well, soon I'll be in a bit of bother, m'dear. Or I think I will. And I'm going to have to make a run for it. I thought I could hold out until I got my hands on your money, but it looks like I was a bit too optimistic." He gave a sigh.

Phoebe wanted to shriek at him like a woman she'd once seen in the marketplace had shrieked at her husband.

Like a fishwife.

"You owe money?" She bit back the scream, forcing it down like too many pillows stuffed into a wooden kist. She'd had plenty of practice. Her voice didn't even wobble.

"'Fraid so. But that's not why I'm running."

"Then why were you hoping to get my money early?" She tried to be calm and logical.

"Living in exile is more comfortable when you have funds." He tugged at his kerchief as if he meant to tear it in half. "I already asked your father's lawyers if your dowry could be made available before the wedding, but it appears not." He sighed again. "And your trustees control it anyway. It's not as if you could help me. They'd have to approve, and I know for a fact they won't because I already asked one of them."

Phoebe stared at him.

"Well. That's that, then. Don't say anything, will you, until tomorrow? About my jilting you and taking off. I'm due to catch a boat to the Continent from Dover tomorrow or the day after, and I'd like to have a clear run."

"You're leaving London tonight?" Phoebe's voice came out lower than usual.

"Yes. The whole thing is coming to a head. If I don't run now, I risk being closed in." He shrugged. "You can put it about later that I was on my skids. Better a bankrupt, money-grubbing cad than a . . . " He jerked his waistcoat. "Well, never mind what."

"Sheldrake, I have no idea what you're talking about."

"No. You wouldn't." He patted her arm, in the way he'd done countless times before. A way that made her want to jerk her arm viciously away and do him some bodily harm.

285

She drew in a deep, deep breath. Pulled her arm very gently from under his grasp.

Oblivious to her fury, he lifted his pocket watch to the thin stream of light coming into the alcove through a gap in the drapes, and turned it this way and that until he could read the time. He gave a grunt.

"My coach will be waiting." He twisted his lips in a grimace. "Sorry, dear thing. Sometimes the best plans turn to ash and well . . . Don't believe everything you might hear about me if this comes out. I was doing something. Taking action. But it's all gone to the dogs. Our puppet has lost his nerve. I'm afraid he'll crack or botch it, and it will all come out. I refuse to be sacrificed." He rubbed his forehead one last time and pushed his kerchief into his pocket. "Be careful for the next few days, eh? Watch your step."

With a last pat, he cocked his head, listening for any sign of someone nearby, and then opened the curtains to step out. Hesitated.

"You should be safe enough." With a little nod of his head, he slipped out between the heavy curtains, leaving nothing behind but the sharp scent of his pomade and his sweat.

Phoebe collapsed onto the deep window seat, her fingers clutching at the thin cushions beneath her.

Her betrothal was over. And from the way Sheldrake had spoken, he was involved in something illegal, or at least immoral. He was running from the authorities.

She lifted a hand and rubbed it over her heart. She touched her face, but the tears she expected weren't there.

After some time had passed, she couldn't say how long, she stood and parted the curtains. Walked slowly back to the light and sound of the ballroom.

Her world, her future as she had thought it would be, was gone.

All she could feel was relief.

A DANGEROUS MADNESS: CHAPTER 2

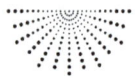

M onday, 11 May, 1812

"MY LORD! HIS GRACE IS IN HIS BATH. YOU CAN'T . . ."

James heard the unusual sound of his valet in full panic moments before the door to his dressing room was wrenched open and Lord Dervish stepped, grim and breathless, into the room.

"It's all right, Towers. Lord Dervish is welcome." James said nothing more, and neither did Dervish until Towers had closed his mouth with a snap, closed the door, and retreated to wherever aggrieved valets go.

He was almost finished with his bath, but James lay back and raised his brows as Dervish continued to stand quite still, head cocked, as if to hear if Towers or anyone else may be trying to listen in.

They probably were.

"Move the water in your bath about so it's harder for

anyone to hear." Dervish stepped closer, something stealthy in the move. He hummed with suppressed energy and adrenalin.

"What is it?" James didn't deign to follow his instructions. Their voices were low enough to make listening at the door impossible.

"The Prime Minister has just been assassinated." Dervish ran a hand over his stark, sharp face, and James could see it shook.

He sat up suddenly, and water slopped over the side with a splash. "You're not joking."

Dervish never joked, but James wondered if he could have made a mistake.

"I wish I were." Dervish walked over to the window and looked out on the garden at the back of the house, his tall, wiry frame barely able to stay still.

James rose from the still-warm water and wrapped a towel around his waist, took up another and began to dry himself in quick, economical movements.

"Who did it?"

"Some fellow called Bellingham. Put the gun right against Perceval's chest as he came through the lobby to the Lower House, pulled the trigger and then went and sat down on a bench nearby. Didn't try to run, just sat, waiting."

"Part of a group? Some conspiracy?"

Dervish turned as James pulled a fresh shirt over his head. "It's the most likely explanation." He turned back to the window, shook his head. "I know a lot of people hated Perceval's politics, and with this current inquiry into the Orders in Council, they've been more front and center than usual, but when the word spread, when it got out that he'd been killed . . ." Dervish ran a hand through thick, dark hair winged with silver at the temples. "I had to fight through cheering, celebrating crowds to get here. They were all but dancing in the street. Calling for the Prince Regent to be next."

James pulled his trousers on and considered things. He'd despised Perceval. It hadn't been difficult to pretend to be a malcontent these last few years, because the sheer pomposity and self-righteousness of the prime minister had been everything he disliked in politics. In life in general.

But rioting in the streets and calling for the death of the regent? How could it end well? "What have you done with the killer?"

"They tried to take him to Newgate, but the crowds were too strong, too wild. Everyone was cheering him, trying to shake his hand. They had to take him back inside, wait for the guards to clear the crowds."

For the first time, James noticed a small bruise high on Dervish's cheek. Realized he'd been speaking literally when he'd said he'd had to fight the crowds.

"What do you want of me?" He'd already pulled on his boots, and was shrugging his way into a coat.

"The problem is, so many people wished Perceval ill. The slave traders. The manufacturers. The Luddites. The shipping industry. Bellingham claims he did it on his own, that it was for personal reasons. But I can't bring myself to believe that. It's too good to be true."

"Yes." James slung his cravat around his neck and started to tie it. His valet would be surprised to see how well he was able to accomplish the task. "A lone man with a grudge would certainly be the most convenient explanation. Leave no one with a cause to take up." He pulled his shirt straight and began to button his jacket.

"We want you to focus on your area of specialization, Wittaker. There are plenty of noblemen who were being ruined by Perceval's Orders in Council and he had such a grip on government—hell, he almost single-handedly *was* government—that some might have seen assassination as the only way to dislodge him."

"I haven't heard even a whisper about something like that." James leaned back against his dresser and crossed his arms over his chest.

Dervish glanced at him sharply. "Yes, but you haven't been hanging around your usual haunts for the past month and more."

No. James had to admit he hadn't.

The lustre had gone off his old lifestyle. Not that there was much lustre to begin with, though he'd felt he was helping in some way. But there was only so long you could wallow in the mire before the mud started to stick.

He shrugged. Let the silence draw out.

Dervish looked away. "Your help was always much appreciated. I know it wasn't said enough." He cleared his throat. "It's not likely, but there are enough idiots in both the Upper and the Lower House who may have thought they were doing England and their family fortunes a favour by taking Perceval out of the running."

"Even more manufacturers, exporters, and slavers who were being ruined." James tapped his lips. "What are Bellingham's connections?"

"He's from Liverpool, apparently. Involved in the shipping trade to Russia."

"Hmm." James and Dervish exchanged a look. "So looking into the young hot-bloods is really just being thorough. If he's from Liverpool——"

"He's most likely working for the slavers or the shipping trade." Dervish gave a nod of agreement. "But it's almost too obvious."

MICHELLE DIENER

"Sometimes," James opened the door to Dervish and waited for him to step out the room, "a thing is exactly what it seems."

~

"I HAVE HEARD THE MOST UNBELIEVABLE NEWS FROM MRS. Jenkins." Aunt Dorothy stripped off her gloves with hands that trembled, and Phoebe paused in the act of pulling the tea tray toward her and looked up at her aunt.

"Something bad, I take it?" She looked down at her hands, suddenly unable to pick up the teapot in case she dropped it. Someone must have found out about Sheldrake and told her aunt.

"The worst news I've ever heard. The Prime Minister has been shot."

Phoebe lifted her head to stare at her aunt's angular, beautiful face for a long moment. "When?"

"No more than a few hours ago. Shot down like a dog in the lobby of the Houses of Parliament."

"Surely that can't be right?" Phoebe picked the pot up at last and poured them both a cup of tea with steady hands.

She should have told her aunt right away about Sheldrake's abandonment of the engagement that had been both their fathers' dying wish. But the shame of it, the humiliation, still stung; an inflamed, pulsing bite out of her pride.

"It's right, all right. Mr. Jenkins was there. Still is there, by the sounds of it. He got a note out to his wife, but as a witness, he's had to stay on while they charge the assassin." Aunt Dorothy lifted the delicate cup to her lips and took a deep gulp.

"They have someone in custody? It wasn't an accident or

something?" Phoebe couldn't imagine anyone actually shooting the diminutive, cherub-faced man.

Dorothy shrugged. "So Mrs. Jenkins understood from her husband's note. The details will no doubt come out soon. Something about him being like a puppet with its strings cut after he did the deed. Just collapsed onto a bench and waited for the inevitable."

"That's terrible. Who would shoot a man in cold blood?" She didn't know why she was suddenly thinking about what Sheldrake had said last night, each word burned into her memory in charred, ugly letters.

The word 'puppet', that was it.

An icy drop of unease snaked down her back and made her shiver.

"More than one person of my acquaintance has threatened to do away with him," her aunt said, eyes avid. "Ruining the country, my dear husband says, almost every morning when he reads the paper. Single-handedly ruining the country." She settled back in her chair and took a piece of Madeira cake. "It's been one of the few things I've not missed about him, being in Town with you for a few weeks. What does dear Sheldrake say about it?"

"Sheldrake?" Phoebe had to force herself to breathe so her voice wouldn't squeak. "He's never seemed to have much of an opinion when it comes to politics."

"Lucky you. Mr. Patterson drives me almost 'round the bend going on about how Mr. Perceval is trying to throw England into a pit of economic ruin and despair."

"Not any more," Phoebe said, and gripped her teacup a little tighter. "By the sounds of it, not any more."

A DANGEROUS MADNESS: CHAPTER 3

"Haven't seen you before, luv." An arm came around James's waist, and a soft, well-endowed body pressed up against his back and rubbed. He smelled rose water and powder, with just a musky hint of old sex.

James turned slightly and stepped away, removing the woman's arm as he did.

Behind him, a room full of well-dressed men shouted and laughed as they played Hazard. The pungent aroma of cigar smoke, along with the sharp-sweet stink of spilled drinks, layered over with sweat, washed over him.

He hadn't missed this.

It amazed him that at one time, he hadn't even noticed the smell.

"I can keep you company, if you like." The woman gave him a saucy wink.

He looked her over. She was dressed in a peacock blue dress, cut so low her nipples were just visible above the neckline. It was nipped in tight at her waist, and she had a peacock feather dressed into her up-swept hair.

"You must be new here." She looked no more than eighteen or nineteen, but he couldn't accuse Jillie Bellows of breaking her deal with him. Her new girl was of age—just—and did not seem to be coerced or afraid.

Of course, coercion was a tricky line to walk. How many of these girls really felt they had a choice in entering this life?

"Your Grace." Jillie stepped into the hall from her little office, the old parlor, James guessed, from when this smart West End house had been a family home, rather than The Scarlet Rose, one of the most profitable gaming hells and brothels in London.

"Madame Rouge." James gave a nod. He called her the name she went by here, although she was well aware he knew all there was to know about her.

"Bessie, don't bother the Duke. He's here strictly for the gaming." Her voice was sharp, gilded with a little fear, and Bessie blushed, curtseyed, and fled down the passage and through a white and gold door.

"A little harsh. She couldn't have known my . . . rules."

"No. You haven't been by for more than a month, and she's only been here two weeks." Her tone was almost as fierce with him as it had been with Bessie, and she looked away, her shoulders stiff.

He didn't respond. He wasn't prepared to answer to her.

"Well, nice to have you back." On that lie, she gave a nod, still not meeting his eyes, and stepped back into her office.

Jillie Bellows hadn't been pleased to see him since the day he'd threatened to close her down for selling a child into sexual slavery, and that had been two years ago.

Since then they'd reached a strange truce. She didn't send any of her girls out to him, and swore never to deal in children again, and he, by the cachet that came with being a duke, lent her establishment an air of high-class sin.

It appeared to be doing quite well without him, though, if the crowd in the gaming room was anything to go by.

"Wittaker. There you are! Thought you'd abandoned this place. I even started enquiring where you'd moved on to." Banford was slumped in a chair near the door, his face flushed with the close heat of the room and the whisky in his glass.

So that was the reason behind Jillie's sharp tongue. She sensed the sheep were getting ready to follow him to what they thought were greener pastures.

"Busy with other things, is all," he said to Banford, slurring his words just a little. He wondered if he'd ever get drunk again—risk actually sounding like this.

Somehow, he doubted it.

"Oh?" Banford sat a little straighter, his eyes lighting at the possibility of something even more dissolute than what was on offer at The Scarlet Rose.

Wittaker didn't hide his contempt at Banford's reaction, flicking him a look before turning his attention to the room without making a reply.

It made him even more popular, even more respected among this lot, he'd found. The more contemptuous, the more dismissive he was of them, the more they tried to please him and follow his style.

"Like that, eh? Keeping all the best secrets for yourself." Banford narrowed his eyes. "What's a fellow got to do to get an invitation?"

James looked back at him. "You hear about Perceval?"

"You'd have to be living under a rock not to hear." Banford got unsteadily to his feet. "Damn disgrace. Shot down in the one place he should have been safe." He tipped slightly to one side and stumbled a little as he steadied himself on the chair.

"Worried about your own neck next time you're at Westminster?" James didn't look at him as he spoke, his eyes on the raucous game of Hazard happening in the middle of the room.

Banford laughed. "Not in the House often enough for that to be likely. Still, some places should be sacred."

James gave him a cool look. "As you say."

It was a hard line to walk. To play aggrieved enough by Perceval's policies to let a possible conspirator know he would lend a sympathetic ear, but also suitably outraged enough that a man, any man, had lost his life by murder.

Almost as hard a line as to know how he genuinely felt about the prime minister. He'd approved of Perceval's practical support of the abolition of the slave trade, but found the man himself objectionable. When facing off against his political opponents, Perceval attacked the individual, not their policies, leading James to think he didn't have the intelligence to argue against them.

Perceval used his obviously genuine love for his family and the Church to garner himself more support, and further his political agenda, thereby sullying any moral high ground he would otherwise have had.

Perceval was a thorny problem of a man.

Unbending, unable to see any opinion other than his own, wholly annoying, and yet, no matter what, he did not deserve to be killed.

James rubbed the back of his neck.

He was on a wild goose chase here.

No one would say anything different to Banford. Certainly not a few hours after the murder itself had been done.

The breech of the sanctity of the Houses of Parliament, the way murder had slipped into a place where all thought they were safe but for a tongue-lashing from a political opponent—that would shock all of them, no matter if they hated Perceval or not.

Nevertheless . . .

He stepped toward the Hazard table, and was surprised to find himself tensing, as if for a blow.

It wasn't so far off.

Forcing a sardonic smile on his face, he waded into the crowd, listening for anything unusual.

By the time he waded back out again, 2000 pounds richer, he had a name.

Sheldrake.

ALSO BY MICHELLE DIENER

HISTORICAL NOVELS BY MICHELLE DIENER

Susanna Horenbout and John Parker series:

In a Treacherous Court

Keeper of the King's Secrets

In Defense of the Queen

Regency London series:

The Emperor's Conspiracy

Banquet of Lies

A Dangerous Madness

Other historical novels:

Daughter of the Sky

FANTASY NOVELS BY MICHELLE DIENER

Mistress of the Wind

The Golden Apple

The Silver Pear

SCIENCE FICTION NOVELS BY MICHELLE DIENER

Class 5 series:

Dark Horse

Dark Deeds

Dark Minds

Sky Raiders series:

Sky Raiders

Calling the Change

Shadow Warrior

Verdant String series:

Interference & Insurgency Box Set

Breakaway

Breakeven

Trailblazer

To receive notification when a new book is released, sign up to Michelle's new release notification list on michellediener.com

PRAISE FOR MICHELLE DIENER'S OTHER BOOKS:

Luxury Reading: Diener has set a standard for what good historical fiction ought to be . . .

Chicago Tribune : With its richly detailed historical setting and intrigue-filled plot, "In a Treacherous Court" is simply irresistible.

Affaire de Coeur Magazine: Awesome! History woven flawlessly into riveting fiction.

RT Magazine, August 2011 issue: Just when readers think there is
nothing new to be learned about Henry VIII, debut author Diener
delivers a taut suspense . . . that will keep you turning the pages.

Readers Entertainment: Diener's writing style is beautiful, to the
point, vivid and exciting. The characters are going to hook you
first, and the intrigue will keep you turning the pages.

Publishers Weekly: Diener (Keeper of the King's Secrets) delivers
a rousing read ...

ABOUT THE AUTHOR

Michelle Diener writes historical fiction, science fiction and fantasy. From the Tudor court, to the streets of Regency London, and into magical landscapes, she's never happier than when she's building worlds and crafting suspenseful plots and unforgettable characters.

Michelle was born in London, grew up in South Africa and currently lives in Australia with her husband and two children.

You can contact Michelle through her website (michelle-diener.com) or sign up to receive notification when she has a new book out on her New Release Notification page.